Wedding Bells at Butterfly Cove

Sarah Bennett

ONE PLACE. MANY STORIES

HQ
An imprint of HarperCollins*Publishers* Ltd
1 London Bridge Street
London SE1 9GF

This paperback edition 2018

4
First published in Great Britain by
HQ, an imprint of HarperCollins*Publishers* Ltd 2017

Sarah Bennett asserts the moral right to be identified as the author of this work.
A catalogue record for this book is available from the British Library.

ISBN: 978-0-00-832771-2

MIX
Paper from responsible sources
FSC™ C007454

This book is produced from independently certified FSC™ paper to ensure responsible forest management.

For more information visit: www.harpercollins.co.uk/green

Printed and bound in Great Britain by
CPI Group (UK) Ltd, Croydon, CR0 4YY

For M. My very own happy ending.

Chapter One

May 2016

'Mummy.' The whispered voice next to her ear woke Kiki. She swam up through the layers of drowsiness, noting the darkness in the room, and wondered what time it was. 'Mummy.' A little shake of her shoulder added this time.

'Matty? Is everything all right, darling?' She matched his whisper, but it wasn't enough to avoid disturbing Neil.

He rolled over with a grumble. 'Whatever it is, take it somewhere else. I've got to be up in a couple of hours.'

Kiki slipped from beneath the quilt and used her toes to locate her slippers. After tucking her feet in the thin mules, she ushered her son towards the sliver of light shining from the landing. She pulled the bedroom door closed behind her, then crouched down to look at her beloved boy. Sweaty strands of dark-brown hair clung to his forehead and his cheeks shone with a feverish glow. He nibbled his bottom lip. 'I didn't mean to wake Daddy.'

The gleam of worry in his eyes stabbed her in the heart. Neil was perfectly capable of making everyone's life a misery at the slightest provocation. She forced a smile as she smoothed the damp hair from his brow. 'Don't worry about that, he'll be fast asleep again by now. Did you have a bad dream?'

Matty shook his head. 'I don't feel very—' He cut himself off with a hand over his mouth and his whole body convulsed in a shuddering heave, sending a stream of vomit through his splayed fingers and down the front of them both. Tears of shock and upset glinted in his eyes and she scooped him up in her arms, swallowing down the echoing hitch in her own stomach.

She carried him quickly into the bathroom and just managed to settle him on his knees in front of the toilet before another gush of bitter-smelling liquid spewed forth. 'Poor poppet. Poor darling,' she murmured, rubbing circles on his back as he shivered and shook. The front of her nightdress clung damply to her body, but she pushed the unpleasant sensation to the back of her mind to focus on Matty. He gasped like a little fish out of water, swallowing and panting. She knew the pattern well. This was just a brief respite in the process.

'Uh-oh,' he muttered and lurched forward again. This would be the last of it now. Kiki stroked his hair until he subsided into breathy sobs, sinking down until his head rested on the cold rim of the toilet.

'Better out than in, that's what they say.' She rose from her cramped position by his side to rinse her hands under the tap. Grabbing a dark-green flannel from the edge of the sink, she soaked it in cold water then bent down to turn Matty towards her. 'Look up, darling.'

He lifted his pale little face and she held his chin in a light grip as she wiped the tears, sweat and other less pleasant things from his skin. A quick rinse of the cloth and she folded it into a square. 'Hold this against your head a minute, can you?' He nodded weakly and clutched the flannel with a shaky hand.

Confident he would be okay for a couple of minutes, she left him to go and check his bedroom and fetch some clean pyjamas. His bedding and carpet were mercifully clean and she sent up a silent prayer of thanks that at least she wasn't faced with changing the sheets at... she glanced at the LEGO Batman clock on the dressing table and winced... three a.m. Pausing at the airing cupboard on the landing, she dug out a T-shirt and a pair of leggings for herself and returned to the bathroom. A quick change and a teeth-clean and they were both soon tucked into Matty's single bed.

'How's your tummy now, still sore?' She feathered her fingers through his silky-soft hair. The deep-brown strands matched her own, but his soulful blue eyes were all his father's. She'd fallen for a bigger version of those baby-blues before she'd known the truth—a twinkling look and a sweet smile could mask a monster. Neil had smiled, flirted and flattered his way into her life and she had lapped up the attention like a parched flower, blooming into a blushing, eighteen-year-old bride.

His earnest focus on her, his need to know her every movement, had seemed exciting. He needed her with him, couldn't stop thinking about her, worried someone else might snatch the prize of her from under his nose. Oh, the lies he'd told her had been music to her innocent ears. Like Helen of Troy and Paris, theirs was a love that would burn through space and time. Like Heathcliff and Cathy, like Jane and Rochester, nothing could keep them apart. Only she'd glossed over the ugly, hard truths of those childhood love stories in her burning need to feel special to someone.

And how exciting for a naïve girl to capture the heart of an older, wiser man. Neil had been in his first year as a postgraduate student when they met, and at twenty-two he'd seemed a fount of knowledge and experience from the moment they bumped into each other in the Ancient Greece section of the university library. Taking a classical studies course had been Kiki's transparent attempt to please her father, and when Neil found out she was the daughter of one of his intellectual heroes, he'd been hooked. He painted a fascinating picture of a man nothing like the withdrawn, preoccupied one who ruled her home with more neglect than care.

A soft snore drew her attention and she eased her arm out from under Matty's head to settle him more comfortably on his pillow. Content he was asleep, she slipped out of his bed to clean up the mess left behind on the landing carpet. Once that was done, she might as well tackle the ironing pile. She cast a quick glance at her closed bedroom door as she passed it. There was no way she wanted to risk waking Neil again, and she could always have a catch-up nap once the kids were sorted in the morning.

'Mummy?' Déjà vu. Only this time the voice was Charlie's sweet, piping tone, still carrying a babyish lisp. And the hard, wooden table beneath her cheek was no substitute for her pillow.

Forcing open her grit-filled eyes, Kiki tried to ignore the sick, groggy pain in her head and sat up. 'What's the time, darling?' A rhetorical question to a three-year-old, but her brain was still too full of cotton wool to think straight.

'It's gone eight o'clock and I'm going to be late, thanks to you,' Neil snapped as he stormed into the room.

She blinked, noting his suit and tie, rather than the casual-jacket-and-jeans look he favoured when lecturing. 'Oh, your meeting. I'm sorry, I must have dozed off.' Jumping up, she hurried over to switch the kettle on and stuff a couple of slices of bread into the toaster. 'Give me a minute, just one minute, and I'll bring your breakfast to your study.'

Neil glared at her, not an ounce of warmth in his blue eyes. 'I already told you, I don't have time. Which part of 'late' don't you understand?' He dodged back to avoid their daughter's attempts to clutch his legs for a hug. 'No, Charlotte! You'll crease Daddy's suit.' He left the kitchen, muttering to himself.

Kiki leaned back against the board, wondering how she'd managed to screw up the day before it had even started. Charlie, lower lip quivering, her dark hair sleep-tangled and knotted, painted a picture of abject heartbreak. Kiki swooped on her, gathering her little girl into her arms for a tight hug. 'Daddy doesn't mean to be cross, Charlie. He's just got a busy day and Mummy didn't help by falling asleep.' Even as the words left her mouth, she wondered why she was making excuses for him. Neil was an adult and perfectly capable of getting himself up and ready for work on time, but the default blame in the Jackson household for any problem fell squarely on her shoulders.

She could just imagine what her big sister would have to say if she could hear her. Mia had never warmed to Neil. Kiki suppressed a bitter laugh. There she went again, painting the situation in a rosier light than it deserved. Mia couldn't stand him. Had even tried to persuade Kiki to leave and bring the children with her to Mia's new home in Butterfly Cove. As if she could just pack up and start again! She hefted Charlie onto her other hip. 'Come on, poppet, let's go and see how your brother is feeling this morning.'

Matty appeared untroubled by his early morning misadventures, so she dropped him off at school, then a bubbly Charlie at crèche for her morning session. Strictly speaking, the rules required her to keep him off for forty-eight hours, but he usually bounced back after an episode and Kiki preferred not to make a fuss about it. His bouts of sickness had started a few months previously, frequent enough for her to have taken her son to the doctor. After a range of tests, they'd not been able to find anything wrong with him, and Kiki was keeping a food diary to see if there might be an allergic connection. She hadn't found an organic link to his problem, and she was beginning to suspect the doctor's other suggestion—stress—might be the real cause.

The resilience the children showed filled her with pride, and not a little guilt. They shouldn't have to tiptoe around their father the way they had been recently. She would have to try and talk to him, ask him to be a little more patient around them. Her stomach churned at the thought, but if she broached the subject when he was in a good mood, maybe she'd get through the conversation without it turning into a shouting match. Not that she did any shouting of her own. Perhaps if she made his favourite meal for dinner... She turned left at the next set of lights towards the supermarket.

***

Brushing the flour off her hands onto her apron, Kiki ran to the hall to fish her mobile out of her bag where it hung over the end of the bannister. The damn thing had found its way to the very depths and she almost dropped it in her hurry to answer before the caller rang off. 'Hello?'

'Jesus, Kiki. Can't you even answer your phone without a drama?'

'Sorry, darling. I was in the kitchen and I'd left my bag in the hall…'

Neil sighed. 'I don't need to hear your latest line in stupid excuses. Just go into my study, will you? There's the name of a hotel and a phone number on my jotter and I need it.'

'Hotel?' She crossed the hall and pushed open the study door. The room reminded her so much of her dad's, and it, too, was off limits unless she was cleaning. The high-backed leather chair behind the desk had cost a fortune, but Neil needed to be comfortable when he was working in the evenings. She nudged the chair to one side and scanned the familiar scribble on the cream-coloured jotter. 'What's it called?'

'If. I. Knew. What. It. Was. Called. I. Wouldn't. Be. Wasting. My. Time. Talking. To. You.' She winced at the deliberate pause he put between each word. 'It's on the left-hand side somewhere.'

Using her finger, she traced the scribbled notes. 'Oh, here. Lilly's Island Hotel? Number starts with a plus-thirty?'

'That's the one. Hurry up, I need to get back to the meeting.'

She reeled off the number, then paused. 'Antiparos? Isn't that near Despotiko?' The island was one of the most famous archaeological treasures outside of Delos. Neil's research focused on the cult of Apollo and he had been trying to get on a dig at the sanctuary for the past few years. 'Did you get your approval?'

'I won't get anything if you don't stop chattering, but yes, looks like I'll be there for the summer.' He hung up without saying another word.

Kiki sank into the deep leather chair. How many times had they talked about a summer trip to the islands when they'd first got married? Curled up in Neil's bed in his tiny flat, they'd spun dreams of days spent uncovering hidden treasures buried deep in the rocks and nights sipping ouzo and eating local delicacies. Then she'd fallen pregnant with Matty and those dreams were put on hold while they struggled to make ends meet. She'd dropped out, knowing there was no way she could finish her degree with a new baby and Neil needing all the help he could get with his research.

Life had got in the way, as it so often did, but maybe this would be a chance for them to spend some quality time together. A tiny bubble of hope stirred in her heart. Away from the stresses and strains, perhaps they could find a way to make things right between them. The kids could run and play in the sunshine, and she could help Neil catalogue his findings. She bit her lip, unable to stop a smile. If they could just get back to the way things used to be…

She reached for the wireless mouse on Neil's desk and shook it gently to wake up his computer. A Word document filled the screen, so she scanned the lower toolbar looking for the browser icon, but accidentally clicked on the email one. The screen changed, displaying an open message and she gave it half a glance, before looking back at the bottom bar.

Darling…

Her finger froze on the mouse as the word registered. Who would be calling Neil darling? Ignoring the little voice in her head that warned he would be furious at her for snooping, Kiki rolled the mouse to the top of the message and began to read. Incredulity became denial, became horror, as she followed the email exchange back over several weeks. She wanted to shut her eyes, refuse to see the truth laid out in black and white, but her finger kept clicking on the previous arrow. Every click was punctuated by the same word, the admonishment Neil threw in her face on a regular basis—stupid, *click*, stupid, *click*, stupid.

He was right.

Chapter Two

The problem with his best friend finding a wonderful girlfriend, Aaron Spenser mused to himself, was the way it emphasised the complete failure of his own love life. Ensconced in his very favourite place in the world—the cosy kitchen at Butterfly Cove—he watched the banter between Daniel and Mia and rubbed the phantom pain in his chest.

'Everything all right?' Mia cast him a little frown.

He stopped his hand, embarrassed at being caught mooning over his poor, lonely heart. 'Fine, thanks. Touch of heartburn, that's all.' He paused to give her a sly grin. 'I blame the chef.'

'Cheeky sod!' The balled-up tea towel caught him on the side of the head when he ducked too slowly.

Rising from his assigned seat around the wooden table, he stretched his arms above his head to loosen the last bit of stiffness from the exertions of the previous day. Mia's project to renovate the rundown old house perched beside a beautiful sandy beach in the picturesque village of Orcombe Sands was going full steam. Three of the five guest bedrooms were complete, and the final two were a few days from being finished. Aaron had spent every spare weekend since Daniel's surprise exhibition in March travelling backwards and forwards from London to Orcombe to lend a hand.

Life in the celebrity hurricane could destroy even the hardiest of souls, a lesson Daniel had learned the hard way. Exhausted, hungover and burned-out, he'd hit rock bottom. Fate, the West Coast mainline and a well-meaning neighbour had delivered Daniel to Mia's doorstep, and into the lonely young widow's life.

His friend's abrupt career change, from successful art photographer to creating a new artistic retreat on the south coast, had set tongues wagging in the gossip-fuelled celebrity circles he'd escaped from one cold, miserable February morning. There was already a huge level of interest and Aaron had helped them set up a mailing list and blog to maintain the buzz.

Every stage of the renovation works on the guest house, as well as the adjoining barns, which would house Daniel's haven for artists needing to take a break, was carefully documented and posted on the blog. They'd gained followers from all over the country and enough booking enquiries to fill the house for the entire summer season. The race was on to get everything ready in time for their grand opening next weekend.

Aaron picked at the remnants of red paint stuck under his nails, before abandoning it as a hopeless task. He still had the doorframe and windowsill to gloss in the country-garden-themed bedroom, so he'd no doubt end up with more on his hands. Saturday had been a washout; a huge squall had blown in off the sea, forcing them to keep the windows closed and dropping the late May bank holiday temperatures by several degrees.

The grey army—Mia's late-husband's parents and her neighbours Madeline and Richard—had battled valiantly in the driving rain to stake the most vulnerable flowers and shrubs in the sprawling garden at Butterfly Cove. The two older couples had become firm friends when everyone rode to Daniel's rescue after his ex-agent stole his work and attempted to put on an exhibition without his knowledge.

Pat and Bill had accepted Daniel into their life with a grace which left Aaron breathless with admiration, and not a little jealous over how well the new family structure was blending together. It had been a quarter of a century and his stepmother still hadn't forgiven Aaron for being a living, breathing reminder of his mum. As though thoughts of Cathy had summoned him, Aaron's younger brother, Luke, wandered into the kitchen, mouth stretched wide in a yawn.

'Morning.' Luke scrubbed his hand through his hair, sending the wayward curls tumbling in an artless display. Women loved those blond curls, not to mention the soulful brown eyes he could widen into a look both innocent and suggestive. Aaron shook his head. The ladies of London Town would be mourning his absence given he was also spending all his free time in Orcombe.

Daniel grinned at him. 'About time you showed up. Get your breakfast down you. Jordy will be here soon and I want to run over the plans for the mezzanine one last time before the builders arrive on Tuesday.' Daniel had hired the local carpenter to project manage the conversion and he was proving a sound choice. With local connections, he'd brought on reliable labour and got some decent discounts on raw materials.

The plan was to install a first floor in the main barn to house five self-contained apartments which could be rented by visiting artists. Each apartment would come with a purpose-built studio on the ground floor to cater for different mediums—pottery, painting, photography, sculpture and the like. A smaller outbuilding would then be converted into a multipurpose support space, housing a kiln, a small forge for iron-working, and even a darkroom for those traditionalists who preferred film to digital. The scope of the facility Daniel and Luke were creating took Aaron's breath away.

In addition to drawing up the design for the barn refurbishment, Luke had jumped in with both feet when Mia asked him to work up a harem theme for a pair of rooms in the main house. Free of the shackles of his junior role at a prestigious firm of architects, Luke had seized on the projects at Butterfly Cove like a starving man. He was happier than Aaron had seen him in a long time. Something had happened to Luke about a year previously, stealing the easy laughter from his eyes, but he'd been tight-lipped about it, claiming it was a work problem and nothing he needed his big brother to sort out.

Being a tiny cog in a big wheel didn't suit his little brother, any more than it suited him if Aaron was honest with himself. Getting a good degree and a placement with one of the big five accounting firms had always been top of his career wish list. But wishes and reality rarely gelled, and without the side work he took on, including looking after Daniel's financial affairs, Aaron would be digging an escape tunnel.

Where had that thought come from? He had a good job, was one of the youngest team leaders in the company. A smart flat in an up-and-coming part of the city, a good pension pot and the beginnings of a decent investment portfolio. His dad had drummed it into him from an early age: work hard, save well, live the best life you can within your means. So why so restless? *Another side effect of all the change in Daniel's life.* Perhaps thirty was the new threshold for a midlife crisis.

Feeling an uncomfortable itch between his shoulder blades, he turned to find Mia watching him with those big brown eyes of hers. She always saw too much. He flashed her a smile and tried to shake off the restless feelings stirring in his gut. Settled, steady, that was the life he had, and the life he wanted, too. No drama, no mad emotional roller-coaster. *Boring*. He frowned.

Introspection was for moody, artistic types. He preferred action.

Luke opened the back door, letting the tangy scents of the ocean fill the kitchen. Aaron breathed deeply. He could almost taste the freshness of the post-storm air on the back of his tongue. The faint sound of birdsong drifted from the garden, making up his mind. It was too nice a day to be stuck in the house. He turned to Mia. 'Leave the cottage, and I'll finish the last bits later.' Apart from glossing the doorframe, everything else was dressing.

She tilted her head, a quizzical look in her eyes. 'If you're sure?'

'I'm sure. Don't let me catch you up a ladder trying to hang those bloody curtains either.' The creamy material, covered in huge cabbage roses, had been edged with a red-checked pattern. Not something he'd ever have put together, but Mia had an eye for design he couldn't fault. Huge stacks of matching bedding, cushion covers and throws sat in neat piles on the dining-room table. He'd learned more about pelmets, valances and padded headboards than he'd thought possible. And it would have taken a braver man than he to point out a fitted sheet, a couple of pillowcases and a duvet cover were all that was required to make a bed.

She gave him a look, like butter wouldn't melt, and he knew she'd be rappelling from the upstairs bannisters if it took her fancy. 'Will you be back for lunch?'

That was something else he liked about her. Even though they were rushing to get everything finished, it never escaped her that everyone was giving up their free time to see her dream achieved. She never demanded, never expected, just gratefully accepted whatever efforts people could put in. 'I won't be long, just fancied a bit of fresh air.'

'Of course. Why don't you take Jamie's bike?'

Daniel glanced up from the drawings spread across the table. 'It's in the garage – help yourself.' The way the two of them had come to terms with the subject of her late husband stunned him anew. He might never have lived in the sprawling house at Butterfly Cove, but Jamie's memory lingered there in everyday objects. Jamie would always be a part of Mia's life and Daniel accepted it without a fuss.

'I'll be back before lunch.' He nudged his brother aside to get out of the back door and Luke's hand fell companionably upon his shoulder. They walked in silence towards the garage where Luke gave him a hand to swing open the rusty up-and-over door and then to lift the silver mountain bike from the hooks on the wall.

'Everything okay?' The edges of Luke's eyes crinkled in concern.

Aaron nodded. 'Yes, Spud. Just need a bit of air, that's all.' He glanced over his shoulder towards the kitchen door. 'Those two…'

Luke squeezed his shoulder. 'Happy as pigs in shit. Nothing like true love to make a man feel hopelessly inadequate.'

Aaron tossed his brother a wry grin. 'You, too?'

A cloud of sadness wiped the sunny smile from Luke's face. 'You have no idea, mate.' He shook himself like a dog after a dip in a stream. 'Don't mind me. Enjoy your ride.' Tucking his hands in the front pockets of his jeans, Luke strolled away. The casual pose might have worked better had his shoulders not been stiff with tension. Aaron frowned. It wasn't like him to keep secrets. Pondering not only what Luke was hiding from him, but the best way to get him talking, Aaron pedalled down the twisting driveway.

Blooms of white cow parsley and shiny yellow buttercups decorated the long grass verges on either side of the country lane, and the fields behind were a sea of pale-green wheat stalks. Reaching the crossroads to the main road, he paused to consider his options. Left would take him along the familiar route towards the main village of Orcombe Sands and the train station. Madeline and Richard lived somewhere towards the right. They'd likely be piling into Richard's sleek Mercedes with Bill and Pat, ready for another day of toil in Mia's garden. Not wanting to get caught skiving, he checked both ways then crossed the road to follow the lane into unexplored territory.

Muscles suitably warm, Aaron flicked the gears a couple of notches higher and increased his effort. A welcome burn began in his thigh muscles. He drew in a deep breath, letting it out on a happy laugh. Who would ever choose the gym if they had this on their doorstep? Cycling in London took a level of bravado he didn't possess, and the car-choked streets around his flat would have filled his lungs with dirty fumes, not fresh air.

Fields gave way to trees, dappling the road with leafy shadows. Weeks away from their full thickness, the boughs offered glimpses of houses tucked a few feet away from the road. Old-fashioned wooden gates bearing carved nameplates told their stories: *Willow Rest*, *Journey's End*, *Honeysuckle Cottage*. He squeezed the brakes and pulled over in the entrance of the last property. A sweet perfume floated on the air, proving the name to be more than a flight of fancy. The corner of a thatched roof was visible, crouching low over whitewashed walls and dark-framed square windows. A trellis covered part of the lower walls, thick with greenery and white-pink flowers. A proper chocolate-box cottage.

A loud thud and a sharp curse shattered the idyllic illusion. 'Bloody hell, Karen. Be careful!' Not a local accent, more the drawn-out vowels of the Midlands.

'I told you it was too heavy for me. We should have got a proper firm in, instead of trying to do it ourselves.' The woman's protest carried a similar twang.

Curious, Aaron rested the bike against the open gate and hooked his helmet over the handlebars. A few strides down the drive brought him face to face with a sweating, frowning man about the same age as him, struggling to hold one end of a heavy-looking chest of drawers. The other end rested on the ground in front of an exasperated blonde. A white box van stood behind them, the tailgate down. He gave the couple a grin and a friendly wave. 'Hey. Sorry to intrude. I was cycling by just now and it sounded like you might need a hand.'

The blonde cast him a tired smile. 'Thank you. We've bitten off a bit more than we can chew here.' She held out her hand. 'Hi, I'm Karen. D'you live around here?'

Aaron stepped forward, shook her hand, then offered his own to the man, who'd placed his end of the dresser down. 'Aaron. My friends live a couple of miles down the road, at Butterfly Cove.'

'Dave.' They shook hands. 'Never heard of it. We're down here trying to sort out Karen's great aunt's place.' He gestured with his head towards the cottage. 'She passed a couple of months ago, left her the cottage and all its contents in her will.'

Karen folded her arms across her chest and rubbed her biceps in a self-soothing gesture. A frown creased between her brows. 'I didn't really know her. She was my nan's sister and I hadn't seen her since I was a kid. She never married, some sad story about a lost love in the war, I remember Nan telling me once. Turns out I'm her only living relative so it all came to me. Not that we can do anything with the place. There's a few things we want to take, but we don't have room for it and we can't keep two houses running.' Colour lit her cheeks and she gave an embarrassed little laugh. 'Not that you want to hear our life story.'

Aaron stared at the cottage. Weeds had claimed the flowerbeds beneath the windows, and the paint was peeling a bit in places, but it looked sound enough. His mind started whirring. Luke would need to take a look, of course, and a proper surveyor. He could ask Richard for details of a local solicitor; Dave and Karen could use the one who'd handled her great aunt's will. The flat in town had a two-month clause on the lease, but he was pretty sure he could find someone to take it off his hands quicker than that. Interest rates on his cash ISA were in the toilet, so it wasn't like he'd be losing any interest if he withdrew it for a deposit…

A rushing sound filled his ears and he could feel his heart thumping in his chest. He didn't do impulsive. Steady, solid, the man with the plan. A house martin swooped past and disappeared into the eaves. Feeling light-headed, light-hearted and thoroughly unlike himself, he turned to the couple. 'So, you're looking to sell the place then?'

Chapter Three

Tap, tap, tap. 'Hellooo? Mizz Sutherland, are you there?' Mia closed her eyes and sent up a silent prayer for patience. They'd been open for guests for two weeks now and their grand-opening weekend had been such a success, it had spoiled her into believing running Butterfly House would be a doddle. Then the Chivers couple had arrived on Thursday for a five-night stay. Ten minutes of Mrs Chivers' pointed disappointment in, well, *everything* had poured cold water on Mia's cocky confidence. From the supposed inferior quality of the sheets on their bed in the beach room... 'One expects at least five-hundred thread count from a quality establishment'... to the disdainful sniff given to the homemade chicken pie Mia had served for the previous evening's supper... 'It's so hard to get an even, thin crust, isn't it, dear?'... Mrs Chivers had picked and poked until Mia was ready to offer a full refund if she would just leave.

'Bugger that,' had been Daniel's response to her suggestion. 'Make the miserable old bat pay.' She would have laughed if he hadn't said it almost loud enough for her awkward guest to hear it. By contrast, Mr Chivers couldn't have been kinder, and Mia wondered if he spent so many hours exploring the little beach behind the house as an excuse for a bit of peace and quiet.

Fixing a smile on her lips, Mia tugged off her washing-up gloves and turned towards the closed kitchen door. 'It's not locked, Mrs Chivers, please come in.'

Looking immaculate in a camel-coloured blouse and matching cords tucked into a pair of spotless walking boots, she looked as fresh as when she'd come down to breakfast that morning. Her highlighted hair, just a shade too perfect to be natural, swung around her face in a millimetre-perfect bob. 'It's such a pleasant afternoon, we thought we'd take tea on the patio.'

'Of course. The scones are just warming in the oven. Why don't you make yourselves comfortable and I'll bring everything out to you shortly?'

'That would be lovely, dear. I don't suppose you have different preserves? Homemade has its place, but when one is used to Fortnum's…' Mrs Chivers heaved a martyred sigh so exaggerated that Mia had to bite her lip not to laugh.

'Lady Begley will be sorry to hear her bramble jelly doesn't meet your expectations.' Mia busied herself removing the scones from the Aga, counting slowly to ten in her head. *One, two, three…*

'Lady Begley?' Was that a slight sputter? God, Mia hoped so.

Schooling her features, she began to lay the scones on the waiting cooling rack. 'Yes, from the Hall. Didn't you and Mr Chivers visit the gardens yesterday? Lady Begley is passionate about traditional homecrafts and most of the pickles and preserves they sell in their farm shop are made by her. I thought it would be a nice touch to cross-promote a local business.'

Mrs Chivers smoothed a nervous hand over her sleek hair. 'Yes, well, perhaps our palates have been slightly spoiled by mass-market products.'

Mia schooled her features into a bland smile. 'I'm sure that's it.'

The faint whirr of a drill sounded from outside. Although they'd made it clear at time of booking that conversion works were taking place in the barns, Daniel worked hard to schedule the noisy stuff for when their guests were out for the day. When they'd spoken at breakfast, the couple had planned to spend the day walking on Dartmoor and Mia hadn't expected to see them much before supper. Afternoon tea had been hastily put together, but her fridge and pantry were well stocked enough to cover it without any trouble.

Mrs Chivers frowned and Mia cut her off before another complaint could be raised. 'Why don't you go and join your husband on the patio, and I'll run out and tell Daniel to pack up for the day? I'll bring your tray straight afterwards.' Mrs Chivers pursed her lips, but didn't say anything else.

'Daniel?' Mia peered around the door of the barn, but didn't venture inside. He stood with his back to her, arms raised a bit above shoulder height as he drilled another hole in the wooden partition. The pose tightened his dusty T-shirt and she took a moment to admire the view. There was just something about a man working with his hands that made her shivery in all the right places. Not any man, though. Him. Daniel had a single-minded intensity he applied to every task, whether working or playing. But she had her guests to think of. Maybe later, when they were alone in their room on the third floor, she could find him some manual labour… She raised her voice over the drilling and called his name again.

The noise cut out, and he turned, tugging down his face mask to reveal his bright smile through the dark hair of his beard. 'Hello, love, everything all right?'

'Oh yes, just admiring your handiwork.' She cast him a fake-innocent look from under her lashes. 'I think the bulb in the bedroom overhead light needs changing.'

His rich, deep laugh curled around her like a caress. 'Behave yourself, woman. Did you come out here to admire the view?' He lifted the bottom of his shirt to wipe his brow, giving her a flash of tanned skin in the process.

'Ha! Now it's your turn to behave.' They shared a smile and the simple joy of the moment swelled in her heart. The art of flirting was yet another thing she'd assumed lost to her for ever when Jamie died. Such a little thing in the grand scheme, but each time they bantered like this, the bond between her and Daniel solidified a bit more. Learning what pleased the other, sharing a secret smile, using a codeword which meant nothing to anyone listening, but everything to them.

Covered in grime, damp hair clinging to his neck, clad in scruffy clothes and with his beard a few days past needing a trim, he looked a far cry from the pale, broken figure who'd landed on her doorstep five months previously. He looked fit and happy, with no trace of the shadows haunting his eyes, and if she could spend the rest of her days watching him grow and change, life would be good. Her stomach fluttered. Soon. She'd ask him soon. That was the deal between them.

Why not now?

She opened her mouth, but the question died on her tongue. Her guests were waiting, she had responsibilities and it seemed ridiculous to propose and run. Something as important as that should be done in a proper romantic setting, not a dusty barn. Calling herself ten types of coward, she rolled her eyes and imitated Mrs Chivers' best put-upon sigh. 'One simply can't enjoy afternoon tea on the patio with this racket going on.'

Daniel frowned. 'They're back early then?' She nodded and he shrugged.

'We knew it would be a balancing act. I'll finish up, then come and give you a hand with preparing dinner.'

Mia blew him a quick kiss. 'I've saved you a scone.'

His eyes lit up. 'And that's why I love you.'

Her tummy fluttered and danced. It was still new, hearing those words from his lips, knowing them to be an echo of her feelings for him. After Jamie, she hadn't expected, hadn't wanted, this again. Loving someone, needing them, meant risking losing them, and she couldn't go through that again. But Daniel had given her no choice. He'd stumbled into her life and into her heart when neither of them had their guard up. A pulse of blind fear struck. He'd been out here on his own, anything could have happened to him and it hadn't occurred to her to check. Accidents happened. That's what they said, and she damn well knew the aching, ugly truth of it.

Needing to break the spiral of her thoughts, she forced a wonky smile. 'It's my cooking you love.'

He closed the distance between them, no answering smile upon his face. 'Don't do that, don't deflect.' She tried to turn her head, but he caught her chin in a firm but gentle grip. 'What is it, what's put that look in your eyes?'

His features wavered through her suddenly watery gaze and she choked on the words. 'Nothing. I'm being silly.'

He pulled her into his arms and she snuggled into his chest, not caring about the dirt and dust covering his T-shirt. 'Talk to me,' he murmured against her temple.

The words came easier when she didn't have to see his face. 'I got scared. What if you fell off a ladder or cut through a cable or something? I didn't think to check and I should have, what if—'

'Breathe, Mia. Take a breath, love, before you work yourself up over nothing.' He stroked her back, rocking them both on the spot. 'I never climb when I'm on my own in here, I promise, and all the power tools are battery-operated. Jordy would throw me out on my ear if he thought I was doing stuff like that.'

She nodded into his shoulder, knowing he was right. Jordy had given them all a serious talking to about what he would and wouldn't accept if they took him on to run the project. 'I'm sorry, I'm being silly.' She sniffled, then laughed at the unattractive, wet sound. 'I think I made a mess on your shirt.'

'It's destined for the wash, anyway. Look at me.' He swiped his thumbs gently under her eyes to catch the tears shimmering there. 'I'm not invincible, love, but I promise to do everything I can to be careful. Being with you is a gift I'm not going to squander if I can help it.' He pressed a kiss to the tip of her nose, tickling her skin with his beard. 'So, you're stuck with me.'

Stretching on tiptoes she caught his lips with hers, for a brief, hot moment. 'I like being stuck with you.'

Keeping an arm around her shoulder, Daniel walked with her back across the yard. He left her with a quick kiss to take his shower, and she gave her hands and face a rinse at the sink. Setting out the tray, she hurried through the dining room and out through the patio doors. Her guests bracketed one of the wrought-iron tables she'd picked up at a local DIY centre. Daniel had glossed them brilliant white and the matching chairs were covered in thick, bright-red cushions, made by Madeline as a surprise gift. Her friend was an absolute marvel when it came to sewing and embroidery. Mia was learning, slowly, but she'd get there. One of the best things about refurbishing Butterfly House had been the chance to learn new skills, to challenge herself in a creative way. Her youngest sister, Nee, was the artist in the family, but it had been a surprise to Mia to find she had her own talents, too.

'This is lovely, dear.' Mr Chivers patted her hand then began to load his plate with sandwiches and scones.

'And not just the food, though I'll be on strict rations when we get home, won't I, Jen?' He winked at his wife.

'Silly old fool,' Mrs Chivers said, but there was real affection in her voice.

Undaunted, Mr Chivers continued. 'You've made a beautiful home here, inside and out.'

Mia smiled as a warm glow started inside. 'I can't take credit for the garden, my thumb is more brown than green. Luckily my friends and my in-laws have plenty of talent in that department. The garden and grounds are down to them. You should have seen the mess out here before.'

'In-laws?' Mrs Chivers' tone held a hint of something sly. 'I didn't realise you and your young man were married.' She nodded at Mia's naked fingers. 'No ring.'

This was another of those things she hadn't taken into account when she decided to open a guest house. Hotels were impersonal, anonymous places, but opening your home to people was different. They expected to get to know you, even over the space of a few days. No one had been rude, but she'd been surprised at how open people were, how much they shared with her, and the kinds of questions they asked in return.

'I was referring to my late husband's parents, Mrs Chivers. Daniel and I aren't married, yet.'

The iron legs of her chair scraped back and Mrs Chivers descended on Mia to gather her into a fierce hug. Shocked, and not altogether sure what to do, Mia returned the embrace with a tentative pat on her shoulder. Mrs Chivers pulled back. 'Oh, my dear, it's an absolute sod of a thing to lose the man you love. And you so young as well. At least I had thirty good years with my Tony.'

Mia couldn't stop herself from glancing between the older couple. She'd assumed they'd been together for years. Mr Chivers gave her a nod, his expression supremely unconcerned. 'That's right. I'm the also-ran. Jen and I had a thing donkey's years ago, but we drifted apart and found happiness with other partners. We ran into each other at one of those U3A clubs and it was like I'd seen her yesterday.'

Was that a blush on Mrs Chivers' cheeks? Mia found herself softening to the woman. Yes, she was an awkward customer, but there was a kind heart under there, too. She squeezed her arm gently. 'I'm glad you've found happiness again.'

Mrs Chivers touched her cheek. 'And you have, too, I hope, my dear?'

'Yes. Yes, I have.' A lump formed in her throat. If she wasn't careful, she'd get all weepy again. 'If you'll excuse me, I'll leave you in peace to enjoy your tea.'

Mrs Chivers gave her one more quick hug then let her go. Needing a few minutes to compose herself, Mia escaped down the path rather than returning to the house. The grey army had done an amazing job with the garden, and the flowerbeds were already bright with colour. The shrubs and bushes edging the garden shone with every shade of green, a verdant promise of more to come. Buddleia lined the back of the lawn, framing the steps which led to the beach. Mia paused, picturing them ripe with white and purple blossom, covered in dancing butterflies.

It would be the perfect backdrop for a late-summer wedding. Chairs on the lawn for guests during the ceremony and a barbecue on the beach afterwards. They could offer a package for couples wanting an intimate, more casual affair, and the harem suite would serve as an unusual wedding-night setting. Daniel might even be persuaded to take a couple of pictures, unique souvenirs of a special day.

Warmth enveloped her back, and his arms encircled her waist. 'I've been watching you for the past five minutes. You've got that look on your face. What are you planning?'

She glanced over her shoulder and the look of eager expectation on his face bowled her over. Whatever mad scheme she came up with, he would be first in line to cheer her on.

Not soon. Now.

'I'm thinking we could hold weddings here at Butterfly Cove. We'd have to give it a dry run ourselves, of course.'

The corners of Daniel's mouth kicked up and he repeated the words he'd said to her just a few feet away on the beach, the first time they'd made love. 'Mia Sutherland, are you asking me to marry you?'

'Yes, Daniel Fitzwilliams, I most certainly am.'

Chapter Four

The miles slipped past the train window, grey urban sprawl giving way to longer and longer stretches of green fields as the train took them east to west from London to Somerset. It was the same route they used when travelling to stay with their friends in Butterfly Cove, and Aaron wished they were heading further south to that peaceful spot on the coast rather than their actual destination. Luke sat opposite him, head resting against the window, eyes closed as he nodded along to whatever he was listening to through his headphones. A study in relaxation, if you could ignore his fingers drumming against his thigh. Aaron swallowed a sigh. Going home shouldn't feel like a duty, but he'd dodged every invitation since Christmas. Maybe Cathy would be too busy being the centre of attention to bother with him.

It wasn't fair. And yes, that made him sound like a whiny little kid instead of a grown man of nearly thirty, but damn it, it *wasn't* fair. He loved his dad, adored his brother and would have loved Cathy, too, if she'd let him, but the time for that was long past. He'd settle for friendship; hell, he'd settle for being politely ignored. Anything would be a respite from the smiling barbs and digs. Each time he crossed the threshold of the one place on earth he should feel safe and happy, he swore he wouldn't rise to the bait. He'd be like Teflon and let it all just slide right off him. Shrug and smile, move past it and let Dad and Luke breathe easier.

His fingers clenched around the small box in his pocket. The sharp corners dug into his skin to the point of pain. He could tell himself a hundred times he didn't care, that he didn't need her approval, her affection, but it was a lie. The cost of the gold Pandora charm in the box proved it. How many times would he do this to himself? Memories flashed of homemade cards hidden behind others on the mantelpiece, of flowers purchased with preciously hoarded pocket money left to wilt without water. Then there was the jumper she'd admired in a shop window which somehow ended up with a hole in it the first time she wore it. All easily explained away as silly accidents, but somehow it only ever happened with gifts from Aaron.

A nudge to his foot startled him and he blinked the burn from his eyes. Luke stared at him across the little table between them, a deep furrow between his brows. His headphones were looped around his neck and faint, tinny music echoed from them. 'You don't have to keep doing this, you know.' As much as he loved his mum, Luke was under no illusions about her animosity towards Aaron.

'Yeah, I do.'

Luke shook his head. 'You really are a glutton for punishment. Ah, sod that, let's talk about something else. Are you going to tell Dad about the cottage?'

Ah yes, in just one week's time he'd be the proud new owner of Honeysuckle Cottage. His offer had been half in jest. He'd assumed, once they'd had a chance to think about it, that Karen and Dave would put the property on the market. Orcombe's location made it a prime destination for eager weekend commuters looking to escape city life. However, they'd settled for a quick, easy sale instead and, thanks to the miracle of two solicitors who had heeded their clients' instructions about concluding the deal swiftly, they were in the final stages of exchanging. His investments had been cashed in for the deposit and he was the sole holder of an eye-watering mortgage. The monthly payments were less than his current rent, so it wasn't like he'd overextended himself. It was just the overall figure that made his knees a bit wobbly.

It had been too good an opportunity to pass up and, if he changed his mind, he could do the place up and put it back on the market. 'If I get some time alone with him, I will.'

Luke leaned forward to rest his arms on the table. 'So, you can tell me to mind my own business, but how are you going to afford two places? The rent on my flat is sucking my will to live, along with the bulk of my salary.'

'I'm giving up the flat.' Saying it out loud, acknowledging the truth of what he'd been doing over the past few weeks, sent his stomach roiling. It wasn't only his flat he'd given notice on.

His brother sat back in his seat. 'You can't be thinking of commuting from Orcombe every day.' Aaron stayed silent, watching the thought process play out on Luke's face. There was a reason he was crap at poker. 'Oh.' Luke glanced out of the window and back again. Red splotches sat high on his cheekbones and, when he spoke, there was a thread of anger in his tone. 'So, when were you going to tell me?'

'Come on, Spud, don't be like that. I've barely got to grips with this myself.' Aaron shrugged his shoulders, not liking the guilt weighing on them. Luke was a grown man, they had their own lives. He tugged at the collar of his shirt. 'Is it me, or is it hot in here?'

Luke had chosen to study and then live in London in direct opposition to his mother's wishes. There'd been tears and recriminations for weeks and his brother had faced it all with remarkable stoicism. He was the only person immune to Cathy's attempts at manipulation, and the only one she would forgive anything. And, in his heart, Aaron knew Luke had chosen London to be near him, an open declaration of support and an enormous *eff you* to his mother. He owed him better than this. 'I didn't plan for this to happen, but the cottage was too good an opportunity to pass up, and I've been feeling out of sorts for a while.'

His brother scrubbed his face with his hands, like he was trying to erase the anger bubbling. 'What will you do for work?'

Aaron shrugged. 'I'll try and increase my freelance stuff, take a financial advisor's course to expand my range. It's a prime area for older people and those looking to retire, and with all the changes the government's been making to pensions, there's a market for it. I might even look at mortgage brokering in time. If going independent doesn't pan out, then I'll look for an accountancy firm in the area.' That was his least-preferred choice, but at least his qualifications were transferable to anywhere in the country. Coming home to his own place, setting down some roots and becoming part of a community would be worth almost any price.

Luke chewed his bottom lip as he stared into the middle distance. His thinking-face, their dad called it. Aaron grinned as a memory drifted up of Luke sitting at the kitchen table, the exact same expression screwing up his little features, legs swinging back and forth as he tried to puzzle his way through his maths homework. He'd sit there for hours before asking for help, stubborn little sod. A fierce rush of love and pride flooded him. 'You could do it, too, you know.' His soft words startled Luke's vacant stare back into focus.

'Do what? Have some kind of emotional breakdown and chuck everything I've worked for away?'

Aaron laughed. 'Nah, leave that to Daniel.' He reached out to cover Luke's hand with his own, holding his gaze as he let the smile fall from his lips. 'I'm serious. I've never known anyone who works harder than you when you set your mind to it. Think about how much fun we've had down at Butterfly Cove. Your designs for the studios are brilliant.'

Luke snorted. 'I can't just open my own firm of architects, I don't have the experience, or the finances, to do it.'

'So do something different, expand your options same as I'm doing. Project management, design jobs for small tradesmen like Jordy and his dad. Lots of little things to keep busy and build a client base.'

Luke shook his head. 'This is your adventure, Aaron, not mine. I can't live in your shadow for ever.'

Is that what he thought he'd been doing? 'Then don't. Take your place beside me where you belong.' His mind raced a mile a minute, building on the possibilities. His voice rose in excitement. 'Imagine it – Spenser Brothers Limited. You and me against the world, Spud!'

Luke shook his head again, but he couldn't stop the broad grin lifting the corners of his mouth. 'You're off your head.'

'Probably. You in?'

'Why the hell not?'

***

Aaron paced the kitchen, checked his watch again and sighed. He hated being late, to the point of irritating friends and acquaintances with his need for punctuality. Those who knew him well often gave him a later meeting time so he didn't arrive miles before anyone else. Laughter carried from the living room where his dad and Luke were watching a sitcom while they waited. The mistress of the grand entrance, Cathy would be at least another ten minutes. Needing to do something, he grabbed a couple of bottles of beer from the fridge and went to join the others.

Luke took the offered beer, then leaned to one side to see the screen when Aaron didn't move quickly enough. Knowing his reputation as an annoying big brother depended upon it, Aaron stood his ground, taking his time to pop the lids off the remaining two beers and handing the spare to his dad.

'Shift your arse!' Luke kicked him none too gently in the shin.

Aaron stayed put. 'It's not like you haven't seen it before.'

'That's not the point.'

He bit the inside of his cheek so as not to laugh. They'd slipped into the same banter routine they'd been throwing at each other for the past twenty-odd years. 'Then what is the point?'

'Daaad!' Luke whined, sending them both into gales of laughter.

'How old are you two?' Brian Spenser made a fair attempt at his best stern-dad voice before giving up and taking a mouthful of his beer. 'Sit down, Bumble, you're making the place look untidy.' Aaron's grandmother had knitted him a black-and-yellow-striped jumper when he was a baby. Mum had said it made him look like a bumblebee, and the name had stuck. He was years past such a childish nickname, but he and his dad both clung to it. A shared connection to his mum, of which they had precious few.

Aaron plonked himself down on the sofa next to Luke, still grinning. The silly moment had loosened the tension from his shoulders and he relaxed deeper into the cushion behind him. Cathy was as Cathy did and it was stupid to get wound up over something he would excuse in any of his friends.

An advert break interrupted the sitcom, and his dad got up and crossed the room to lean out into the hallway. 'Come on, darling. The table was booked for five minutes ago,' he called up the stairs. The local pub was only a few minutes' walk down the road and boasted an exceptionally good restaurant. They were regular customers so the landlord wouldn't give away their booking at least.

'All right, all right, you don't have to shout.' Aaron lifted his head, following her progress through the familiar creaks of the upper floorboards. He could still remember the location of each loose one—one step outside the bathroom, two from his bedroom door. There'd been more than one late night/early morning when he'd tiptoed around them because he was out past his curfew.

His dad stepped back into the centre of the living room, a smile on his face and a brightness in his eye. 'You look lovely, darling.'

Cathy wafted in on a cloud of her signature perfume and did a little twirl. Aaron had to admit, his dad was right. Still slim and fit from her regular sessions in the gym they'd installed in the spare bedroom, Cathy always made the most of herself. The coffee-coloured silk blouse she wore brought a warmth to her skin and looked good tucked into a pair of slim-legged taupe trousers. Wedged sandals gave her a bit of extra height, something she needed because the three of them topped out at six feet. Her deftly highlighted hair was caught up in some kind of fancy knot at the nape of her neck. Jewellery shone at her ears, throat and wrist.

Brian caught her hand and drew it to his lips in a courtly gesture, and a delicate blush highlighted her cheeks. Whatever issues Aaron and she might have, the love his father and stepmother shared for each other was honest and true. His dad held on to Cathy's hand, turning it left and right with a frown. 'Where's your new bead?'

The comment drew Aaron's attention to the charm bracelet on her wrist, and a familiar icy sensation gripped his stomach. The glittering band around her arm was the one Luke had bought her for Christmas, the one Aaron had spent ages making sure he'd selected the correct style of bead for. Cathy tugged her hand, trying to free it, but Brian refused to let go. She heaved an aggrieved sigh. 'I don't know what you're making a fuss about. I said thank you to Aaron for my gift. It just didn't match my outfit.'

But the mix of blue, red and silver beads threaded onto the thin band did, apparently. Aaron took a deep swig from his beer to keep the sarcastic snap in his head.

'Mum.' Luke sounded exasperated, and not a little angry.

Christ, if he didn't do something, they'd be having a full-blown argument. Aaron heaved himself up from the deep cushions and stepped to Cathy's side. Bending his head, he brushed a quick kiss on her cheek. 'You look great, Cathy. It's your birthday and you should wear whatever you want.' He managed to keep his tone light, but anyone who looked at him would be able to see the muscle he could feel ticking in his jaw. Aaron escaped to the kitchen to dump his bottle and gather his cool.

The rest of the evening stretched out before him. Dad and Luke would carry the conversation, expanding it to include Aaron because Cathy would focus almost exclusively on her son and his life. He could picture her reaction to his and Luke's plans. Wide-eyed shock that Aaron would expect Luke to risk his promising career and fall in with him. She'd tilt her head, and purse her lips as she pleaded with their dad to talk sense into them. His excitement over the future turned sour in his mouth. And just like that, he was done.

Getting upset over the bead was pointless. It was just one more thing in a lifetime of small snubs. It was always his cards to her that somehow ended up at the back of the mantelpiece; the flowers *he* gave her that drooped and died in a few days. His gifts which lay neglected and forgotten, tucked away in the back of her drawer. She'd always done her duty by him, helped with his homework, nursed him when he was sick, keeping him at arm's length all the while. The ever-hopeful child within him had never quite given up, though.

Until now.

Cathy would never do more than tolerate his presence, would never fill the void his mum had left in his life. He didn't know why she couldn't love him, but it was past time he stopped trying to win her over. He pushed away from the sink, skirting the three of them where they waited in the hallway. Tension hung thick in the air, a strain none of them would be feeling if he wasn't there. Things between Aaron and Cathy would never be better, so why keep trying when Dad and Luke got caught in the crossfire?

'I don't feel too well and I don't want to spoil dinner, so the three of you should go without me.'

'Aaron...' His dad stood in the hallway, hands shoved in his pockets, confusion and sadness on his face.

'It's all right, Dad. I've been trying to ignore this headache all day, but I think it's going to be a bad one. I'll have an early night and we can catch up in the morning.'

He glanced past his dad to Cathy, forcing an empty smile. 'I don't mean to be a party pooper. Make sure they spoil you properly, okay?'

She managed a faint look of concern, but it didn't disguise the flicker of relief in her eyes. 'Do you need anything before we go?'

'I'll grab a couple of tablets and a drink of water.' Avoiding the suspicious gaze of his brother, Aaron shooed them out with repeated assurances, then closed the door with a sense of finality. After thirty years, it was time to acknowledge the truth. This house wasn't home any more. It was time to make his own.

Chapter Five

If anyone had asked her two weeks previously, Kiki would've told them she was an honest person. She'd never learned the art of lying, even as a self-defence mechanism. If she'd taken to heart the lessons in deceit her mother had demonstrated to her, perhaps things might have turned out differently. But no, Kiki had had to be the one to try and see the best in everyone, to build bridges and mend fences, taking on the blame more often than not in the process. How she'd envied Mia's determination and Nee's fiery spirit. When they'd been dishing out backbone, Kiki had somehow stood in the wrong queue.

The change, when it came, was so sudden, so surprising to her given all the times she'd turned the other cheek, she understood what people meant when they talked about reaching 'breaking point'. Even at his worst, when the words he spat wounded her deeper than the occasional slap or punch, she had assumed Neil loved her. A twisted, ugly kind of love, but love just the same. So, she'd convinced herself that trying a little harder, finding another excuse for him when he had none of his own to give, would nurture their stunted relationship into something beautiful.

But she was like the little pig in the storybook, building her house of love from straw, stacking the fragile stalks into piles to be blown down again and again. Fear, doubt, and not a little jealousy had prevented her from examining why Mia's relationship with Jamie had been forged in brick and stone, solid enough to stand against everything except the cruelties of fate. She listened instead to the other mothers at the school gate, who moaned about their husbands and convinced herself all relationships had troubles.

Two words.

Two words had been all it took for the scales to fall from her eyes. Two stupid little words. Two precious little words she'd tucked away in her heart the first time Neil had whispered them into the ear of an innocent, lovestruck girl. *My Helen.* Having been raised on the tales of the ancient Greek heroes, there was only one Helen. The woman so beautiful that men had burned the world for her. When Neil had likened her to that mythical siren, it had turned her head and won her completely. Two words meant only for her, she'd assumed until she'd read those bloody awful emails and seen the truth—her husband was a liar, his declaration of true love nothing more than a tawdry cliché designed to get her, and God only knew how many other women, into his bed.

And so, for the past two weeks, she'd smiled her way through the frantic preparations for Neil's trip, washing, ironing and packing his clothes. Not a word of dissent had passed her lips as she collected the lists of books he left her, marking the sections that would most help with his research. It was like the old days, when she'd given up her own studies to help him through his PhD. Only this was no labour of love. Volunteering to help him gave her the perfect excuse to spend precious hours in his study without raising suspicion.

For every piece of information she prepared for him, she squirreled away one of her own. Passwords, account details, balances; all the things she'd been 'too stupid' to deal with, according to Neil—she made them her own. For every shirt of his she neatly folded, she packed something belonging to the kids into the boot of her car. Like the little mouse everyone believed her to be, she burrowed and sneaked around, a dull little thing, not worthy of notice. Soon, the little mouse would roar.

Being underestimated by everyone had turned out to be the perfect cover. Clad in her usual tidy uniform of a matching skirt and blouse, hair rolled into a discreet bun at the nape of her neck, she sat on a visitor's chair in the school office and waited for the head teacher to be free. She clenched her fingers around the handle of the bag resting in her lap to prevent herself from fiddling with the hem of her skirt.

'She shouldn't be too much longer.' The secretary offered an apologetic glance at the clock on the wall as the minute hand clicked loudly to mark quarter past the hour.

All those years of being subjected to her mother's play-acting were finally paying off. Kiki pictured Vivian supine on the small couch beneath her window, a soft blanket over her legs, and an empty glass resting on the table beside her. *'Mummy needs her special drink, darling. I've got such a terrible pain in my head.'*

Kiki gripped her handbag until her knuckles turned white. With hindsight, the catch in her mother's voice, the flutter of her hand as it gestured to her glass, had been a performance worthy of the stage. To a worried six-year-old girl, though, it had been all too real. Vivian could even cry on demand—nothing too drastic in case it spoiled her delicate complexion, just enough for a few tears to shimmer on her lashes as she whispered, *'You want to help me, don't you, Kiki? You want to be a good girl for Mummy.'*

Swallowing the bad taste in her mouth, Kiki fixed her mind on her end goal and let her voice drop almost to a whisper. 'I hope not. We still have so much to put in place.' She returned the woman's sympathetic smile with just the right amount of wavering in her own. Vivian at her manipulative best couldn't beat the performance she'd been laying on since she'd hurried into the office. Angela Baines was a pleasant enough woman, but a notorious gossip—always had been. If you wanted a rumour to race around the playground, a word dropped in her ear was all it took.

Angela had lapped up Kiki's tale with alacrity. A contemporary of theirs, she remembered the details of Jamie's death, *'so young, such a tragedy.'* It hadn't taken much to convince her Mia was struggling to come to terms with it still. Swallowing down the lump of guilt, Kiki had taken her sister's name in vain, dropping enough vague hints for Angela to fill in the gaps and assume Kiki had no choice but to carry out a mercy dash to the coast before the very worst happened. She could only hope Mrs Wilson was as gullible.

The inner door swung open and Kiki stood. She paused to place a silent hand of thanks on Angela's shoulder, and to accept the returning pat of sympathy, before following Mrs Wilson into her inner sanctum. Nothing appeared to have changed in the twenty years since she and her sisters had been pupils here. The carefully drawn pictures pinned to the noticeboard were different, but the sentiment behind them struck a chord of memory.

Following Kiki's gaze, Mrs Wilson cast a glance over her shoulder. 'I had one of Nee's drawings up there back in the day. It's in the cupboard somewhere. Perhaps I should dig it out and boost my retirement savings.'

Kiki allowed herself to smile. She couldn't image Mrs Wilson cashing in on any of her beloved mementos. 'You might need to hang on to it for a few more years, but we have great hopes for her. She's studying in New York, did you hear?'

'No, I hadn't. How exciting for her.' Mrs Wilson sat back and folded her arms. 'I understand Mia is making a new start for herself.'

Kiki stared down at her lap. Here was the perfect opening she needed, a few choice words and she could conclude her business. Another item ticked off her secret to-do list. So what if she couldn't look the woman in the eye and lie? Kiki Jackson, the timid little mouse, rarely did eye contact at the best of times. She opened her mouth, then closed it again when the words stuck in her throat. It didn't seem right, to diminish her sister when she had shown nothing but courage in the face of so much suffering. Maybe there was no need for lies.

'She is. I need to go and stay with her and, with Neil going overseas for work, I can't leave the children. I know it's not long until the holidays, but it can't wait. A person can only endure so much before they buckle under the weight of things. A person's life shouldn't feel like it's over before they're thirty, right? It shouldn't be impossible for a person to ask their family to help them correct a mistake.' Words spoken from the heart, they could be interpreted by the listener in myriad ways.

The springs in Mrs Wilson's chair creaked as she shifted around, and Kiki risked a quick glance up through her lashes. The older woman rested her arms on the blotter in front of her and folded her fingers together. 'No, my dear. Family should come first, above all things. If you need to join your sister, then I'm sure we can reach some accommodation with Matthew's schooling. We try to wind the children down over the last couple of weeks before the holidays. I'll consult his teacher and we'll forward you anything he needs to catch up on.'

Kiki swallowed around the lump in her throat. 'Thank you, Mrs Wilson. I'd wait if I could, but I've almost left it too long as it is.' Another truth. If she didn't stand up for herself now, she never would. The children deserved better. What example was she setting to them, and what legacy would they inherit, if she continued to mimic her own parents and remain in a failed relationship?

'Can we expect to see Matthew back for the new term?'

No. 'I'm not in a position to confirm that. It depends how things go over the next few weeks. I'll notify you as soon as I can.' Even that prevarication tasted bitter on her tongue.

The glint in Mrs Wilson's eye said she'd caught it, but her tone remained as mild as her words. 'You just let me know when you know. If you need recommendations for schools in the area, don't hesitate to ask and I'll make some enquiries.' She leaned further across the table, brows drawn together, no sign of the sweet, soft lady in her sharp eyes. 'A change of scenery might be just what Matthew needs, he's been quite withdrawn lately.'

Guilt wrenched Kiki's insides. It shouldn't have taken the shattering of her own dreams to spur her into action.

She should have been braver, acted sooner. Matty and Charlie needed her to protect them and, so far, she'd done a terrible job of it. No more. She sat up straight. 'I think it's going to be exactly what we all need.'

***

Neil stepped out of their bathroom, a towel wrapped around his waist. He played squash several times a week during his lunchbreak and had retained the same attractive physique she'd once marvelled over. He paused at the sight of his clothes laid out across the bed, the steaming cup of coffee waiting on his bedside cabinet. Kiki bit the inside of her cheek to keep a bitter smile at bay. In shattering her to pieces, Neil had finally achieved the perfect wife. She'd not set a foot wrong in the past two weeks, anticipating his every need before he'd even thought about it. 'I've double-checked with the taxi company; your car will be here in half an hour.'

'Good.' He let the towel drop and began to dress. The wet tangle on the carpet taunted her, and Kiki forced herself to turn away, knowing if he glanced her way he would see the hatred seething inside her. The perfect wife would scuttle forward, pick it up and hang it back in the bathroom. The perfect wife wouldn't imagine grabbing the cup of coffee and dashing the scalding contents into his eyes.

She'd never be perfect, it seemed. 'Do you want anything to eat?'

Neil glanced up from the act of knotting his tie. 'What? No. I'll get something at the airport once I'm through security.'

Washed down with champagne, probably. He'd never spared his wallet when he'd been wooing her. No doubt *the new Helen* would receive the same treatment. A better person would warn the foolish girl, would contact the university and report Neil for exploiting a position of trust. Kiki had considered it, but at the end of the day, a roaring mouse was still just a mouse. A better person would confront her husband, tell him the truth and walk away with her head held high. She'd scuttle away once the coast was clear and count herself lucky for it.

She watched him turn left and right, checking the hang of his jacket. A piece of fluff clung to one shoulder and she stepped forward to remove it. Their eyes met in the mirror and she searched for one hint of the man she'd thought to spend the rest of her life with. His even, handsome features were as familiar to her as her own, and yet she knew nothing about the person beneath the flesh. How was it possible? How could she have devoted the past nine years to a stranger? Unbidden, her fingers traced the top of his shoulder, seeking proof there had once been a connection between the two of them. A frown creased his brow and he shrugged off her hand. 'Don't fuss, Kiki. I hate it when you fuss.'

Don't fuss. How many times had he said that to her? About as many times as he'd accused her of neglecting him. No matter what she did, she'd always be on the wrong side of him. She folded her fingers into a fist and pressed it into the top of her thigh. 'I'll wake the children and we'll see you downstairs when you're ready.'

'Let them sleep. I can't be doing with them whining around me.'

The perfect-wife mask slipped a little. 'You're going to be away for three months, Neil. I thought you might want to say goodbye to them.'

'Christ, Kiki. I can do without a fucking guilt trip. What do you want me to do, give up the opportunity I've waited my whole career for?' He took a step towards her and she shrank back, an instinctive response intended to defuse the situation, but it only served to stoke his temper. 'I've licked your father's boots for years to get this grant, given you everything you needed even after you hung the weight of a family around my neck, but you can't let me enjoy one thing that isn't about you. You stupid, selfish bitch—' The beep of a car horn outside cut him off, the promised taxi having arrived early.

Neil straightened up, ran a hand over his hair to smooth it back into place and rolled his shoulders. He snatched his wallet and keys from beside the bed and stuffed them into his pockets. 'Great job, Kiki. All I wanted was a calm, quiet departure and you couldn't even give me that.'

'I'm sorry.' He'd already shouldered his way out of the door, but the words weren't meant for him. They were for herself, for the idealistic girl who'd deserved a man who loved her. For her children, who meant everything to her and yet so little to him. For Mia, whose love and support she'd almost thrown away.

The front door slammed and quiet voices drifted from the street below her window. Checking her watch, Kiki gave the departing taxi five minutes in case Neil had forgotten anything in his haste to leave. Satisfied he was gone, she crouched beside the bed and dragged out her own already-packed case. Her self-imposed timetable gave her two hours to finish loading the car, get the kids up and ready and their journey started. She wanted to be on the motorway the moment the rush-hour traffic eased.

She left Matty to supervise Charlie's breakfast while she ensconced herself in Neil's study. They didn't know what was happening beyond the fact there would be no school today. She hadn't wanted to get their hopes up until she knew for sure what the next step would be. Her hand clenched around her mobile, hard enough for the corners to dig into her palm. By rights, the call she was about to make should have been made two weeks ago, but she hadn't dared. Escaping to Mia had been her only plan, and belief there was a place for them in Butterfly Cove the only thing that kept her moving forward.

Whispering a silent prayer, she scrolled through her favourites and tapped on her sister's name. It was early to be calling, but she hoped Mia would be up. The ringtone echoed in her ear just long enough for the nerves to start dancing in her stomach, and then a deep voice answered. 'Butterfly House, hello?'

Kiki cleared her dry throat. 'Hello, can I speak to Mia, please?'

'You've just missed her, I'm afraid. Gone to catch the early train to Exeter. Is there something I can help you with?'

She hesitated. The voice of the man at the other end of the phone had a soft West Country burr to it. Hadn't Mia said Daniel came from somewhere in the north of England? 'Daniel?'

'Nope.' A kind chuckle softened the denial. 'This is a really bad game of twenty questions. My name's Aaron, I'm a friend of theirs, a neighbour, too, I suppose you could say. What did you say your name was?'

She hadn't. 'I'm Kiki.' She hesitated for a second. 'Mia's sister.'

'Ah, yes.' The way he said it sounded like he knew who she was, which left her wondering what else he knew about her. She sank back into her chair. In all the scenarios she'd played out in her mind, she hadn't once assumed her sister wouldn't be there when she needed her.

Heat prickled behind her eyes and she bit her lip when it started to wobble. 'Do… do you know when Mia will be back?'

'She's gone dress shopping with Madeline, so it could be all day. Butterfly House is booked solid for the season, so this is one of her few chances to get out and about.' *Dress shopping?* Mia's wardrobe ran to jeans and jumpers in the winter and shorts and vest tops in the summer. There was something about the inflection in his voice, the way he had stressed the word. If she was *dress* shopping… A sob escaped her as the realisation struck. They'd become so estranged she didn't even know her sister was getting married again. She'd waited too long to respond to the messages of support. The unanswered texts lurking in the inbox on her phone.

At first, she'd been too angry, too blinded by her own shame to reply to Mia's overtures after the fight they'd had during her recent visit home. As the days slipped by, the anger had faded and she'd promised herself she would answer… tomorrow. Pat and Bill had called, even taken the children out for the day, and she had taken it as a sign Mia still cared. That she still had time to build bridges between them.

Of course, Mia still cared. Brushing aside her hurt, she focused on the more critical piece of information Aaron had imparted. It sounded like Mia's new venture was already a success. Fully booked could mean only one thing—there would be no room for her and the kids. She shivered, as though a cold wind had blown over her and her plans scattered like straw on the wind once more. The last thing Mia needed was her barging in and causing chaos. Kiki tried to stem her tears, but it was like she'd opened the flood gates and didn't know how to close them again.

Chapter Six

Aaron cursed a blue streak in his head as he listened to the quiet, desperate sobs in his ear. He should have left well enough alone and let the answerphone catch the call. Head buried in the plans for the barn while he sipped his coffee and waited for Daniel to return from running Mia to the station, he hadn't even thought about what he was doing when the handset on the table started to ring. He didn't know much about Kiki; Daniel had mentioned some estrangement between the sisters to do with Kiki's marriage, but hadn't gone into details. Instead of minding his own business, he'd blathered on, shoving both feet firmly into his mouth, it seemed, by mentioning the reason behind Mia's trip to Exeter.

A harsh, wracking noise ripped from her throat, so pain-filled it hurt to listen to it, and Aaron couldn't help himself. 'Is there anything I can do to help you?'

'He… he's gone now. Gone for the summer and I waited… I thought it would be best to wait… and I just assumed it would be okay…'

He tried to make sense of the jumble of words. 'Who's gone? Your husband?'

'Yes... yes, with his new Helen.' More tears followed and he gave up trying to understand the broken sounds she was making.

Feeling wretched and useless, he offered what comfort he could. 'It's all right, Kiki. Everything will be all right. Don't try and talk, just let it out for a minute. Shh, now.' He continued to mutter whatever soothing nonsense words came into his head until she finally grew quiet.

'I shouldn't bother you with this,' she managed at last.

'Just talk to me, Kiki. You sound like you need a friend.'

She laughed, a hollow little sound that stabbed him deep, as though the concept of a friend was alien to her. When things had gone to hell on Cathy's birthday he'd jumped on the train to Butterfly Cove without a second thought, knowing Daniel and Mia would be there for him. What must it be like to not have a security net of friends you could turn to? He tried another tack. 'Mia has her mobile with her. Why don't you call her?'

'I can't. She doesn't need me spoiling her day.' The hopelessness in her tone stirred something ugly in his gut. Someone had done a real job on this woman if she honestly believed her sister would resent her reaching out when she was in such obvious need. If Luke ever tried to hide anything like this from him, he'd wring his bloody neck.

'Then tell me. Whatever it is, we'll find a way to fix it.'

She laughed a second time and if he never heard the bitter, mirthless sound again it would be too soon. 'I'm leaving my husband. Well, I'm trying to, but I can't even manage to do that properly. I assumed there would be room for me and the children at Mia's, but you know what they say about assuming anything… Oh God, Neil was right, I am *stupid*.'

When he had time to think about it later, he couldn't decide what made him say his next words. Whether out of loyalty to his friendship with Daniel and Mia, or his horror at hearing another person speak about themselves with such self-loathing, or his own vulnerability after losing the only place he'd ever really thought of as home, he didn't know. 'You can stay with me.'

Shocked silence. Then, 'Don't be ridiculous.'

He tucked the phone under his ear and leaned back in the kitchen chair. 'What's ridiculous? I'm the proud new owner of a four-bedroom cottage, which is less than two miles from your sister's doorstep. I'll be out most of the time, either meeting with clients for work or here helping Daniel with the barn. I can probably move into one of the attic rooms at Butterfly House if you'd rather have the place to yourself.'

'I couldn't possibly turn you out of your own home.' She sounded thoughtful, though, which was a step up from outright rejection.

'You have two children to think of, Kiki. You can do whatever you need to. When were you hoping to travel down?'

'The car's already packed.' Her sheepish admission settled it as far as he was concerned.

'Then come.' The back door opened and his eyes met his best friend's. 'Daniel's here now and he agrees with me. Get in the car and drive. You've made the hard decision and everyone here will help you in whatever way you need.' He let his absolute conviction ring through his words. He knew Mia and Daniel would back him, Madeline and Richard, too. They'd pulled together when Daniel had needed them to resolve the crisis at the gallery caused by his former agent trying to sell his photographs behind his back, and they would do so again to help this poor lonely woman.

'You make it sound so easy.'

Aaron shook his head, even though she couldn't see him. He'd never had a serious enough relationship to endure a messy break-up, but he understood loss better than most. 'It'll get worse before it gets better. But at least you won't have to face it on your own.'

'Mummy? Who are you talking to?' The faint voice of a young boy reached his ears.

'I'm talking to a new friend of ours, Matty. How would you like to go and stay near Aunty Mia for a while?' Relief flooded him at her words. She was going to come.

Aaron listened to the excited chatter for a few moments before interrupting. 'Kiki, do you have a pen?... Good. Write down my number and send me a text when you're on your way.' He reeled off the digits, making her repeat them back to him before ending the call.

He looked up at Daniel who was standing next to his chair, arms folded across his chest. His friend inclined his head towards the phone. 'Mia's sister?'

Aaron nodded. 'She's in a bit of state, trying to leave her husband and had a bit of a panic when she couldn't get hold of Mia.'

He took the pronouncement more calmly than Aaron expected. Clearly, he knew more about the circumstances surrounding Kiki's decision to leave her husband. 'And she's definitely coming?'

'She's promised to text before she sets off.'

Daniel scrubbed a hand through the close-cropped beard covering his chin. There might be one or two threads of silver showing in the dark hair, but Aaron didn't think he had looked better in years. Mia had saved him, taken him in when he hit rock bottom and given Aaron something invaluable back in return—his best friend. If he could do even a fraction of the same for her and Kiki, he'd move heaven and earth in the process. Daniel stood. 'Let me know when you hear from her and I'll speak to Mia.'

Aaron nodded. 'Of course. I meant what I said to her. She can stay at Honeysuckle Cottage for as long as she needs to.' It was fully furnished, even if the décor was outdated and a little tired. Dave and Karen had left the bedrooms mostly intact and the contents of his flat had been enough to fill the gaps created by the furniture they'd taken with them. Single man and spinster might be a clash of styles, but he doubted the children would notice, or that Kiki would care about any decorative shortcomings. There was plenty of food in the fridge and it would take five minutes to make the beds up if Kiki took him up on the offer of a place to stay.

Daniel nodded. 'Cheers, mate. We'll let them sort it out between them when she gets here.' He checked his watch. 'Jordy will be here with the lads any minute, might as well get on while we can.'

Aaron had just crossed the yard to the barns with a thermos full of coffee when the phone in his pocket began to vibrate. He fished it out, unable to stop a sigh of relief at the three-word message from an unknown number. *On our way*. Continuing inside, he showed the message to Daniel, then made his way over to where their young project manager waited. 'Where do you want me?'

'First floor, if that's all right with you? Plaster should be dry enough to start undercoating in Suite One.' Suite sounded grand for the studio apartments which would house visiting artists, but the specs Daniel planned for them were of a high enough quality to carry it off. The main painting would be carried out by qualified contractors, but Aaron was happy to turn his hand to the grunt work where a strong back and decent work ethic were all the skill a man required.

He grabbed a pair of loose-fitting white overalls and tugged them on over his shorts and shirt, then made his way up the temporary staircase to the mezzanine above. Some helpful soul had already taped dust cloths across the newly laid laminate flooring. A box of disposable shoe covers sat on the table next to an industrial tin of undercoat and a set of rollers. Music drifted from an adjacent room, a familiar song already threatening to be one of those catchy summer hits the stations seemed to play every five minutes. It was still just the right side of new enough not to be annoying and he hummed along to the tune as he started to work. If he tried hard enough, he might even convince himself it was just a day like any other, though the flutter of anticipation in his gut told a different story.

He received two more texts during the day from Kiki, noting her progress when she stopped for petrol and a break. Richard had been dispatched to the station to collect his wife and Mia, and the two women were busy in the kitchen cooking up a welcome meal. Mia was insistent that Kiki should stay at Butterfly House, and Aaron had left Daniel to argue it out with her. Personally, he agreed with his friend that cancelling guests was a bad move so early into a new venture, but it wasn't his call to make.

Richard had agreed with him and they'd retreated to the barn to tidy things away. It was make-work really, as Jordy ran a tight crew and they kept the work area in good order, but it would keep them out of trouble. Madeline had no such qualms about voicing her opinion and agreed with Daniel that Honeysuckle Cottage would be the best place for the new arrivals.

She'd even gone so far as to offer Aaron a room at their place, and a small, selfish part of him hoped Kiki would take the cottage just so he could have Madeline fussing around him. She was a force of nature, a whirlwind of kindness who'd swept both Aaron and Luke into her makeshift family. Her affection for him was a bittersweet balm to the wounded boy who lurked in his soul. If only Cathy could do the same.

'If wishes were horses, beggars would ride,' he murmured under his breath. Gravel crunched outside and he and Richard gravitated towards the open door of the barn. A dark-blue hatchback sat on the driveway. Sunlight reflected off the windscreen, making it impossible to see the interior. Aaron started towards it, but hung back when the kitchen door of Butterfly House flew open, disgorging Mia, with Daniel and Madeline close on her heels. She ran for the car and tugged the driver's door open with a cry of welcome.

'Stand back, darling, give poor Kiki chance to get out.' Daniel placed his hand on Mia's shoulder urging her to make some space.

A slender figure emerged, and Aaron found he'd closed the distance between himself and the car without noticing. The woman, *Kiki*, skirted the open door and half fell into her sister's waiting arms. Her profile afforded him teasing glimpses of her features, a button nose, the same slightly prominent chin which gave Mia's face a heart shape. Same deep-brown hair, although Kiki's looked a lot longer than Mia's spiky mop from the tangled knot at the back of her head.

Gentle sobs rose from the pair, but when Kiki lifted her head to glance at him over her sister's shoulder, her cheek was tear-free. He raised a hand, and she offered him the ghost of a smile. His chest grew tight; the tiny tilt of her lips transformed her face. Too pale, too haunted with those dark shadows ringing her eyes, but damn, she might just be the most beautiful woman he'd ever seen. A beautiful woman who wasn't even a day free of her unhappy marriage. *Get a bloody grip, Spenser.*

'Mummy?' A little boy, his pale skin and wounded eyes a match for his mother's, clambered out of the back of the car.

'I'm fine, poppet. Can you give your sister a hand?' Kiki tried to disentangle herself from Mia, but Madeline was quicker.

'I've got her.' The older woman opened the opposite door as Richard hurried to her side to lend a hand. 'Hello, darling. Look at your pretty dress, don't you look gorgeous? Shall I help you with your buckle?' Keeping up a constant stream of light chatter, Madeline fussed and flattered the little girl as she helped her out. Perched on Madeline's hip, brown hair a riot of curls around her head, Charlotte cast a wary eye over the gathered group of strangers. Her lower lip wobbled and her face screwed up in an expression Aaron well remembered from when Luke was that age. A heart-rending wail split the air and fat tears began to roll down her plump cheeks.

'Oh, Charlie, don't cry, sweetheart.' Kiki broke free from Mia's arms and rushed to her daughter's aid. She gathered Charlotte into her arms and rocked her back and forth, kissing her head and whispering endearments to try and soothe the fractious child.

A light touch on his arm caught Aaron's attention and he stared down into Matthew's big blue eyes. 'She needs Mr Bunny.'

Aaron crouched down so they were the same height. 'Mr Bunny?'

The boy nodded. 'He's magic, he takes all the sad things away. Mummy packed him in the boot by mistake.'

'We'd better find him then, eh?' Aaron rose, turned to grab the keys from the ignition, then circled to the rear of the car. He pressed the unlock button and slipped his hand under the handle to release the catch.

'Careful! It's a bit full…' Kiki's warning came a fraction too late and Aaron found himself grabbing for half a dozen overflowing carrier bags as they tumbled from the top of the haphazard pile crammed into the small space. His lightning reflexes, honed on the rugby pitch, saved the day, or so he thought until the thin material of the supermarket bag hooked on his little finger began to tear. With his arms spread, trying to hold everything else in place he couldn't do anything other than watch the orange plastic turn white as the weight of its contents stretched it beyond breaking point. Shoes, clothes and, *well, hello,* a flamingo-pink bra fell to the ground.

Tearing his gaze from the scrap of lace trailing over his foot, he looked up into a pair of horrified, amber-flecked eyes. The little girl resting on Kiki's hip let forth another howl of utter wretchedness and Aaron had to bite his lip to stifle an inappropriate laugh. He looked from the embarrassed woman, past the tear-stained moppet, down to the solemn-faced boy at his side and back again. If he did nothing else, he'd put smiles on all their faces before the summer was through. 'Welcome to Butterfly Cove.'

Chapter Seven

There was no God, Kiki decided, when the sinkhole she silently prayed would swallow her up failed to materialise. Charlie's fingers were tangled in her hair, tugging painfully at Kiki's scalp as she worked herself up into a rare old state. She winced and pulled her head away, half of her hair tumbling free from its loose bun in the process. Heat warmed her cheeks as she considered the terrible first impression they must be making. She'd given herself a pep talk over the last hour of the journey and had been so determined to hold it together. And then Mia, of all people, had started crying the moment Kiki stepped out of the car, and it had been all she could do not to collapse into her arms and let her take the weight of everything. Everywhere she looked, kind smiles greeted her and she knew they only wanted to help, but for once, just for one damn minute, she'd wanted to control a situation.

Aaron, and it had to be him, with that same deep, reassuring voice she'd heard on the phone earlier, just kept smiling at her. Her world was tumbling at his feet—literally, if you took into account the contents of the spilled carrier bag and that ridiculous bloody bra hooked around his shoe. She didn't know why she'd packed the damn thing; she'd bought it after cringing her way through an Ann Summers party one of the other mothers had thrown. The hot-pink set had been the least shocking thing she could find in the catalogue, and she'd felt obliged to buy something… Kiki closed her eyes. She wasn't standing in her sister's driveway looking at an attractive stranger and thinking about a sex-toy party. *Where the hell was that sink hole when she needed it?*

Perhaps sensing her discomfort, Aaron broke the awkward moment. 'Give us a hand will you, Daniel?'

She opened her eyes, intrigued to get a good look at the man her sister had chosen to follow in Jamie's footsteps. Tall and lean, with a close-cropped dark beard which gave him a stern appearance, Daniel was nothing like the laughing, sandy-haired boy Kiki remembered Jamie being. He took one look at the bra dangling from Aaron's shoe and a huge grin split his face and Kiki saw instantly what had attracted Mia to him. Without any of the embarrassment creasing Kiki's insides, Daniel bent down to scoop up her scattered belongings and stuff them into the tops of the other bags in the boot. A few hard shoves, and the two men had the overflowing contents mostly contained. She hadn't meant to pack *quite* so much.

'And who do we have here?' Kiki sighed in relief when Aaron pulled his arm from behind his back and waved a bedraggled-looking stuffed toy at the still-crying Charlie. Caught mid-wail, her daughter opened and closed her mouth like a little red-faced fish, clearly trying to decide if the prize of her favourite toy was worth abandoning her tears for.

'Mr Bunny!' Charlie held out her arms and Aaron took a step closer, waggling the droopy brown rabbit in encouragement. The little girl giggled and strained forward. Caught off-guard by the sudden shift in her body weight, Kiki loosened her grip to adjust her hold and Charlie took full advantage. She flung herself across the small gap and straight at Aaron. His arms closed instinctively and Kiki wanted to laugh at the look of abject shock on his face as Charlie grabbed Mr Bunny and settled herself into the crook of Aaron's neck.

Daniel laughed. 'He's always had that effect on women.'

'You've got the wrong brother there, mate. Luke's the ladies' man of the family.' A faint spot of colour showed on Aaron's tanned cheek, adding a sweet shyness to his smile, and something wound tight inside her loosened a notch. They all seemed so confident and put-together, it was a relief to see a little chink in his armour. He met her eyes over the top of Charlie's head and mouthed, 'Is this all right?'

She nodded. Charlie's long lashes were lower than half-mast and she looked utterly at ease with one little arm looped around Aaron's neck. 'I don't think she's going anywhere for a while. If you don't mind?'

Aaron shifted his hold until Charlie was perched on one broad forearm, freeing his other hand. He rested his broad palm lightly on Matty's shoulder and looked down at him. 'Your smart thinking saved the day. Your sister is lucky to have a big brother like you to look after her.' Some of the tension in Matty's frame loosened and he stood a little bit taller. Kiki's heart stuttered. How starved of praise must he be for a simple remark like that to have such an impact? She tried to imagine Neil's reaction and shuddered. It would be her fault for not controlling the children. He'd have clenched his jaw and forced a smile, saving his anger for behind closed doors. A cold trickle of fear ran down her spine, stealing the soft warmth of the early summer sun.

'What's wrong?' Aaron's brow creased in concern and she forced herself to shrug off the malignant presence. Neil was hundreds of miles away, so wrapped up in his dig and his pretty new girlfriend Kiki doubted he would spare any of them even a passing thought.

'Nothing. I'm just a bit tired. Not used to driving so far, I suppose.'

A familiar warmth looped around her waist and Mia tugged her in for a one-armed hug. 'Come inside and I can get you all settled in. I've got three couples arriving tomorrow, but the forest room is free tonight. I'll make some calls and start cancelling the bookings we have for that room.'

Kiki resisted the pressure from Mia to move towards the house. 'You shouldn't be turning away paying guests because of me. I thought we were staying with Aaron.' She bit her lip. What if he'd had second thoughts? She shot Aaron an apologetic look. 'But if you've changed your mind, that's perfectly understandable.'

He shook his head. 'There's more than enough room for the three of you at Honeysuckle Cottage, for as long as you need it.'

'But then…' Kiki caught the determined jut of her sister's jaw and understood. Now her brief flurry of tears had passed, she was in full-on protection mode. If Kiki let her, Mia would take over everything. For a fleeting moment she indulged the idea. But if she wanted to live in someone else's shadow for the rest of her life, she could have stayed with Neil. Not that Mia would be anything other than loving and supportive, but Kiki would still be surrendering responsibility to someone else. 'I think staying at the cottage makes more sense.'

Mia shook her head. 'Don't be daft, Kiki. Family should stick together.'

Kiki yanked her shoulder free from Mia's hand and stepped back. The barb had struck too close to home, too similar to Neil's constant undermining of her with his accusations of stupidity and incompetence. It was clear from the way the colour drained from her face that Mia regretted her hasty words almost as soon as she'd said them. 'Kiki Dee… I didn't… I'm sorry…'

'Why don't Aaron and I take the kids for a walk on the beach?' Daniel's tone was light, but Kiki didn't miss the pointed stare he fixed on his fiancée.

Richard chimed in. 'Good idea. I think I spotted a ball in the garages somewhere. I'll dig it out and we can leave the ladies to sort things out between them.'

Kiki crouched down in front of Matty. Little furrows creased his brow and she smoothed them with her thumb. 'Would that be okay with you, little man? Do you fancy a kickabout on the beach with Aaron and the others before we go and see our new home?'

He stared up at Aaron, who'd kept that reassuring hand clasped around his shoulder the whole time. 'We're coming to stay at your house for a while?'

Aaron nodded. 'If that's what you, Charlie and your mummy would like. It's a bit lonely there on my own, and it would be nice to have some new friends to spend time with. We'd only be down the road so you could come and see your Aunty Mia every day.'

'I'd like that.'

Mia stepped forward to touch his cheek. 'I'd like that too, poppet. Why don't you let Uncle Daniel and Aaron show you the beach, and when you come back you can have some chocolate cake with your tea.'

'Do we all get cake?' Aaron batted his eyelashes at Mia and Kiki felt another one of those tight notches loosen.

Mia laughed. 'Only if you're a good boy.'

'No chance of that!' Richard snorted as he returned from his foraging. Dust clung to the leg of his crisp chinos, and he looked to have a cobweb clinging to his silvering hair. He held a bright-red ball aloft like a champion brandishing a trophy. 'Come on then, last one to the beach is a rotten egg!'

The two men looked at each other for a split second before sprinting after Richard's retreating back. Matty glanced once at Kiki and she gave him a nod. 'Wait for me!' His boyish giggles drifted back to them on the light afternoon breeze and Kiki let herself relax for a moment. It would take time, but she'd make sure he laughed like that every day.

A light touch brushed her arm. Mia. 'I truly am sorry, Kiki Dee. I've just been so worried about you.'

'I know, Mimi, but this is my mess to sort out, not yours.' Hurt clouded her sister's expression and Kiki turned away, unable to cope with that on top of everything else. This wasn't working out how she'd expected it to at all.

'Let's go inside and have a cup of tea.' Madeline held her hands out to the two of them and made a beckoning motion. Kiki allowed herself to be herded along by the older woman. Unlike her husband, there was no trace of silver in her vibrant bob, and her white linen trousers and lime-green T-shirt were fresh and crisp even this late in the afternoon. Kiki glanced down at the creases in her navy cotton skirt with a sigh. The hair Charlie had pulled free dangled past her cheek and she winced. If she wanted them to believe her capable, then she needed to start looking like it. Pulling the elasticated band free, she wound her hair back into a neat bun and secured it at the nape of her neck as she followed the others into the kitchen.

The scents of fresh baking filled the cosy room. She paused for a moment, pride filling her as she admired the beautiful space her sister had created. From the flag-stoned floor, to the solid pine furniture, the checked curtains at the windows and the huge Aga taking pride of place along the back wall, it was the epitome of a country kitchen. A space made for family and friends to gather and share a meal and laughter. 'It's fabulous, Mia. Is the rest of the house like this?'

Madeline smiled over from the white butler's sink where she was filling the kettle. 'I love it in here. And the rest of the house is even better. Our Mia has such an eye for design.' *Our Mia.* Said with such casual affection, it could only come from her heart. Mia's bravery struck her anew. Heartbroken and alone, she'd uprooted herself and relocated to a place where she hadn't known a living soul and in less than a year had made a beautiful new home for herself filled with friendship and love.

Comparing herself to Mia in the past had always been an exercise in futility, and Kiki expected jealousy to stab its poisonous barbs into her as usual. The envy twisting inside her when it came to Mia had always been her most shameful and carefully hidden secret. There had even been occasions in the darkest hours before dawn, huddled still beside Neil, afraid to move in case she disturbed his sleep and caught the worst of his temper, when she'd resented Mia for being a widow; resented the freedom Kiki could never have. Ugly, sneaky thoughts, they horrified her in the cold light of day, creating a tension between them which Mia had never understood. *Because she'd never told her.*

There were no excuses now, though. Kiki looked around at the new life her sister had woven from the ashes of heartache and the rotting bones of an old house and, instead of questioning why she couldn't have this, too, she had only one thought. How could she make something like this for herself and the children?

She took a seat at the table and let Madeline pour her tea from a rainbow-striped teapot into a matching mug. The crockery was sturdy, a breath away from being perfect, telling her they were handmade rather than mass-produced. She wrapped her hands around the wide body of the mug, loving the way it filled them. 'These are beautiful.'

Mia smiled. 'I found a local guy who makes his own stuff. I can't wait for the studios to be finished.' She took a sip of her tea and settled back in her chair. 'Daniel is hoping some of the artists will allow us to display and market the work they produce while they stay here. The Butterfly Cove Collection, or something like that. We're thinking of converting the garages into a gallery, with maybe a tearoom attached to it. And then there was my bright idea about using the garden as a wedding venue.' She laughed. 'Although how we'll find the time to run all these things is another matter.'

Madeline laughed. 'You two will have a mini empire running here before you know it.' There was nothing but admiration in the fond way she watched Mia, though.

Mia sipped, then shook her head. 'Our ambitions might outstrip our capabilities. Daniel is going to have to put all his energy into the studios if he wants to meet his target opening date. All that effort I put into teaching him how to make the beds properly wasted.'

Kiki smothered a laugh as she took a drink from her mug, letting the strong brew warm and soothe her. There were claims the British had won wars on the back of nothing more than stubbornness and an ever-flowing stream of tea. It was more than the drink—it was the ritual, the giving and receiving of a small, familiar comfort. She gave Madeline a grateful smile. 'Thank you for the tea.'

Her sister raised her mug in a toast. 'Yes, Mads, thank you for your timely suggestion.' She turned to Kiki. 'I am sorry.'

This time, it wasn't so hard to accept. 'I know. I'm sorry for making you worry about me.'

Mia grinned. 'It's what big sisters do. Comes with the territory.' She extended her free hand across the table and Kiki placed hers on it.

The connection between them had frayed around the edges, but coming to Butterfly Cove would give them both a chance to repair it. *If* Mia could be persuaded to give her a bit of breathing space. 'I'll be all right, you know? Once I find my bearings and get myself a job, I should be able to find my own place. I'm not saying I don't need your help, Mimi. God knows, I do. But I want you to help me help myself, if that makes sense.'

The legs of Mia's chair scraped against the kitchen tiles and Kiki found herself enveloped in a tight hug. She let herself cling to the strength her sister offered for a few moments. Face muffled against Mia's shoulder, she let herself say the words that proved there was no turning back. 'I've transferred enough money from our savings account to see us over the summer. My solicitor suggested it as a precaution, in case Neil turns ugly when he gets the divorce papers next week.'

Mia loosened her hold enough for Kiki to see the shocked expression on her face. 'You've filed for divorce? How long have you been planning this?'

Her lips twisted in a grim smile. 'Every single minute for the past two weeks.'

Chapter Eight

With his elbows resting on his knees, Aaron sat on the beach and watched the children play football with Richard. Daniel sprawled beside him, head propped on one arm, a broad smile fixed on his lips. Childish laughter and whoops filled the air, mixing with the squawking of the gulls circling over the white caps of the incoming tide. Matty rolled the ball to his sister, then raised his arms above his head in a victory cheer when the little girl kicked it all of three feet. She beamed at him like he was her hero, stirring memories in Aaron's head of Luke grinning up at him with the exact same expression on his face.

Daniel scrambled into a sitting position and fished his camera out of the side pocket of his cargo shorts. The children played on, oblivious to the fact some people would drop thousands of pounds for the privilege of having Daniel Fitzwilliams take their photo. A few months in the fresh air and sunshine had wiped the last of the grey pallor from his friend's skin. 'London feels a lifetime away,' Aaron observed.

'You're not kidding. On the rare occasions I think about it, it's like watching a movie. Like it happened to a different person. I'll always be grateful for the opportunities being Fitz brought me, but I never want to be him again.' Daniel took a few more shots of the children then turned his full attention on Aaron. The piercing gaze that served him so well in his art made Aaron want to squirm from the intensity of it. Daniel cut straight to the chase. 'Do you know what you're letting yourself in for?'

He watched Charlie take a tumble in the soft sand. Matty was on her in seconds, scooping her up and brushing her arms and legs. Her face scrunched and Aaron pushed to his feet, ready to run over and check on her, but Matty had the situation in hand. He tickled her tummy, making her giggle and squirm, and in a couple of seconds they were running around again. He sank back onto the sand, rubbing his chest to ease the flutter of worry there. Half an hour and he already felt responsible for them. 'I haven't got a clue, to be honest, but they seem like good kids.'

Daniel nodded in agreement. 'Father's a bit of bastard, by all accounts.' He held up his hands when Aaron swung his attention back to him. 'Like I said, I don't know details, but you have to wonder when she ups and leaves the moment he's out of the country.'

A bite of anger gnawed Aaron's gut. Slight and willowy, he doubted it would take more than a strong breeze to knock Kiki over and the children struck him as being well-behaved, given how well they'd taken being thrown in with a group of strangers. Every relationship had its stresses and strains, to be sure, but you'd have to be a special kind of wanker to mistreat a vulnerable woman and two small kids. 'They'll be safe with me.' The words resonated through him, a promise and a vow.

'It's not just them I'm concerned about, mate. You've turned your entire life upside down on a whim. That's not like you at all. You've always been so steady and methodical.' Daniel placed a hand on his forearm to take any sting out of his words, but they still struck home. Steady; methodical. *Boring.*

Aaron stood up, brushing the sand from the back of his legs. 'Perhaps you're not the only one in need of a change, mate.' He jogged over to where the game of football was winding down. 'Who's ready for some tea? Aunty Mia and Madeline have been baking all afternoon.'

'I'm ready for some cake, how about you, Matty?' Richard ruffled the boy's hair then bent to pick up the ball.

'I like cake,' Matty said, giving his sweet smile.

'Cake! Cake! Cake!' Charlie bounced at Aaron's feet, arms raised, hands opening and closing in that universal *pick-me-up* sign all children seemed to instinctively know.

He bent down and lifted her into his arms. 'Is this how it's going to be from now on, Miss Charlotte? Me carrying you everywhere?' Her little hand patted his face as she gave him a solemn nod.

Richard chucked the little girl's cheek before giving Aaron a sympathetic pat on the shoulder. 'Looks like you've found yourself a new job.'

'Looks like.' Charlie settled against his shoulder and a sense of rightness eased over him. He'd never wanted children of his own, and he was self-aware enough to know it stemmed from his own childhood experiences. At least Cathy had provided him with a template of what not to do while living under the same roof as vulnerable little hearts and minds.

Daniel crouched in front of Matty. 'Fancy a lift, Matty?' He turned, offering the boy his back. The boy hesitated for a moment, then placed his hands on Daniel's shoulders. Daniel hoisted him on his back and hooked his arms around his legs to anchor him in place. With Richard leading the way, they trooped back towards the house.

'The wanderers return!' Madeline greeted them with a sunny smile and a kiss on her husband's cheek. 'We were about to mount a search party. Hands and faces washed and then up to the table, everyone. You too, Daniel!' She added with a cheeky wink.

'I'll take them.' Kiki looked better; less pale and with a firmer set to her shoulders. Aaron and Daniel set the children down and they ran to their mother who ushered them towards the downstairs cloakroom.

Mia snuggled into Daniel's side and he pressed a kiss to the top of her head. 'All sorted?'

'Getting there.' She looked over at Aaron. 'I've been persuaded that your place is the most sensible option for all of us.' A fierce frown creased her forehead. 'You look after them, you hear me?'

'I hear you. I know what it's like to be the eldest, Mia. I also know what it's like when your world turns upside down. I'll do right by them all.'

The corner of her mouth gave a sceptical twist, but she nodded. 'Let's see how it goes.' She meant no offence, and he took none. He'd seen Mia in full protective mode before and admired her fierce spirit.

Tea was a riotous affair with everyone pitching in to make Kiki and the children as welcome as possible. By the time they were sprawled around the kitchen table with a final cup of tea, Matty was half asleep with his head lolling on Kiki's shoulder. With too many interesting new people to show off to, there was little sign of Charlie doing the same. She perched on Madeline's lap, chattering away like a magpie. Richard had moved his chair closer and seemed equally enraptured by the little girl.

Aaron rested a hand on his full stomach, grateful once again for the good food and better company he always found at this table. It would be easy to while away the next couple of hours in idle conversation, but he still needed to show them the cottage. He caught Kiki's eye. 'Ready to make a move?' Her relaxed smile disappeared beneath lines of worry and he could've kicked himself. 'There's no rush.'

She shook her head. 'No, you're right. It's been a long day and I need to get these two sorted out...' The way she hesitated, he knew what she was about to say.

'It's really fine for you to stay. I promise.'

With a soft touch to his cheek, Kiki got Matty to sit up. A wry smile tweaked the corner of her mouth as she got him to his feet and leaned across to retrieve Charlie. 'I'll remind you of that when these two are making a racket.'

They rounded up the children and headed out to the car. Aaron held the door for Kiki while she leaned in to strap Charlie into her car seat. A soft touch brushed his leg and he glanced down. A worried frown creased Matty's brow. 'I promise we won't make too much noise.'

Aaron took him by the hand and walked him around to the other side of the car. He opened the door and ushered Matty in. Crouching beside him, he helped the boy with his belt then touched a finger to his cheek. 'It will take us all a bit of time to adjust to being under the same roof, Matty. You mustn't be worried about being yourself and having fun. It's your home, too, and I want you to be happy while you're here. Promise me, if I do something you don't like, or say something that worries or upsets you, that you'll tell me or your mummy. I won't be cross, and I never shout.'

He wasn't sure the boy believed him, and he couldn't blame him under the circumstances. He knew all too well what it was like to live somewhere you had to walk on eggshells. Matty gave a little nod and Aaron decided to be satisfied with that for the time being. A quick tug assured him Matty had secured his seatbelt properly, so he stood up and pushed the door closed.

Kiki's eyes met his across the roof of the car. 'Thank you.'

'You're welcome. Are you happy to drive or do you want me to? It's only a couple of minutes down the road.'

A look of relief crossed her face. 'You drive, if you don't mind. I'm not very good at following directions.'

Realising she was deadly serious, he swallowed a laugh. She'd found her way to Butterfly Cove without any problems and the M5 was nobody's idea of a great driving experience. He wondered how many other things were on the list of stuff she wasn't very good at, and who the hell had made her believe it. *Her bloody husband, no doubt.*

Aaron pushed back the driver's seat to accommodate his long legs, then took the car keys from Kiki's outstretched hand. The engine started at the first attempt and he turned the car carefully in the driveway. Richard had parked their old estate car well to the side so there was plenty of space. He lowered his window and raised an arm to acknowledge the chorus of goodbyes from the others who'd come out to see them off.

'You giving us a hand again with the painting tomorrow?' Daniel called out.

'Depends how things go. I'll text you.' It was his last free day for a week, and he'd promised to put as many hours in on the studios as possible, but getting Kiki and the children settled would have to come first.

'No worries.'

With a final wave, he steered them along the winding driveway. The worst of the potholes had been filled in as soon as the weather had dried out. Mia had winced at the cost of the resurfacing, but better that than a guest bursting a tyre trying to navigate their way back and forth to the main road.

Main road gave the country crossroads a grandeur it didn't deserve. Aaron gave a cursory glance left and right then accelerated over and into the narrow lane leading to his home. The setting sun cast a warm glow over the thatched roof of Honeysuckle Cottage, brightening the faded straw to a deeper yellow.

He parked just forward of the front door, to help with unloading the boot. 'Here we are.'

Kiki ducked her head lower to peer out of her window. 'It's beautiful.'

'You say that now, but you haven't seen the interior.' Maybe her taste ran to cabbage-rose-covered wallpaper, but his didn't. Most of the changes he wanted to make were cosmetic, the building itself having been well maintained. A full redecoration, outside and in, and maybe an update of the kitchen and bathroom fixtures and fittings when he had the time. *And the budget.*

The cut in his salary hadn't started to pinch yet, and he hoped to add to his client base soon. He had meetings lined up in Exeter and a couple of potential new artist clients he'd met at Daniel's exhibition. Luke had promised him use of his sofa for a couple of days so Kiki and the kids would have some space to find their bearings and settle in.

He retrieved his door key from his front pocket and handed it to Kiki. 'Why don't you three go and explore the place and I'll unload the car?' Not giving her a chance to refuse, he climbed out. It was important she feel comfortable in the place and a guided tour might make her feel like a guest.

Taking care to open the boot slowly and prevent a repeat of the earlier spillage, he waited until Kiki unlocked the front door, then loaded up with the first handful of bags. She hesitated on the threshold, but he nodded his head. 'Go on in. I'll put everything in the dining room for now. You can sort out essentials for tonight and then we'll move the rest upstairs once everyone has decided on a bedroom.'

'That's probably a good idea. We'll have a quick look around and then I think I need to get these two settled.' She brushed her hand over Charlie's chestnut curls. 'It's nearly your bedtime, isn't it, poppet?'

The little girl looked full of beans, but it wasn't for Aaron to deal with. 'Living room is on the right, kitchen's the next door after it. Bedrooms are upstairs, of course.' He nodded towards the staircase on the left side of the red-tiled hallway.

She shepherded the children before her, and they moved into the living room. Aaron used his elbow to open the dining-room door and dumped the first load on the floor. Three more trips and the car was empty. He surveyed the pile of bags and cases for a moment then decided it was best to leave it to Kiki to sort out what she needed. Quiet voices could be heard from the kitchen so he headed there to join them.

The three of them were clustered by the open back door, looking out at the garden. The old lady who'd lived there had obviously taken pride in it and a bit of weeding and a good mow of the back lawn would have it looking shipshape. 'I had a quick look the other day. I think there's a vegetable patch down the bottom end.'

Kiki glanced over her shoulder at him. 'I always thought it would be nice to grow my own veg, but I never got organised enough to do it.'

'Now's your chance then.'

She blinked, as though the idea hadn't occurred to her. 'I suppose it is.'

He bit his tongue against the urge to push other suggestions on her. She had time. They all had time to find their way along this new path life had laid out before them. 'Shall we look upstairs?'

The ceilings in the cottage were lower than he was used to, and Aaron ducked beneath the thick plaster of the upstairs landing as he led them up. He'd tested it at his full height and there was a couple of inches clearance, but his instincts hadn't quite caught up to the logic of it. He took a couple of steps to the side and waited for the others to join him.

Small and square, the landing looked gloomy thanks to the single small window at one end. The thatch overhang blocked the last of the evening sunshine and he flipped the switch on the wall, flooding the space with harsh light. He needed to get a shade to cover the bare bulb. He clapped his hands together and smiled at the children. 'Ready to pick a bedroom?'

Chapter Nine

She couldn't fault him for trying. From the moment they'd arrived in Butterfly Cove, Aaron had done his best to put them all at ease. His gentle touch with the children helped calm some of the nerves fluttering in her stomach, but being there in the house, made her wonder if she'd made a mistake. It had been selfish of her to put her own needs first, to uproot the kids with no thought to their future other than removing them from Neil's malign influence. She'd had the whole summer to plan and make her move, and trying to cram everything into two weeks didn't feel like such a good idea any more. It felt more like the panic of a weak and foolish girl, not a strong, organised woman.

'Kiki?'

She jumped about a foot in the air at the soft touch on her arm. 'Sorry, you startled me.' Her shaky laugh sounded brittle to her ears. *Hold it together.* Aaron stepped back, hand up in apology. Damn, she was making such a hash of everything. Matty had that look about him, all big eyes and worried pout. Poor boy, he always saw too close to the truth.

'I'm just tired. I think that drive took more out of me than I realised.' Forcing a smile, she took Charlie by the hand. 'Shall we find you somewhere to sleep, darling?'

Her daughter shook her head and buried her face against Kiki's leg. 'I want my bed, Mummy.'

'I know, poppet, but you'll soon get used to things here.'

Charlie sniffled and shook her head again and the fluttery feeling in Kiki's stomach expanded. If there were any more tears today, she would end up wailing along. The thick white walls of the landing seemed to close in on her and her breath hitched in her throat. She needed to move. How hard could it be to take a couple of steps forward to look at the first bedroom? It was as though her feet were glued to the floor. *Bloody useless.* Neil's mocking sneer rang in her ears and a tremor started in her fingers and began to work its way up her arm.

'Mummy?' She didn't dare look at Matty. If she acknowledged the worry in his face it would finish her off.

'The spare room is already made up. It's a king-size bed. Why don't you all sleep in there tonight and we can sort things out in the morning?' There he was again. This practical stranger offering the lifeline she needed in his calm, reassuring voice.

'That sounds like a brilliant idea.' She bent to pick Charlie up and settled her on her hip. 'Would you like that, darling? We can all snuggle in together like you did with Aunty Mia when you stayed with her. You liked that, remember?'

Charlie gave her a wary look, but nodded. She couldn't blame her. Neil had refused to allow the children into their bed. He'd pointed out that, as the only one who had to work for a living, he was entitled to a decent night's sleep. How many other normal things had she deprived the children of to suit his selfish demands?

'What do you say, Matty? Shall we all pile in together? I promise not to snore.' Her smile came easier when he responded to her forced silliness with a giggle.

'Charlie snores.'

'Do not!'

'Do too!' Matty grunted and groaned and snuffled like a pig until Charlie started to laugh.

The ball of tension in Kiki's stomach loosened a fraction more and she met Aaron's eyes over the children's heads. He winked, just the tiniest flicker of movement, and it filled her with renewed hope. She wasn't on her own, it seemed to say. Maybe he had a speck of dust in there and she was reading too much into it, but she'd take it anyway.

He pointed over her shoulder. 'The spare room's the door behind you. Bathroom next to it. I'm at the other end of the landing. Do you need me to bring anything up for tonight?'

Thankfully, she'd had the foresight to put together a little overnight bag while she'd still believed herself in control of everything. 'There should be a blue holdall somewhere. If you don't mind?'

'I know the one you mean. I'll be right back.' He started back down the stairs. 'Just don't blame me for the wallpaper.'

Kiki nudged open the bedroom door and set Charlie back on her feet to free her hands to find the light switch. The warm glow from an old-fashioned peach-coloured fringed lampshade filled the room with soft light. An honest-to-goodness four-poster bed with a carved headboard dominated the middle of the room. A matching dark-wood chest of drawers and wardrobe filled the spaces on either side and a smaller dressing table sat under the window.

Huge pink roses covered the faded wallpaper, making her smile at Aaron's earlier remark. Matching curtains, including a frilly pelmet, framed the windows and lighter patches on the carpet showed where the furniture had been rearranged. It was definitely not a room designed for, or by, a man, but she found it altogether charming. Just how a country cottage bedroom should look.

Aaron tapped on the open door and peeked in. 'I'll leave your bag here. Have you got everything you need?'

She looked at the children who were already clambering onto the bed. 'I think so.'

He tucked his hands in his pockets and rocked back on his heels. 'I'm going downstairs to sort a few things out. Just shout if you need anything, otherwise I'll see you in the morning.'

A lump formed in her throat. Thank you seemed a barely adequate response to his unwavering support today. Taking in a complete stranger and her two children didn't seem to have fazed him in the slightest. Regardless of his casual assurances, they would be a huge disruption to his life, even if the children were as good and quiet as church mice. The bed behind her started to squeak and Charlie giggled in a way Kiki knew meant she was doing something naughty. *Church mice, eh?*

The corner of Aaron's mouth quirked up. 'I'll leave you and the Butterfly Cove Formation Trampoline Team to it then. Night.'

Heat prickled the top of her chest and up her throat. 'Thank you. Sorry. Night.' She waited for Aaron to leave then closed her eyes and drew in a deep breath. She'd made this new bed and they would all have to make the best of it. The future could wait until tomorrow. Sleep first, think later.

'Right, I'm counting to three and by the time I finish there had better be two children ready to put on their pyjamas. One...' The squeaking stopped, and Kiki swallowed her sigh of relief. Never mind all the things on her list she wasn't sure about, being a good mother was the one thing she did know how to do.

***

Sharing a slightly sagging mattress with two wriggling little bodies might have been a far cry from the top-of-the-range orthopaedic king-size bed she shared with

Neil, but Kiki couldn't remember the last time she'd slept so well. She rolled her shoulders, aware only by its absence of the aching knot of tension that usually rode the top of her spine.

Tugging a powder-blue T-shirt on over her head, she scooped the mass of her hair out from the collar and began to weave it into a thick plait. Impractical it might be, with the ends trailing to the base of her spine, but she couldn't bring herself to cut it. One of the few good memories she had of growing up was the hours her mother spent brushing and playing with her hair. The rhythmic strokes from the silver-backed brush had seemed to soothe Vivian, and Kiki had sat at her feet relishing the calm moments.

Appearance had been everything to Vivian, and when Mia proved too wilful to be moulded into a perfect little doll, it had fallen to Kiki to meet their mother's expectations. Ribbons and frills, even lace-edged socks—she'd let Vivian style and dress her exactly as she wanted, desperate to be a good girl, to make her mummy happy and keep the smile on her face.

If the tears started, then the begging started, the insidious little whispers that put Kiki in the worst dilemma possible. Ignore them and Mummy would work herself up into a terrible state; obey them and Daddy would give her that look of disappointment and despair. He never told her off, never raised his voice; he just looked sad and that was somehow worse than anything.

Splashing and laughter from the bathroom next door dragged Kiki from the shadows of the past and she shook her head to dispel the last of them. Drawing back the delicate floral curtains, she let the blue skies and promised warmth they heralded soak into her.

Today would be a good day.

Another, bigger splash. Then, 'Char-*lie!*' and she hurried from the bedroom to see what devastation the children had wrought in the bathroom.

A soggy towel, now bundled up in the bathtub until she could find the washing machine, and a change of dress for her daughter had been the only casualties of the children's bathroom antics. They sat next to each other at the round kitchen table, munching away at their cornflakes. It was a day of miracles, apparently. The basic cereal would have caused mutiny at home, but neither had batted an eyelid when Aaron looked up from his own half-eaten bowl to offer the box to them.

Sipping a weak cup of coffee, Kiki tried to plan out the things she needed to do. Each item added to her mental list prompted two more until the squirmy feelings of panic were stirring in her belly. She glanced around the room, wondering where she'd left her bag the night before. A sharp sting from the raw skin on her lower lip reminded her chewing it was a bad habit she kept meaning to break.

'Now's your chance.' Aaron's three words from the previous evening echoed in her mind. If she was serious about making a new start then perhaps it was time to

make another list. A private one, of things she wanted to change about herself, as well as goals to aim for. She needed to find her daybook and write them down.

'Have you seen my bag?'

Aaron swallowed his final mouthful of cereal and frowned for a second. 'On the sofa, maybe?'

She left the cosy kitchen and padded down the hall. The red tiles were cool under her bare feet and she added finding her slippers to her mental to-do list. Turning left, she entered the living room. The dark-leather three-piece suite looked out of place against the flowery walls and pale yellow carpet. A bit like Aaron himself, a huge masculine sprawl in the delicate, feminine cottage. A giant flat-screen TV hogged the space between the fireplace and the window and the sofa and chairs were orientated to face it.

Her bag nestled in one corner of the three-seater, in the exact spot she'd dropped it when they first arrived. She could hear Aaron's low voice from the kitchen and the higher tones of the children as they chatted with him. Taking advantage of the peace and quiet, she sat on the sofa. The supple leather gave beneath her, inviting her to sink deeper into its comfortable depths. Curling her legs underneath her, Kiki dug in her bag until she found her daybook and slid the pen out of the holder in the book's spine.

She scribbled a quick list of the most important things to do that day—sorting out the children's rooms, unpacking, food shopping for the next few days. Mia would be able to point her in the direction of a supermarket. There was bound to be a local paper she could pick up while she was there to see what jobs were available. She made a note of it on her list.

'Mummy?' Charlie called, and Kiki clicked her pen with a wry smile. The self-improvement list would have to wait until that evening once the children were asleep. She clicked the end of her pen again and scribbled 'wine' at the end of her impromptu shopping list. Neil didn't approve of drinking during the week, and Kiki had always shied away from strong spirits, fearful that whatever weakness Vivian carried might have been passed down to her. But sitting in the garden with a cold glass of white wine while she tried to map her future didn't sound like the worst idea she'd ever had.

'I'm coming, poppet.'

***

They piled out of the car at Butterfly House just as Madeline and Richard's old estate pulled up behind them. Kiki found herself engulfed in a fragrant hug from Madeline while her husband reached over to pat Aaron on the shoulder before hunkering down before the children. They chattered a mile a minute, telling him all about the cottage and the sleepover in Mummy's bed the night before. He had such an easy way with them, asking questions and listening closely to their responses.

Madeline disengaged from their embrace, but kept a loose arm looped around Kiki's waist. 'I think he was nearly as excited as them about today,' she said with a fond smile.

Glancing up from his crouch, Richard sent them both a wink. 'I'm looking forward to a beach football rematch.'

The children bounced around him like a couple of eager puppies, and Kiki knew when to surrender to the inevitable. 'Half an hour on the beach, and then you must come inside. Matty, you have some reading to catch up on for school.'

Richard pushed to his feet. 'If you give me his books, I'll make sure it gets done.' He held out his hand to Charlie. 'And you can draw me a picture while Matty does his work, can't you, Sweetpea?' He shouldered the small rucksack Matty used for school and off they went down the garden.

'Well, that's the last you'll see of them for the morning. I should have warned you Richard is a complete softy when it comes to little ones.' There was something wistful in Madeline's tone and Kiki noticed a sheen in her eyes. The two of them were such bright, vibrant characters, it would be easy to forget they must have seen their fair share of the ups and downs life brought to everyone.

Aaron rubbed his hands together. 'Right, while he's distracted by the children, I'm going to steal you away, Madeline, my love.' He gave her an outrageous wink, chasing the sadness from her face in an instant.

She raised a hand to her throat, fanning her face and fluttering her eyelashes. 'Are you going to whisk me away on a hot date, darling boy? How exciting!'

Before Kiki had time to ask where they were going, or when they might be back, she was standing alone on the driveway watching Madeline's grubby old car rumble away. She glanced around; a flat-bed truck full of equipment and tools sat outside the open door of the barns, the noise of construction and men's laughter ringing in the clear air. Richard and the children had vanished from sight down the steps leading to the beach, leaving her alone and feeling a little surplus to requirements. The back door to the house stood open so she turned towards it, hoping to find that her sister at least wanted her company.

The kitchen was empty. Bowls and mugs stacked on the draining rack beside the sink and a teapot in a bright-pink cosy sitting on a cork mat in the middle of the table were the only signs of recent occupation. Dumping her bag on one of the wooden chairs, she wandered into the hallway and rested her foot on the bottom of the stairs. 'Hello? Mimi?' she called out.

'Kiki Dee? I'm in the beach room, darling!' Mia had shown her the four guest rooms on the first floor the previous day, so she understood the reference and began to climb the stairs. Each one had been decorated according to a different theme—beach, forest, traditional country cottage, and a breathtaking master suite of rooms filled with bright silks and opulent furnishings they were calling the harem.

She paused on the threshold of the fresh, bright room and marvelled at her sister's style and ingenuity. Mia had never shown much interest in interior design before moving to Butterfly House, but she'd put together four unique and beautiful spaces. Maybe Kiki should take up Aaron's suggestion of reviving the vegetable patch. She would enjoy the research around what to plant and when as much as digging her hands into the soil. It would be the first thing she added to her self-improvement list that evening.

Mia was trying to wrestle a huge feather quilt into a taupe-and-gold-striped cover and Kiki hurried over to give her a hand. The colours captured the different shades of the sand on the beach to perfection. A gauzy white canopy floated over the bed, like gentle clouds against the pale-blue ceiling. Together they made short work of dressing the bed, piling a mountain of pillows and cushions against the white-pine headboard.

Mia stepped back to survey the completed bed with a critical eye, moved forwards to tweak a couple of cushions, then gave a small nod of satisfaction. It looked so comfortable and inviting, Kiki could have happily crawled between the sheets there and then. 'Just the day bed and then it's all finished in here.' Mia pushed her spiky fringe off her forehead. 'Thanks for your help. Now Daniel is so busy with the conversion, it's a rush to get all the rooms ready in time.'

'I'm happy to help any time you need it. Housework is one of the few things on my skills list.' She hesitated, wondering if it was too cheeky to ask, but then ploughed on anyway. 'I don't suppose you'd be looking for a chambermaid?'

Chapter Ten

Madeline climbed out of her car and arched an eyebrow at the large green DIY store in front of them. 'When you promised me a hot date, Aaron, I'd set my sights a bit higher than a trip around Homebase.'

He held out his arm for her, and tucked her hand into the crook of his elbow. 'I'll buy you a cappuccino and a slice of millionaire's shortbread from the café when we're done.'

She laughed. 'You know the way to a lady's heart, dearest. Now, what exactly are we doing here?'

The children had been good sports that morning when it came to choosing their rooms, but it hadn't occurred to Aaron until he'd tried to see through their eyes how unsuitable the décor was for them. He hadn't looked beyond the practicalities of enough rooms with beds when he'd offered them a place to stay. He couldn't do much about the wallpaper, not in the next couple of hours at least, but he wanted to try and make it a bit more welcoming for them.

Unfortunately, he had no clue where to start. 'I want to spruce up the rooms for Matty and Charlie, everything is a bit impersonal and old-fashioned. Something nice for them to come home to tonight.'

Madeline squeezed his arm. 'You're a good man, Aaron Spenser. Did anyone ever tell you that?' He ducked his head to hide the sudden rush of colour to his cheeks. It wasn't a big deal, just a few bits and pieces. Nothing more than any half-decent person would do.

She dropped his arm and stepped in front of him. A fierce glint shone in her blue eyes. 'Bloody hell, no one has, have they?'

He scrubbed the back of his neck, trying to ease the sudden knot of tension there. That was the trouble with Madeline—she saw too much. It was easy to get caught up in the funny, flirtatious façade and forget the razor-sharp mind that lurked behind her smile. 'Dad's great.'

Hoping that would put an end to it, he grabbed a trolley and tried to steer around her. Uncaring that they were blocking the entrance doors, she grasped the side of the trolley, leaving him no choice but to stop. 'But not your mum?'

He wasn't going to do this here. Not in front of a load of random strangers, maybe not even if they were somewhere more private. '*Luke's* mum.' Tugging the trolley free, he shoved his way through the automatic doors. His long stride carried him away from her and he entered the first aisle he came to. Trying to calm the rapid beating of his heart, he stared blindly at a collection of plumbing fittings and pipework. It was one thing to tell himself he'd let the past go and moved on; it was another thing to actually do it. He hadn't stopped caring that Cathy kept herself distant from him; he'd just shoved it to one side and ignored it. The way he always did.

The soft squeak of Madeline's deck shoes alerted him to her presence a moment before her soft touch on his arm. 'I'm sorry, darling boy. Like Mia says, I'm a meddling old bag. I won't say I didn't mean to pry, but the last thing I want is to upset you. To upset any of you. You're all so precious to us, it brings out the worst in me.'

Sincerity and concern shone through her words, chasing the anger and upset away. It was hard to be angry with someone for loving you. He covered her hand with his own. 'You hit a nerve, Mads, and it was a lot more raw than I expected.'

'I'll leave it be, then. But not for ever. I won't have you hurting if there's something that can be done about it.'

He sighed and lifted her hand to press a kiss into the centre of her palm. 'I don't think there's anything to fix, and that's the hardest part to deal with.'

Madeline studied him for a few moments more and he fought the need to flinch away from her uncompromising stare. He'd done nothing wrong, done everything he could to bridge the gulf between himself and Cathy, and yet the little boy inside still squirmed. His relationship with his stepmother was a failure, and Aaron liked to win. Top of the class, first pick for a sports team, outstanding work appraisals. His whole life felt driven by the need to prove his worth to the one person who would never acknowledge it.

After an interminable moment, Madeline shook her head and took charge of the trolley. 'One of these days you'll let me know what's going on in that head of yours.'

'It's mostly filled with thoughts of rugby and cakes, Mads.' He added an extra dose of Somerset burr to his voice.

She snorted. 'Don't think you're fooling anyone with that country bumpkin act, my boy. Come on, let's see what we can find to brighten those rooms up.' Grateful for the reprieve, he let her lead the way.

***

Aaron straightened the corner of the fluffy white rug they'd found for Charlotte's room then checked his watch. *Damn.* It had taken him longer than he expected to get everything unwrapped and installed. A high-pitched beep sounded from the kitchen, and he jogged down to answer the demanding summons of the tumble dryer. Hauling out the new sheets he'd purchased for Matty's bed, he gave them a shake and studied them for creases. Madeline had insisted on ironing the pretty set they'd picked out for Charlie's room—all bright smiling flowers with cheerful bees and butterflies dancing around them—and he supposed he should do the same for these.

Madeline had left him to finish off about half an hour before and he'd thought they'd been about finished then, but he'd kept finding things to fiddle with and reposition. Anything to avoid the nervous feeling building inside. What if he'd overstepped the mark? Maybe he should have left it to Kiki to choose what she wanted for their rooms. The last thing he wanted was for her to think he was trying to take over. He just wanted the place to look a bit more welcoming for them all. He shook the duvet cover again and sighed, picturing the perfectly dressed rooms at Butterfly Cove. Shoving clean sheets straight back on the bed might be fine for him, but he suspected that wouldn't pass muster with either of the two sisters. He dumped the still-warm bedding onto the kitchen table and went to retrieve the iron.

The phone in his pocket started to vibrate while he was in the middle of folding the ironing board away. Distracted from his task, he fumbled for the phone and the legs on the board began to slide open again. The ratchet clattered and he yanked his hand free just in time to avoid trapping his fingers. 'Bugger!'

He gave the board a baleful glare and a kick for good measure. It collapsed to the floor with a crash and he cursed again.

A faint voice echoed from the handset still clutched in his palm. 'Hello? Aaron, is that you?'

'What? Oh, sorry, Kiki. Everything okay?' He flipped the phone to speaker mode and balanced it carefully on the neat pile of ironed bedding before scooping the bundle into his arms.

'Yes, we're fine. I'm just leaving the supermarket and wondered whether you needed a lift or not?'

He paused on the stairs. Hadn't he been supposed to go with her to the shop? He really had let time slip away from him. 'You should have let me know you were going. I would have given you a hand.'

Kiki laughed. 'And interrupt your hot date? I might not be good at lots of things, but the day I can't manage a trip to the supermarket on my own will be the day I give up for good.'

There she went again, running herself down. He bit back the need to say anything. Making a joke, even a self-deprecating one, was a damn sight better than being on the verge of tears every five minutes like she had been the day before. 'You're right. I'd probably be more hindrance than help, unless you wanted a guided tour of the ready meals section. I'm back at the cottage so you can come straight home if you're ready.'

Silence greeted him for a long moment. 'Home. Yes, I suppose it is. Well, assuming I can find my way back, we should be there in about twenty minutes.'

Which would leave him just enough time to make Matty's bed and add a few final touches. 'Perfect. See you soon.'

***

The sound of Kiki pulling up outside gave Aaron the perfect excuse to abandon his aimless flicking through the TV channels. It was closer to forty minutes since they'd spoken and he'd driven himself mad second- and third-guessing whether changing the bedrooms had been a good idea. What was done was done, and he hadn't exactly broken the bank in the process. Anything they didn't like could be replaced easily enough. Cursing himself for making a fuss over nothing, he shoved his feet into an old pair of flip-flops and met Kiki on the doorstep just in time to relieve her of a handful of carrier bags.

'Planning on feeding an army?' he said over his shoulder as he carried the first load into the kitchen.

She laughed. 'I got chatting to Mia and we decided to expand my job description a little bit.'

He followed her back out to the car. 'I'll get the rest, you sort the kids out.' A couple of the bags gave a metallic clank when he picked them up and he peered inside. They were full of trays, cake tins, and other baking paraphernalia. *If she cooks anything like Mia...* His stomach gave a rumble of anticipation. 'You said something about a job description? Have I missed something?'

Kiki straightened up, with Charlie attached to her hip. The little girl gave him a wave and he blew her a kiss. 'Hello, gorgeous. Have you had a nice day?'

'We made sandcastles. Mine was the bestest!'

Matty had let himself out of the other side of the car. He turned to his sister. 'Mine was bigger.' Her lower lip stuck out, and he grinned at her. 'But yours was prettier.'

'Pretty!' Charlie agreed with a clap of her hands.

'Yes, darling. Very pretty.' Kiki settled her more firmly on her hip and followed Aaron into the house. 'I'm going to do some work for Mia. Help her with some cleaning a couple of mornings a week and a full day on Tuesdays to turn all the bedrooms. I'll also bake a couple of times a week to help her keep on top of everything. It's not much, but it's a start, and I'm hoping to find something else in the paper to supplement it.'

Aaron placed the rest of the shopping on the table and waited while Kiki set Charlie on her feet and sent the children into the living room to play. There was a lightness about her, a flicker of confidence as she talked about her job. It looked good on her, he decided.

Making a start on unpacking, he paused in front of the cupboard he'd randomly picked for food storage. 'If you want to rearrange things in here, you'd be welcome to.'

She shook her head. 'I couldn't do that. I'll work with whatever system you've already got in place.'

He smiled. 'That assumes there is a system. You're going to be in here more than me so it makes sense to have things where you'd prefer them.' *Did that sound sexist? Like he assumed a woman's place was in the kitchen?* 'Not that I won't be in here, of course. I don't expect you to wait on me, or anything like that. I just meant that if you're going to be baking stuff for Mia...' He forced himself to stop speaking. Really, he should just get a shovel so he could dig himself deeper.

Her bright laughter assured him she hadn't taken offence. 'Show me where everything is for now and I'll see how I get on, okay?' Relieved, he pulled open the cupboard doors and gave her a quick run-through of what was where. They had the shopping bags emptied in a couple of minutes and all that remained on the table was a handful of ingredients.

Kiki took a large frying pan and placed it on the hob. 'I thought I'd make pasta for dinner. Is that all right with you?'

A carb addict since his younger rugby-playing days, Aaron's mouth began to water at the thought of a home-cooked spag bol. From the bundles of fresh herbs and vegetables, it looked like Kiki intended to make the sauce from scratch, not dump a jar of processed gloop on a bit of mince. 'Sounds heavenly.'

He folded his arms and leaned back against the counter next to the cooker. They were facing each other and he waited to speak until she glanced up from watching the olive oil she'd poured spread across the surface of the pan. 'I meant what I said. I don't expect you to cook for me. I didn't invite you here to become a glorified housekeeper for me.'

'I get it, but I'll be making meals for the three of us anyway, so it's really no trouble. Besides, I love to cook.' She lifted the frying pan from the heat and eased the oil to the edges with a deft twist of her wrist. 'I wouldn't say no if you wanted to give me a hand, though.' She nodded to the onions, mushrooms and herbs.

'I'm on it.' Aaron shifted to the other side of the hob, grabbed a knife and a wooden board and began to chop. 'So, tell me more about what you'll be doing for Mia.'

He worked his way through the preparation tasks, handing each set of completed ingredients to Kiki as he listened to her outline her new job. The familiar task left his mind free to wander and he started a mental list of things she would need that he could help her with—a costing sheet for each of the different items she would make, a basic spreadsheet to keep track of income and expenses, a rating sheet for different cleaning tasks.

'Mia has an account set up at the local wholesaler's, so you should speak to her about getting an extra card to use. You don't want to be paying retail prices for ingredients.'

'Oh. I never considered that.'

He smiled. 'I'm a numbers freak, it's what I do. I can put a couple of things together for you when I get back at the weekend.' She cast him a quizzical look and he racked his brain, trying to remember if he'd mentioned his trip. 'I've got business meetings the next few days so I'll be staying with my brother in London until Friday. It'll give you a chance to settle in a bit without me underfoot, sort out your routine and that kind of thing.'

Kiki bit her lip. 'I… umm… I'll need a key for the front door.'

Stupid idiot! Fancy keep telling her this was her home and not even bothering to give her a key! Aaron raised his hand to smack his forehead and nearly poked himself in the eye with the knife's handle in the process. 'Sorry! Sorry, that should have been the first thing I gave you yesterday.'

He quickly rinsed his hands under the tap then dug around in the drawer he'd been using as a dumping ground for things he hadn't wanted to lose. Bits of paper, screwdrivers he'd meant to put back in his toolkit and a handful of foreign coins were all shoved aside as he searched. The drawer had taken on the properties of a TARDIS given the amount of crap he'd managed to cram into it. His fingers finally closed around the ring of keys. He pushed the top of the pile down and forced the drawer shut again.

'I think every kitchen in the land has a junk drawer like that,' Kiki said with a wry smile as he unhooked the spare key and handed it to her. She tucked it in her pocket then turned back to give the sauce a stir. 'This is ready to go in the oven...'

Matty rushed into the kitchen, eyes bright with excitement. 'Mummy, Mummy, come and see!' He hopped about from foot to foot, showing more animation than Aaron had seen from him even when they'd been playing on the beach the previous day.

Kiki gave him an enquiring glance and Aaron schooled his features into as blank an expression as he could manage. She tapped her spoon on the side of the pan, then set it to rest on the edge of the sink. 'I'm busy, darling, can't it wait a minute?'

Aaron had more than a sneaking suspicion the boy had been upstairs and seen his room. He bit his cheek to stop a smile and picked up the oven gloves. 'I'll sort this out. You'd better go and find out what the excitement is all about.'

Chapter Eleven

Kiki wiped her hands on a dish cloth and let Matty grab her hand and tow her out of the kitchen. 'All right, little man, slow down a minute.'

'There's stars, and a racetrack, and Charlie's got a bumblebee!' He tugged her arm, urging her towards the stairs.

'A bumblebee? Is she all right?' Kiki followed on his heels, ears straining for any sounds of distress. She'd been stung by a bee once when she wasn't much older than Charlie and it had hurt so bloody much she'd thought she was going to die. She'd been okay, but the poor bee had died, which had made her cry worse than the pain from the sting. Tender-hearted—that's what her father had always called her. Neil used less pleasant terms for her natural sensitivity. *Weak. Pathetic.*

'Look, Mummy!' Matty tugged her through the doorway of Charlie's room, his face wreathed in smiles. He was like her, her darling boy, so sweet and sensitive to others that it left him wide open to harm from cruel and careless words. At least he'd be guarded from those while living under the thatched roof of this pretty little cottage.

He let go of her hand and ran forwards, taking a flying leap to land in the middle of Charlie's bed. His sister giggled and bopped him on the head with the bright yellow-and-black fluffy bumblebee cushion she'd been cuddling. Kiki could only stare in wonder at the transformed space. The wallpaper was still a dowdy smattering of cornflowers, but it paled into insignificance in comparison to the bold, bright splashes of colour filling the room.

Her eyes roamed, drinking it in, from the sunny bedding to the hot-pink lampshade covering a new bedside lamp, to the sunshine-yellow paper shade shielding what had been a bare bulb hanging from the ceiling. Bright, fuzzy blankets had been draped over the basket-weave chair in the corner, and a selection of Charlie's favourite toys were perched on the pink-and-yellow-striped cushion covering the seat. Mr Bunny had been given pride of place. The fluffy white rug beside the bed looked so soft and inviting that Kiki wanted to kick off her sandals and bury her toes in it.

With a handful of well-placed accessories, the room had been transformed from a plain, uninviting adult space to a sunny haven. The stairs creaked, and she looked over her shoulder to see Aaron waiting one step below the landing. His sheepish, slightly uncertain expression brought out a devilish side she hadn't previously been aware of. She folded her arms across her chest and tried to use her sternest tone, the one the children called her *uh-oh* voice. 'Is this your doing?'

Aaron stuffed his hands into the front pockets of his jeans, looked down at his feet and back up. 'I just wanted to brighten the place up a bit.'

He looked so crestfallen she couldn't keep up the pretence for another second. 'It's wonderful. You're wonderful. Thank you.'

He let out a gasp of what could only be relief and a shy grin lit his face, showing a pair of dimples she'd never noticed before. His normal mega-watt grin quite distracted from the rest of his features, but this softer version amplified rather than smothered the pleasing lines and planes of his cheekbones and wide forehead. In the dim light of the landing, his pale eyes looked more grey than blue. Scruffy hair, casual clothes, broad through the chest and shoulders—such a marked contrast to Neil and his need to be immaculately turned out at all times.

Handsome.

The inappropriateness of the thought warmed her face and she turned away before he could notice. They were practically strangers, housemates and hopefully soon to be friends. *But nothing more.* She didn't want any more, didn't need any more. God knew she'd been through enough heartache with Neil; she should be relishing the thought of being on her own for the first time in her adult life.

Matty ran over and hugged her around the waist, providing a welcome distraction from the embarrassing train of her thoughts. 'You haven't seen the best bit yet.' He scampered away and fiddled with something next to Charlie's bed. Kiki couldn't hold back a gasp of delight as the tiny coloured LEDs entwined in the brass rails of the headboard lit up.

'There's a nightlight here by the door, too.' Aaron's voice sounded close to her ear, and she glanced back to find him peeking over her shoulder. His smile had kicked up about a thousand watts. 'I thought it might help if she wakes up in the night, at least until she's used to being here for a while.'

'That's very thoughtful, thank you. I can't believe what you've done to the place in a few hours.'

He shrugged one shoulder and the shy smile was back. 'I had Madeline's help and it was really no trouble. I want you all to be happy here.'

She looked across at where her children were wrestling on the bed again, play-fighting over the smiley bumblebee cushion, more happy and relaxed than she'd seen them in weeks. 'I think you've already seen to that.'

Aaron straightened up, spots of colour high on his cheeks, like she'd made him blush with the simple truth. 'Hey, Matty. Did you show Mummy your room?'

Surrendering the prize of the cushion for something much better, Matty jumped off the bed. 'Not yet!'

Kiki couldn't believe her eyes. If Charlie's room was great, then Matty's was perfect. The blue bedding was covered in every mode of transportation possible—from a bicycle to a spaceship and everything in between. A huge poster covered one wall, displaying a map of the basic constellations and their relative positions in the night sky. A blue and grey rug covered a huge square of the dull carpet. She tilted her head to better study the design and realised it was the racetrack Matty had referred to.

'I've got lights, too!' He flicked the switch beside his bed and soft-blue LEDs shone from the rails of the headboard, which matched the one in his sister's room. He pointed above them. 'Look up!' Stick-on glow stars were scattered across the ceiling.

'I used to love looking at the stars when I was his age,' Aaron said. 'And the sky is so clear here because we're far enough away from any of the big towns or cities to avoid light pollution. I thought Matty might fancy a bit of stargazing one night.'

'Can we? Can we, Mummy?'

She looked between the two expectant faces, and really, what else was there to say other than yes? 'It sounds exciting. But not tonight.' Matty's face fell and she held up her hand before he could start to protest. 'You need to go to bed at your normal time. I know you're not at school, but it isn't the holidays yet. Ask Aaron nicely and he might find some time at the weekend after he gets back from his trip.'

Matty's brow creased and he drew his lower lip between his teeth and started to nibble it. Kiki sighed. She needed to tread more gently. His smiles and excitement had fooled her into forgetting how much change she was throwing at him in rapid succession.

Aaron crossed the room and placed a hand on Matty's shoulder. 'Don't look so down in the mouth, bud. We can hang out on Saturday and I'll show you some of the books my dad gave me, which are all about the planets and constellations.'

Matty stayed silent for a few moments as his gaze danced back and forth between Kiki and Aaron. The cogs in his little mind were clearly whirring, but he kept his face still. A lash of guilt laid a hot stripe across Kiki's shoulders; little boys of six shouldn't have to guard their thoughts like that. Aaron must have had the same idea.

He lifted his hand from Matty's shoulder to cup his cheek. 'What's going on inside that clever brain of yours, kiddo?'

'Daddy went away on a trip, too. He didn't say goodbye.'

Oh God. Kiki took a step towards them, but Aaron forestalled her by crouching down so his face was at the same level as Matty's. 'Your daddy had to go away for his work, but he'll be back, and I will be, too. I'll be gone for two nights, that's all. Did you know I'm a big brother, just like you?'

Matty shook his head, but he looked more interested than worried now.

Aaron shifted position to rest on one knee. 'I've got a little brother and his name is Luke. One of the things I need to do while I'm away is make sure he's all right.

You understand that, don't you? I see the way you look out for Charlie.'

'She needs my help, she's too little to take care of herself.'

Kiki crossed the room to kneel next to her son. 'And you do a great job. I'm so proud of you, little man.'

Aaron shared a smile with her then turned back to Matty. 'Luke is a lot bigger than Charlie, but I still need to look out for him, make sure he's not getting into any trouble without me.'

Matty took a breath and straightened his shoulders. 'You should go and see him then. I'll take care of Charlie and Mummy until you get back.' He sounded so solemn and serious Kiki wanted to snatch him into her arms, but that would ruin their little man-to-man moment.

'I know you'll do a fine job.' Aaron straightened up and dusted off the knees of his jeans. He raised his head and sniffed loudly. 'Something smells good. Let's go downstairs and set the table ready for dinner.'

Kiki watched her son trot away at Aaron's heels in amazement. With just a few words, his worries had been alleviated and his confidence bolstered. Between Aaron, Daniel and Richard, perhaps he would finally have the positive male role models he needed. He should have been able to rely on his father for that, but Kiki knew from bitter experience how sadly lacking parents could be. She had her own responsibility to bear for all this, too. She'd let it go on for too long, allowed Neil to hurt her and bully the children.

Memories of all the cruel jibes she'd endured, the hurt and fear flashing in Matty's eyes as he heard his father call her stupid, and worse. *Much worse.* She was as bad as the rest of them. Neil, her own parents. Humiliation, shame and self-loathing rocked her and she covered her face with her hands. *No tears, no tears.* She needed to own this, to make it right, and there was no time for self-indulgence.

'Mummy?'

She pinched her cheeks hard with her thumbs to stem the fluttering in her throat, then forced her head up with a bright smile. 'Yes, poppet?'

Charlie snuggled into her side, the bumblebee cushion tucked under her arm. 'I'm hungry.'

'Me, too. Let's go downstairs before those boys gobble everything up.'

***

Kiki smoothed her hand over the edge of her daughter's quilt and smiled. Already asleep, Charlie still maintained a firm grip on the bee cushion. Mr Bunny was tucked in next to her, but the tatty old rabbit had a rival now. The soft lights twinkled around the bed and she reached down to switch them off, then changed her mind. She could do that when she came to bed later.

Treading softly, she left the room and pulled the door until a small gap remained. Soft voices drifted from the bedroom next door. Leaning against the frame, she raised her hand to wave when Matty glanced up from the book he and Aaron were studying. 'Did you know there are nine planets, Mummy?'

'Yes, I did. Although I heard some people don't think that Pluto is really a planet.'

Aaron made a rude noise, which made Matty giggle. 'Pluto is too a planet.'

'I never said it wasn't!' Kiki laughed and held up her hands in mock surrender. 'Five more minutes, you two.' She left them to it before either could argue with the deadline.

Settling back into a slightly rickety garden chair, Kiki raised her glass and took a sip of cold white wine. She'd avoided alcohol until Mia had pointed out they were both guilty of allowing their mother to dictate their actions. They'd shared a bottle of disgustingly sweet fizzy wine and stayed up half the night giggling. It had been just a few weeks before Mia married Jamie and they'd shared their hopes and fears for the future. It seemed like half a lifetime ago.

She took another sip, savouring the crisp, dry flavour. Whatever they might say to each other about escaping the past, neither she nor Mia were regular drinkers. Kiki stuck to a single glass, and only when she had an occasion to mark. Never to numb, never to forget. Even at the worst times with Neil, she'd never been tempted to fall into a bottle.

Swapping her glass for her daybook on the garden table, Kiki nibbled on the end of her pen and rested her head on the back of her chair. The setting sun turned the sky into a wash of reds, oranges and pinks. Evensong danced from tree to tree, the chorus picked up by different birds as they gave thanks for the day.

Her eyes drifted closed. For all the ups and downs, it had been a good day. The first day of her new life. She was safe, the kids were safe, and Neil was hundreds of miles away. She had time to breathe at last.

Opening her eyes, she folded back the spine on her book and drew a line down the centre of a clean page. At the top of the left column she wrote 'changes' and on the right 'goals'. She started to add points to each side—*stop lip-biting, no crying, backbone!* all went in the change column. *Second job, veg patch, read a book a week,* she listed under goals. *Second job.* She allowed herself a smile. Mia had been delighted at her suggestion, surprising Kiki with how quickly she'd added extra responsibilities.

'I think I might have started your son on a new obsession.'

She jumped in her seat, sending the plastic chair rocking precariously. Aaron leaped forwards and grabbed the back to steady it before she tumbled over onto the grass. The warmth from his fingers soaked into her skin, and goose bumps raced down her arm. It must have grown cold without her noticing. Kiki pressed a hand to still her racing heart. 'You startled me.'

He took a step back, tucking his hands in his front pockets. 'No kidding. I didn't mean to disturb you, just wanted to let you know I finally persuaded him to go to sleep.'

Kiki checked her watch. It was closer to half an hour than the five minutes she'd stipulated. 'I lost track of time.' She started to get up, but he waved her back down.

'Charlie's out like a light. I've loaded the dishwasher and put it on so you can take your time and finish whatever you're working on. I just wanted to see if you needed anything before I get on with my packing.'

Was there anything he didn't think of? How on earth had she wound up beneath the same roof as someone so kind and thoughtful? *And handsome.* She rubbed her arms to warm them, and drive out the errant thought. 'It's cooler than I expected. I think I'll come in.'

'Stay there, I'll grab you a jumper.' He loped off before she could protest, returning a few seconds later with a thick, Guernsey-style sweater.

The soft wool eased the chill in an instant, though she had to roll the sleeves a couple of times to leave her hands free. 'Thank you.' She tugged the thick length of her hair free from the high neck with a laugh. 'I really should do something about this. It's more trouble than its worth.'

'I like it.' His eyes widened in surprise as though he hadn't meant to speak aloud. He scuffed his toe in the grass. 'Anyway, lots to do before tomorrow, so I'll leave you to it. G'night.'

She blinked at his rapidly retreating back, not sure how she felt about the idea Aaron had noticed her hair enough to form a liking for it. She shook it off. He was probably just being polite and, besides, didn't most men prefer long hair on women? 'Don't let your imagination run away with you,' she muttered to herself and bent back over her list.

Chapter Twelve

By the time Aaron let himself into Luke's flat with his spare key, he was ready for a shower and a cold beer. Not necessarily in that order. His suit jacket hung like a damp rag from his shoulders and his tie flew at lower than half-mast. The tube had been rammed, worse than he remembered it. Between the sour sweat and foul-smelling junk food filling the carriage, he'd been lucky to keep his long-since-eaten lunchtime sandwich down.

He sniffed his sleeve, wrinkled his nose and shrugged off his jacket. The dry cleaner's would need to work a miracle to freshen it up. Unbuttoning his sleeves, he rolled them to the elbow and gave his hands a quick wash at the kitchen sink before opening the fridge. A wry smile tugged his mouth. The contents could be displayed at the Tate Modern—Portrait of a Single Man. His own hadn't looked too dissimilar a couple of days previously. No child-sized yoghurts, a vegetable drawer stuffed with beer rather than salad and vegetables. With just one trip to the supermarket, Kiki had transformed his sorry shelves into a cornucopia of delights. He knew which version he preferred.

Popping the tab on a can, Aaron took a deep drink and smacked his lips as the bitter, refreshing taste hit the perfect spot. He dragged his small wheeled suitcase towards the back of the flat to satisfy the second-most-pressing need, now the first had been temporarily sated. Stowing his case in one corner of Luke's bedroom, he fished out a change of clothes and dragged his weary body to the shower.

A fresh beer sat on the edge of the sink when he stepped out of the cubicle feeling much more human. 'Hey, Spud!' he called out as he wrapped a towel around himself and swiped the condensation off the mirror.

The bathroom door pushed open. 'Hey, yourself. I've phoned for pizza. It'll be here in about twenty minutes.'

Aaron's stomach rumbled. Salad and vegetables had their place, but an extra-large spicy with double mushrooms was hard to beat. He studied his brother through the mirror. Luke looked as knackered and bedraggled as Aaron had felt. 'Give me two minutes and the bathroom's all yours.' Luke toasted him with his own beer and left him to get changed.

***

Belly full, a third beer rejected in favour of a Diet Coke, Aaron dug out his phone and checked for messages.

Matty says to tell you the big red spot on Jupiter is really a storm.

He shook his head. It was the fourth text he'd received from Kiki since leaving that morning. Each one a different fact about one of the planets. The kid was a sponge.

'Got yourself a girlfriend?'

The sly question from Luke blindsided him. 'What? No! Nothing like that. Mia's sister needed a place to stay so I offered up the cottage.'

'Sister? Which sister?' Luke's sharp tone was in marked contrast to the lazy teasing of his previous question.

Aaron put his phone to one side and sat forward. 'Kiki. The middle one. She's left her husband and needs a bit of moral support. Turned up with a boot full of stuff and two kids in tow. Matty, the eldest, is a sweet boy, a bit shy and nervous. I showed him one of Dad's space books and he's hooked. Keeps sending me facts and figures.'

Luke frowned, blew out a breath and sat back. 'So, you just opened your door to them? How long are they staying?'

'Yes. Do you have a problem with that? Jesus, Spud, she looks fit to cry if someone looks at her the wrong way and the boy is a bag of nerves. The daughter seems more resilient, but she's only a tot. They needed help, so I'm helping them. Husband's a bastard, according to Daniel.' His brother's odd reaction was very unlike him. Luke would be the first to give the coat off his back to a stranger in need. 'What's got into you?'

Luke shook his head. 'Nothing, I just want you to be careful, that's all. You always were a knight in shining armour and broken girls have always been your speciality.'

Broken girls? What the hell was that supposed to mean? A few of the girls he'd dated had had a tough time, but didn't everyone these days? 'You're talking out of your arse, Spud.'

'Sure, sure,' Luke scoffed. 'Out of interest, how many of your ex-girlfriends end up in a serious relationship after they break up with you? You've been to at least two of their weddings that I know of.'

Irritation pricked his skin. His brother didn't know what the hell he was talking about. 'What about you, Casanova? You're not exactly one for finding the future Mrs Luke Spenser and settling down, are you? Have you dated anyone for longer than a week or two?'

The colour drained from Luke's face. He stormed from the room towards the small kitchen. Aaron listened to him slamming around for a few moments while he ran back over their exchange trying to work out what had set Luke off. They picked at each other, sure, but that's what brothers did. And there was nothing he'd said that wasn't true. His brother changed girlfriends like he changed suits. No harm, no trail of broken hearts, but he was a serial dater. Better find out what the dramatic exit was all about.

Leaning against the open kitchen door, Aaron drained the last of his Diet Coke and held out his can to Luke as he stalked past him to pummel the poor, unoffending pizza box into the recycling bin. Luke dropped the can on the floor and stamped it flat, sending a spray of liquid and his own curses into the air. He had to pass Aaron again to get to the cloth in the sink, but this time he wouldn't let him past. 'Talk to me.'

'I'm really not in the mood for your big brother shit, just leave it.' Luke jerked his arm, but Aaron held tight. Bigger and bulkier than his younger brother, there was no way he could be shaken off if he didn't want to be.

'Not happening.'

'You really are the most infuriating wanker.' Luke clenched his fists, but at least he didn't try to pull his arm free of Aaron's grip this time.

He shrugged the insult off. He'd been called much worse. Mostly by Luke. 'Big brother's prerogative.'

All the fight seemed to leave Luke in a single sad huff of breath. 'It's nothing. It's stupid.'

Aaron shifted his grip from Luke's arm to his shoulder. 'Not if it has you this upset, Spud. Talk to me.' He softened his voice to make it less of a demand this time.

Colour spotting his cheeks, Luke cast a quick glance up at him through the tumble of curls shading his eyes. 'Do you believe in love at first sight?'

The question stunned Aaron. Funny, flirty, devil-may-care Luke had never been one for such flights of fancy. There was no humorous glint in his eyes, though. Aaron bit back the teasing comment on the tip of his tongue and searched for the right response. 'Do you?'

A rough laugh rasped from Luke's throat. 'If you'd asked me a year ago, I would have laughed in your face.'

'But not now?'

His brother twisted away and Aaron released his shoulder to let him go. Luke paced back and forth across the fake-wood flooring, keeping his face averted so Aaron couldn't read his expression. 'It was last summer. I saw her in the beer garden behind The George. There was something about her, like she drew all the light down, and I couldn't keep my eyes off her. It took her two drinks to notice me watching her. When she did, she walked away from her friends mid-sentence, like she felt it, too.'

Aaron cast his mind back twelve months. The George was a popular pub with the art crowd and it had become their regular haunt by default of his friendship with Daniel. Aaron had been seeing Natalie, a girl he worked with, and they'd been pretty tight for a while. With Daniel up to his neck in booze and sycophants, the three men had drifted apart. Natalie had been struggling with a difficult performance review from her boss and Aaron had been too focused on helping her through it. Chris Atkins was a notorious misogynist and he'd knocked her confidence badly.

Things had picked up in the autumn—he'd persuaded Natalie to apply for a job in a new department and she'd aced her interview. With both of them busy, they'd drifted apart. Luke's pointed comment about his preference for broken girls drifted to the surface. *Or had he deliberately let her go once she didn't need him any more?* Aaron shrugged off the unwelcome thought. This was about Luke's love life, not his own. *Way to avoid the difficult introspection, tough guy.*

'I never realised.'

Luke stopped pacing and leaned back against the counter with a sigh. 'I hardly saw you. We were so wrapped up in each other, it was like the rest of the world vanished for a couple of months. I thought she was 'the one'. I thought she felt the same until I woke up the morning after we…' He swallowed so hard, Aaron could see his Adam's apple move. 'I woke up one morning and she was just gone.'

Jesus. Aaron had been on the end of his fair share of 'it's not you, it's me' conversations. If he thought about it, most of his relationships ended that way. Not that it bothered him who left who, and it wasn't like any of them had ended badly. He wasn't attracted to the kind of women who thrived on drama. A hug, a kiss on the cheek and a kind parting word was the best way. He'd certainly never dated anyone who just walked out on him. 'Have you seen her since?'

Luke shook his head. 'Not once in all the months since she left. It was like she vanished off the face of the earth. Her mobile number was disconnected and she never responded to any of the emails I sent her.' He scrubbed his face with his hands. 'I thought I'd got over it, and then a few weeks ago I could have sworn I caught a glimpse of her. By the time I crossed the road she was gone. It happened again in the supermarket, but I checked every aisle and the queues at the tills…'

'Oh, Spud. Why didn't you say anything?' Aaron crossed the room and drew his brother into a hug.

Luke's next words were muffled against his shoulder. 'I dunno. At first I was too shocked, like she'd walk through the door any minute. Then I was so angry, I didn't want to waste another second thinking about her. And now, it's like I'm going crazy—seeing her, or girls that remind me of her. It's probably all that time we've been spending with Mia.'

Aaron pulled back to frown at his brother. 'What's Mia got to do with any of this?'

'What? Oh, nothing.' Luke shoved his hands in his pockets and looked away. 'I just meant seeing her with Daniel… you know… seeing them happy together… it triggered a few memories, that's all.'

Aaron shrugged. Everything Luke said made perfect sense, and yet he got the feeling he was missing something. 'Did you speak to her friends, ask them if they knew where she went?'

'I never really met them. Like I said, we got so wrapped up in each other we hardly spent time with anyone else. It was just a mad fling.' He shook himself like a wet dog. 'Enough of that sentimental shit. I met a girl, she broke my heart, I'll get over it. Fancy another beer?'

It was tempting to push for more information, but Luke's body language, as much as his words, made it clear he didn't want to say anything else. 'Sure, why not, but make it a small one, okay? Hey, do you want to come back with me tomorrow night? I'm sure Daniel can find something for you to wallop with a hammer until you feel better.'

His brother gave him a funny look over his shoulder before turning back to examine the contents of his fridge. 'Nah, I wouldn't want to intrude on your new project. Besides, it sounds like you've no room for me.'

Aaron bristled at the jibe. Kiki wasn't a bloody project; she was just a friend of a friend who needed a place to stay. 'Give it a rest, will you? There's always room for you. Mia and Daniel have a spare room on their third floor. If you don't fancy that, I'm sure Madeline would be thrilled to put you up for a few days.'

'Ugh, I'm being an idiot. Just ignore me, all right?' Luke held out a beer as a peace offering.

He stared at it for a couple of seconds before taking the stubby bottle and clanking it against Luke's. 'You're an idiot.' They both laughed and the tension between them broke. Aaron took a sip and sighed. 'So, let's talk about something fun instead. How's Cathy?'

Luke choked on his own mouthful of beer. He wiped his chin with the back of his hand. 'Jesus, Bumble. If we kick that hornet's nest we'll both end up in the funny farm.'

They laughed again. Luke had never pulled any punches when it came to his mum. He knew her faults, called her out on them even when Aaron would've preferred he kept quiet. Well, it wasn't his problem any more. 'Have you spoken to Dad?'

'Sunday night. Your fake headache at Mum's birthday weekend fooled no one. He's racked with guilt about letting you walk away like that. As he should be.' Luke mumbled the last around the mouth of his beer bottle, but Aaron caught the bitter aside.

'You blame him?' Dad had always done his best to play fair by all of them.

Luke took a long drink, eyes fixed hard on Aaron. He lowered the bottle and shook his head. 'And you don't? Get real. If he'd faced up to her indifference towards you, then we wouldn't be in this mess. But of course he won't, because he feels guilty about how much he still loves your mum. If one or other of them would just let her rest in peace they might actually move on.'

'You think that's still the problem, after all this time?' Bloody Hell. Dad and Cathy would be celebrating their silver wedding anniversary in a few days. How had they managed twenty-five years together without clearing the air over their feelings about his mum?

'I'm sure of it, and they've kept you stuck between them from the very start.' Luke sighed. 'You're as bad as he is, always so bloody reasonable. I've watched you take every time she slighted you, turning the other cheek so many times I'm surprised you didn't give yourself whiplash.' He checked his watch. 'Look, I've got an early start tomorrow so I'm going to turn in. Are you sure you'll be all right on the sofa?'

Still trying to absorb everything his brother had said, Aaron trailed around after him while they sorted out the spare quilt and a pillow for the sofa. His first meeting in the morning wasn't until nine-thirty—his artistic clients weren't exactly early risers.

Luke shook the pillow and laid it on the sofa. 'You've got everything you need?'

'Yes, thanks. Do you fancy going out tomorrow evening? We could go to the pictures and then on to Chinatown for dinner?' It had been too long since they'd just hung out together and that had been one of the reasons for his visit. The family stuff would still be there, had always been there, but they'd never let it come between them and Aaron was damned if he was going to let that happen now.

The sunny smile that lit his brother's face made everything else fade into obscurity. They weren't just brothers, they were best friends, and he gave thanks for it every damn day.

***

'Just here will be great.' Aaron indicated the top of the driveway to Honeysuckle Cottage and his new-found friend pulled over. They'd got chatting on the train when the last of the other passengers in their carriage had alighted a few stops before Orcombe Sands. Simon had made a joke about civilisation abandoning them and it had gone from there. Once he'd realised they had the same destination, Simon had insisted on giving him a lift home.

Aaron slid out of the car, grabbed his case from the back seat, then leaned down to speak through the open passenger window. 'Thanks again, I really appreciate it.'

'No worries. It's good to meet someone our age, Nancy will be thrilled. We'd heard about the changes down at Butterfly Cove and she's been dying to have a nose around.'

'I'll have a chat with Daniel and arrange a tour. You can bring the kids and we'll have a bit of a barbecue or something.'

'Sounds great. I'll email you the details of that holiday club we've enrolled Christopher in. Have a good weekend.'

Aaron waved him off then turned towards the cottage. A light glowed at the living room window and another upstairs in Charlie's bedroom. A sense of rightness settled over him. He'd lived on his own since leaving university, had always been fiercely protective of his own space, but the cottage had felt too big for him to fill by himself. He picked up his case and hurried forward, eager to see how Kiki and the children had managed in his absence.

The smell of roast chicken hit his nose the moment he turned the key and pushed open the door, making his mouth water. No frozen dinner chucked in the microwave or greasy takeaway tonight. He didn't mind cooking, but it was hard to be creative for one. He always made too much, and eating the same thing for three days on the trot could be tiresome.

Letting the light spilling from the front room draw him down the hallway, he poked his head around the door. Kiki sat on the sofa. Her hair was down, the rich-brown length tumbling over her shoulder like a silken waterfall. Charlie sat cross-legged next to her—rosy-cheeked and clad in an adorable onesie with fluffy ears on the hood. Matty was sprawled on the carpet in front of them, tongue poking out of the corner of his mouth as he coloured in a picture filled with planets and stars. On the TV, a Disney princess swirled around her ice palace telling herself and the world to 'Let It Go'.

Witnessing such an intimate family moment made his heart thud painfully in his chest. What would it be like to be part of that scene, to belong to that little tribe? To be able to claim a place among them… He knew better than most what hid behind the perfect tableau. He'd appeared in enough of them over the years—the happy, smiling group out enjoying a meal together. The children running happily around the park watched by adults with indulgent smiles. Everyone put on a façade, a performance for external consumption. This was different, though. No one was here to watch them. Except him, and he didn't belong there.

He pushed the deep sense of longing away, and forced a bright smile to his face. 'I'm home.'

Three sets of surprised eyes turned towards him, followed rapidly by three happy smiles and competing greetings.

'Aaron's home!'

'Look at my picture! Richard bought me a book and it's full of stars and spaceships…'

'Hello, you should have called, I would have come and fetched you from the station…'

Not sure who to answer first, he chose Kiki. 'I met someone from the village on the train. He offered me a lift.'

Crouching down, he let the children surge around him like eager puppies as they vied to tell him a hundred vitally important things. He reached out to steady Charlie when she overbalanced and she cuddled against his thigh as Matty showed them the pictures in his colouring book. He spared a quick glance at Kiki, stopped and looked up again when he caught the expression on her face. One hand over her mouth, her damp eyes were glued on the oblivious children.

Noticing him watching her, she straightened up and blinked a few times to clear her eyes. 'I'll just go and check on dinner. Give Aaron room to breathe, you two, he's only just got in the door.' She tugged the ears on Charlie's onesie as she walked past, making the little girl giggle.

He stood up. 'I'll give you a hand. Just give me two minutes to get changed.'

She laughed. 'You're fine. Matty has already set the table, and dinner is all done bar the gravy.'

Feeling equal parts grateful and guilty, he nodded. 'Okay, if you're sure. I told you before that I didn't expect you to do everything.'

Her lips pursed and a light gleamed in her eyes. 'I'm sure there'll be plenty for you to do, don't worry.'

Matty tugged his sleeve, and he looked away from Kiki's departing back. 'Mummy's made you a list of chores,' he said, eyes full of sympathy.

'Has she now? Is it a very long list?' The boy nodded, and Aaron battled to keep his face straight. Clearly chores were the worst thing Matty could think of, but they sounded pretty bloody brilliant to him. Kiki was not only making herself at home, she had thought of things he could do to help her. It probably shouldn't please him as much as it did that she'd been thinking about him whilst he'd been away. Even if it *was* only to fix things around the place.

He let Charlie lead him further into the room and over to the sofa. 'Elsa!' She pointed at the TV, clambered back onto the seat and patted the cushion next to her.

Aaron sank down with a happy sigh and let the images on the screen flicker before him. This might not be his family, but maybe he could pretend it was—just for a little while.

Chapter Thirteen

Hands full of Tupperware boxes, Kiki used her elbow to open Mia's kitchen door. 'Sorry, sorry I'm late!' The top box in her pile began to teeter and she hurried to the table to set them down before the Victoria sponge could tumble to the floor.

Wiping her hands on her jeans, her sister turned towards her with a smile. 'It's only five minutes, Kiki Dee, no need to panic.' She glanced past Kiki's shoulder. 'Hey, where're the kids?'

Kiki shrugged off her light cardigan. With the Aga on full blast, the room was already growing warm. She crossed to the sink to wash her hands. 'Aaron took Matty to check out some kids' club they're running in Exmouth over the summer. Charlie insisted on going, although I think she's too little for the kind of activities they're putting on.'

Aaron's new friend, Simon, had sent through an email the previous weekend with details of an adventure club run in conjunction with the local schools and the lifeboat team. The main aim was to have fun, but there was a strong emphasis on teaching safe behaviour on the beach and in the water. Matty hadn't been entirely sure about it, but she hoped, once he'd had a chance to meet the organisers, his enthusiasm would grow. It would be a good way to make some friends and boost his confidence. *Maybe they do a course for adults, too.* Kiki sure could do with a dose herself.

Her solicitor had sent a text advising, now she knew Kiki was at least temporarily settled, that she'd dispatched the divorce papers and expected them to be delivered that morning. It was ridiculous really, but they'd been so busy settling in at Honeysuckle Cottage, she'd almost allowed herself to forget the harsh reality of her circumstances.

Neil hadn't done more than send her a quick email advising of his safe arrival, and instructing her not to bother him unless there was something urgent to be dealt with. Proof of his self-centredness had been a relief and she'd tried to push him to the back of her mind. The solicitor had made it clear Kiki was not to talk to Neil if he attempted to contact her, but it didn't help with the growing queasiness in her stomach. The only answer was to keep busy. She opened the fridge and began to shuffle things around to make room.

'If there's anything without cream in it, you can store those in the pantry. It stays cool enough in there.' Mia touched her shoulder and Kiki flinched away in surprise. She swallowed a sigh at her own involuntary reaction. Not jumping like a rabbit anytime someone came near her needed to go on her self-improvement list. 'Hey, everything okay?' her sister asked.

'Yes. No. I don't know.' Kiki laughed at her own nonsense. 'Neil is going to get the papers today.' As though saying his name out loud summoned him, her mobile began to ring. She rushed to where her cardigan hung from the back of a chair and pulled it out. 'It's him.' Her hand shook so much, she dropped the phone on the table.

'Leave it. Let it go to answerphone.' Mia hurried to her side. 'Hey, you're shaking. Sit down, Kiki Dee and I'll make us some tea.'

Six. Seven. God, how many rings before her answerphone cut in? 'Just piss off, will you?' she yelled at the handset. The double-ring ended halfway through and she slumped into the chair in relief. Aware of the sudden silence in the room, she glanced up to find Mia staring open-mouthed at her. 'What?'

A broad smile split her sister's face. 'I think that's the first time I've ever heard you raise your voice to him.'

Heat warmed her face. 'Shouting at the phone doesn't exactly count, does it? It's not like he can hear me.'

Mia crouched beside her chair and took Kiki's hands between her own. 'It counts, darling. You're being so brave about all this, I'm so proud of you.'

Kiki swallowed the lump in her throat. 'Don't be nice to me, Mimi. I'm trying not to cry so much, I even wrote it down on my to-do list. Or should I say my not-to-do list.'

They laughed, both a little watery, and Mia straightened up. 'Get to work, slacker! Those toilets won't scrub themselves.' She cocked her head. 'Better?'

'Much. Thank you.'

Kiki made to get up, but Mia pressed her back down into the chair. 'Hey, I'm kidding. There's no rush. Everyone is having a late start today so they're still having breakfast. Just let me drop this fresh pot of coffee next door and we can have a chat while we wait for them to head out for the day.' She nodded towards a stack of bridal magazines. 'I'm in dire need of some input.'

The beautiful images proved the perfect distraction and Kiki found herself engrossed in an article urgently explaining why homemade favours were the must-have decoration for every fashionable bride's reception. Mia leaned over her shoulder. 'I *hate* sugared almonds. I've been dreaming about the bloody things.'

'I don't remember all this being such a big deal.' Her wedding to Neil had been a small affair—intimate, according to him. '*Cheap,*' her mother had sniffed after too much wine at the reception in the back room of a local pub. Mia and Jamie's a few months earlier had been bigger; Kiki hadn't realised they knew so many people. Neil had sneered about the ostentation, leaning over to whisper in her ear how they didn't need an audience to prove their love for each other. She wondered now whether he'd just been jealous. Jamie always had such an easy way with people, drawing them into his circle, making them feel special without any effort. It hadn't been a performance with him—he'd just been a friendly soul.

She looked up at her sister. 'Does it feel strange, doing this all over again?'

A sad smile quirked one corner of Mia's mouth. 'It did a bit at first, but I love Daniel and I *want* to be his wife. It's his first time, and he deserves a proper wedding. I don't want him to ever feel like he's an also-ran. What I had with Jamie was wonderful, but we were little more than kids back then. This is different, deeper, no holds barred.'

Kiki swallowed. 'I'm so pleased for you. It was hateful of me not to let you tell me about him when you came home.' She looked away, uncertain whether she could explain without sounding as awful as she suspected she was. 'I was jealous.'

A soft hand stroked through her hair. 'Oh, darling. You were having such a bad time of it, I don't blame you for not wanting to hear me gush about my new boyfriend.'

Kiki shook her head. 'No. You don't understand.' The words caught in her suddenly dry throat and she took a quick mouthful of her tea. Hotter than she'd expected, it burned her mouth and she welcomed the pain as some kind of retribution for her ugly thoughts. 'Before. When Jamie died. There you were, broken into pieces, and all I could think of was how I wished it was me. How I wished it had been Neil driving—'

'Kiki Dee…'

She pushed her chair away, undeserving of the tender sympathy in her sister's voice. 'I need to get on with those bathrooms.'

'Please don't. Stay and talk to me. You know you can tell me anything.' Mia moved towards her, but Kiki held up a hand to ward her off.

'You don't want to hear this. I don't want to hear it. I don't even want to think about how much I *hate* him.' She was crying now. God damn, she'd sworn there would be no more tears, but she couldn't stop them pouring down her cheeks any more than the words pouring from her mouth. 'I hate him. I hate his perfect suits, those bloody striped ties he always insists upon. Matty chose a cartoon one for him for Christmas last year, and he made me return it! God forbid anyone shouldn't take Dr Neil Jackson, Ph-bloody-D seriously enough.'

On and on and on, all her darkest secrets tumbled out. 'The stink of that gel he puts on his hair makes me retch; the way he gargles after he cleans his teeth, sounding like he's choking. I used to cross my fingers and pray he would choke on it. I used to lie there, smelling that gel and the mint on his breath, wishing one or other of us would just die so it would be over and I'd never have to let him touch me again.' She turned away, covering her mouth to physically prevent herself from saying any more.

'Oh, shit, Kiki...'

A cheery rat-tat-tat sounded on the closed kitchen door and Kiki dashed for the dark haven of the pantry. Bad enough she was displaying her worst self to her sister without showing her up in front of a paying guest. She curled her hands around one of the thick wooden shelves and clung on, the feel of the hard wood the only thing preventing her from flying apart. *Breathe. Just breathe.* Swallowing her tears, she focused on bringing her breathing under control. In… hold…out. She pushed all her focus into those three words over and over until her racing heart slowed and the fluttering panic subsided.

'Kiki?'

She groaned at the tenderness in her sister's voice. 'Don't, Mimi. Don't be nice, I don't deserve it.'

'Bollocks!' Mia's arms engulfed her waist and the warm heat of her body soaked into Kiki's shivering spine. 'If anyone deserves a bit of nice in their life, it's you, darling.'

Kiki shook her head. 'You can't mean that. You heard me, you heard the horrible things inside me.' All this time she'd been lying to everyone—including herself. Trying so damn hard to make her marriage work when it was the last thing she'd wanted. Pretending if she said the right thing, or finally found a way to make Neil happy, then the ugliness would vanish and they'd be like the Waltons, or the Ingalls, one of those perfect happy families she'd grown up watching on Saturday morning television.

Laughter was the last response she expected. Taken off-guard, she didn't resist when Mia disengaged her arms and spun Kiki to face her. 'I'm glad you hate

Neil. God knows that slimy bastard deserves nothing else from you after everything he's done.'

She really didn't get it, did she? If Neil deserved to be hated, then Kiki deserved that and more for putting up with him and his awful treatment of her. 'I let him do it.'

Mia's hands cupped her face, forcing Kiki to meet her worried gaze. 'Is that what this is about? You still think it's *your* fault?' Kiki opened her mouth, but Mia pressed her thumbs to Kiki's lips to keep her silent. 'After the way Mum groomed you, you were easy prey for him. He saw that vulnerability in you and, instead of protecting your beautiful, tender heart, he exploited it for his own selfish weakness.'

Groomed? Such an ugly word with all its connotations of abuse. 'She was sick, Mia. She didn't know what she was doing.'

Mia snorted. 'She knew exactly what she was doing, Kiki Dee. Why do you think she never tried it with me? She took everything sweet and gentle in you and twisted it around to get you to do what she wanted. Stop making excuses for her, Kiki. Vivian never loved us the way a mother should. Can you imagine treating your sweet Charlie like that?'

Horror filled her. 'Never!'

'Exactly. Try as they might, those two haven't stifled the goodness in you.' Mia dropped her hands and stepped back. 'I know you don't want me bossing you around, but I really think you should find someone to talk to about all this.'

'I'm talking to you...' Kiki understood what Mia meant, but the idea of sitting down with a stranger made her cringe inside.

'Hello? Mia, darling?' Madeline's voice carried from the kitchen, and they both jumped at the sudden intrusion.

'We'll be right there, Mads,' Mia called. She dug in her pocket and handed Kiki a folded tissue. 'Think about it, that's all I'm saying.'

'Think about what? Why are you two hiding in the dark?' Kiki looked past Mia's shoulder to where the older woman stood in the doorway of the pantry. 'Yes, I know I'm being nosy, dear. Ask your sister, and I'm sure she'll be only too glad to tell you what a meddling old bag I am.' There was no shame or censure in her cheerful tone.

Mia laughed and turned towards her friend. 'I'm trying to persuade Kiki to talk to someone professionally about her soon-to-be-ex-husband.'

'Bloody good idea. There's a Relate service in Exeter. I used them years ago when I lost all those babies and Richard got himself snipped without telling me. I know they're still there because we make a donation to them every year. Let me put the kettle on and I'll find their details.'

She left the two of them alone again and Kiki glared at Mia. 'You shouldn't have said anything to her!'

'Of course she should, dearest. We're your friends now, too, and we want to help you,' Madeline called out.

Bloody hell, the woman had ears like a bat! Feeling disgruntled and outnumbered, Kiki trailed after Mia out of the dark pantry and back into the airy kitchen. Madeline had already set fresh mugs on the table and was poking around in the fridge. 'Ooh, is this chocolate cake?'

'That's for the guests, for afternoon tea,' Kiki protested as Madeline bore a familiar Tupperware container to the table with a triumphant smile.

Mia rubbed her hands together with glee. 'Cake sounds just the ticket. I'm only expecting the Pritchards back this afternoon so we've plenty to spare. The Morrises and the Shenleys are making the most of their last day and going for a hike on Exmoor. They won't be back until dinnertime.'

Which was no help at all. Kiki didn't want tea and cake. She wanted to escape to the quiet safety upstairs and get on with her work before these two steamrollered her into making an appointment. She didn't want to dig around in the past any more than she already had. The skeletons in her closet were rattling enough to drive her to distraction. She tried a different tack. 'It's only nine-thirty, a bit early for cake.'

'Nonsense!' Madeline said briskly, a large knife already poised over the double-chocolate fudge cake Kiki had made the night before. It had taken all of her willpower not to surrender to the pleading looks and fluttering lashes of Aaron and the children when the rich smell of cocoa filled the cottage. It seemed a bit mean to them to eat it herself now.

The shiny blade sank into the thick icing and she surrendered. 'Just a tiny slice.' Madeline tilted the knife and slid a huge wedge of cake onto a side plate, then plonked it down in front of Kiki. 'Or maybe not.'

Mia placed the striped teapot on a mat in the centre of the table and accepted her own enormous slab of cake with a grin. 'Cheers, Mads.' She raised the plate to her nose. 'God, this smells heavenly, Kiki Dee. You always were better at cakes than me. I'd better not let Daniel taste this or he'll throw me over. He only loves me for my baking.'

Kiki couldn't help but laugh at the absurdity of it. She might have only been in Butterfly Cove for a fortnight, but it was patently obvious Mia hung the moon and stars for the big, gruff northerner. She forked up a mouthful of the cake and closed her eyes as the buttery-sweet icing melted on her tongue, followed by the darker, headier taste of the plain chocolate she'd added to the batter mix. 'Oh, that's good.'

'Good? It's better than sex,' Mia moaned.

'If a bit of cake is better than sex, my girl, you're doing it wrong,' Madeline snorted before taking her own bite. 'Oh… you're right. It *is* better.' The worshipful tone of her voice set Kiki laughing again and the other women joined in.

They ate the rest of their cake with relish, each trying to outdo the others with sighs and moans of faux-ecstasy until they were giggling so hard, tears leaked from the corners of Kiki's eyes. 'Stop! Please, stop, I'm getting a stitch.'

She pushed away her plate, which was empty apart from a small smear of icing. Feeling a bit sick after eating so much didn't stop her licking her thumb and wiping up that last trace. Her mobile phone vibrated on the table and the cake began to churn around in her stomach. The rising fear subsided when she swiped the screen down and saw the incoming text was not from Neil, but Aaron.

Clicking to open it, she couldn't help but smile at the picture he'd sent. Matty's head poked out of the top of a pile of sand which Charlie was patting down with a bright-red plastic spade. She held up the screen to show Mia and Madeline and they both chuckled at the sunny, funny image. 'He's really taken to them, hasn't he?' Madeline observed.

If he'd taken to the kids, they were entirely smitten with him. His gentle patience and seemingly endless good humour had drawn them to him like a magnet. Charlie wouldn't leave him alone for a moment, pestering him for cuddles and clambering into his lap to watch *Frozen* yet again over the weekend. Matty had been a little more circumspect, but he was never more than a couple of feet from wherever Aaron happened to be—even claiming a corner of the desk in Aaron's office for his colouring book when he went in there to catch up on some paperwork.

The whole week since he'd returned from his trip to London, they'd been like one of those TV families with their idealised picture of domestic bliss. Funny how the thing she'd striven and strained for with Neil had slotted into place with Aaron with no effort whatsoever. They'd fallen into an easy routine without any real thought. At times, she'd found herself holding her breath, waiting for a problem to arise, for her or the children to do something to irritate Aaron and bring them all down to earth with a bump. It hadn't happened yet. By the time they'd settled in a post-dinner lazy sprawl around the living room yesterday evening, she'd even let herself relax for a minute and believe it might be genuine. That Aaron really was as kind and easy-going as he appeared.

And that had scared her half to death.

'They've formed a mutual appreciation society.'

Mia eyed her over the top of her mug. 'You don't sound entirely pleased about it.'

'I don't want them to get hurt. Aaron's great with them, really wonderful.'

'But…?'

She sighed and propped her chin on her hands. 'But, no one is *that* nice. It's all a bit too easy at the moment, but we're obviously in some kind of honeymoon period. The novelty will wear off. They're bound to annoy him at some point, and I couldn't bear it if their new hero turned out to have feet of clay.'

Madeline frowned at her. 'I don't think that's very fair on Aaron. You might find it hard to believe, but he really is a very nice guy. Perhaps instead of waiting for him to disappoint you, you should ask yourself why he's thrown himself so wholeheartedly into things. You might find it's not just those children who are in dire need of a little love and affection.'

The comment took her aback. Aaron was so robust, so full of life and energy, he filled every space he entered with his warmth and wit. It had never occurred to her the confidence she'd taken for granted in him might be hiding something. 'What are you saying?'

'I'm saying big hearts are every bit as tender and vulnerable as little ones. Yours as well as his. Circumstances have thrown you all together. While it's all right to let him support you through this difficult time, make sure you don't take advantage of him in the process.'

Kiki shook her head. Madeline was getting things confused. She and Aaron hardly knew each other and she wasn't looking for anything more than friendship with him. Sure, she might have peeked when his T-shirt rode up to display an impressively toned stomach when he'd changed one of the burned-out spotlights in the kitchen on Saturday. But it had been nothing more than a fleeting glimpse, an uncontrolled biological reaction, an objective moment of admiration for his toned physique.

She needed to put a stop to this nonsense before the entire conversation derailed. They were talking about the children's needs, not her own. 'I don't need a man in my life, Madeline. I'm not ready for one, even one as attractive as Aaron.' *Why had she said that?*

'I hate to tell you this, dearest, but you already have a man in your life, whether you're ready for him or not.'

Madeline slid a number scribbled on a piece of paper forward, a serious glint in her eyes. 'Go and talk to a counsellor. Put the past to rest and then be honest with yourself. If you don't want anything more than a friend, you need to find yourself somewhere else to live sooner rather than later. Two attractive, lonely, *available* people under the same roof is a recipe for disaster.'

Kiki gaped at Madeline. She couldn't honestly think she and Aaron were likely to jump into bed with each other. Could she?

Apparently ready to kill Kiki with embarrassment, Madeline ploughed on. '*If*, however, you're only rejecting the thought of a potential relationship with Aaron because convention states you must wait a certain period of time, then to hell with it. You're a nice girl, and he's a lovely boy. If you can put each other together again the way Mia and Daniel have, then what's to stop you?'

'The fact that I'm still married?' She retreated behind the sarcasm to cover her utter shock. Madeline must be crazy to think she could stagger out of one relationship only to tumble headlong into another.

'Semantics,' Madeline responded tartly. 'Unless you're having second thoughts about the divorce.'

'No bloody chance.' Kiki turned to Mia. 'Help me out here.' But Mia tapped her lip with one finger, as though considering Madeline's words.

Unbelievable.

Kiki dragged the pile of wedding magazines towards her. 'Let's all focus on this happy ending instead of trying to conjure one up out of nothing. Aaron and I are housemates. *Friends*. That's all.'

Thankfully, they took the hint and each grabbed one of the thick, glossy tomes from the pile. The mood lifted as they laughed and swooned over huge meringue frocks and elegant silhouettes. They touched on what Daniel might wear, but Mia said she was leaving it for him to choose. Having never seen Daniel in anything other than paint-stained jeans and a T-shirt, Kiki found herself wondering if he would look as good in a suit as Aaron did on those occasions he dressed up for a client meeting. The jackets emphasised the width of his shoulders and the trim line of his waist. Funny how she could hate the sight of Neil in a suit and yet be drawn to the image of Aaron in one.

He was bound to be acting as best man and Mia had already asked her to be matron of honour. Her mind's eye painted a picture of them arm in arm as they followed the happy couple down the aisle. The contented smile on her face reflected the happiness of celebrating her sister's wedding day—nothing more.

Chapter Fourteen

Aaron sat back in his office chair, stretching the kinks out of the muscles in his lower back. One day he would remember to sit properly in his chair, but it wasn't going to be today. Cocking his head, he listened for sounds from upstairs, but the cottage was silent other than for the hum from his laptop. He'd been banned from the bedtime routine on the grounds of being too much of a disruptive influence. His favourite times as a child had been curled up under his covers, fighting heavy eyelids as he pleaded with his dad for one more page of his book.

Perched beside Charlie's bed, putting on silly voices as he read her stories of princesses and dragons helped him remember those good times. Luke's harsh words had forced Aaron to reflect on things he'd rather have ignored about their dad. Aaron didn't possess the same ability Luke appeared to have to view their parents objectively, and a slow-burning anger threatened to overwhelm him if he dwelled on the idea his dad could have done more to bridge the gap between his first-born son and his second wife. He didn't want to think about it, didn't like the unfamiliar anger, so he buried it deep under layers of innocent sweetness as he focused his attention on the children. Which wasn't fair on them either. *What a bloody mess.*

Part of him recognised he was using the kids to avoid the mess in his own life, but he couldn't deny his genuine affection for them. They'd found a special place in his heart without doing anything other than being themselves. How their father could just ignore them both was beyond him. Minding his own business when it came to Neil might be the hardest thing he would have to do.

Needing a cup of coffee, Aaron shut down his laptop. He paused at the door to the living room, frowning when he found it empty. Checking the kitchen, he found it empty, too. He shrugged. Maybe Kiki had decided on an early night for herself. Though she normally said goodnight. A noise came through the open back window, and he glanced out into the fading evening light. Kiki was down at the bottom of the garden, working in the vegetable patch. It seemed a bit late to be planting potatoes, but she had embraced bringing the scruffy stretch of soil and weeds back to life

With a mug in each hand, Aaron made his way down the path. He had to concentrate on his footing in the growing gloom, so didn't look up until he was almost level with her. She slashed her spade into the ground with such force a grunt of sound escaped her mouth. A divot of earth flew through the air, landing inches from where he stood. The spade swung again, and he realised she was muttering something over and over again.

'Useless. I'll show you useless.' The square blade slammed into the ground.

A sob escaped her, and he set down the coffee, then stepped forward, grabbing the wooden shaft of the spade before she could lift it again. 'Hey, hey, what's the matter?'

'Leave me alone.' She yanked on the handle to budge his grip, but the difference between their sizes made it a wasted effort. Breathing hard, she stared up at him. Strands of hair clung to her forehead and he could just make out a dark smudge on her cheek. 'Go and be bloody perfect somewhere else, Aaron. Leave us pathetic, useless, stupid mortals in peace.'

Wow. The sheer invective in her voice forced him to move back. 'I brought you a coffee.' He nodded to where the cups rested on the path. 'I didn't mean to disturb you.' He scooped up his own mug and turned on his heel, fighting not to rub his chest against the pain flaring there.

He barely made it three steps before she called out. 'Stop. Stop! I'm sorry.' The desperate anguish in her voice paled any hurt he felt into insignificance.

Slumped in the dirt, hair spilling around her hunched shoulders, she cut a pitiful figure. 'I'm sorry,' she whispered, covering her face with her dirty hands. His heart went out to her.

He set his mug on the flagstones and hurried back over. 'Here, here now. Up you come. It's all right, Kiki. It's all right.' With gentle hands beneath her arms, he coaxed her to her feet. 'Come and sit down a minute.'

Whatever fight had been in her had deserted her now and she allowed him to guide her to the plastic table and chairs. He left her momentarily to retrieve their drinks, then pulled the spare seat close to hers. Pressing the mug into her hands, he kept his own curled around hers, until he was sure she had a proper grip on it. In the light spilling from the kitchen behind them, he could see the tremble in her arms as she raised the coffee to her lips. Turning his attention to his own drink, Aaron kept Kiki in his peripheral vision, but made a show of looking elsewhere.

'I shouldn't have listened.' Kiki drew her knees up and tugged the length of her skirt down until it covered her toes.

'To what?'

She lifted her hip slightly to pull her mobile from a pocket and handed it to him. Aaron stared at the screen then back at Kiki. She waved her other hand, still holding the mug, towards the handset. 'The answerphone.'

Feeling like he was prying, even though she'd given him the phone, Aaron selected the correct icon and raised the phone to his ear. The first message was little more than an ugly, angry snarl. *'Pick up the fucking phone.'*

Aaron clenched the flimsy arm of his chair and tried to school his features. The automated voice announced the next message, received earlier that afternoon, and then the angry male voice was back. *'Is this some kind of joke, you stupid bitch? Do you think I'll drop everything and come running after you? I've waited years for this opportunity. Call me back!'*

The recording announced the final call, received an hour previously. When the man spoke this time, he sounded different—calmer, much more controlled, with a mocking, forced humour in his tone. *'Kiki, Kiki, what are you thinking? Did that sister of yours put you up to this? How long do you think it will be before she regrets helping you? How long before she finds out how useless you are. You're a burden, Kiki. A waste of space. You can't even look after yourself without my supervision.'* A cold laugh echoed down the phone. *'Have your little rebellion then. You'll never manage on your own. And when everyone is fed up of your stupidity and failure, you'll be begging me to take you back.'*

Letting his hand fall away, Aaron took a deep breath and counted silently to ten. It didn't help much so he repeated the action several times until the immediate urge to smash the phone subsided. God, was Neil always like that towards her? He counted one last time to be sure he could speak with some modicum of control. 'He's wrong.'

Kiki laughed, a bitter, painful bark of sound. 'About what? Staying with a man I hate and who clearly despises me—that's pretty stupid.' She ticked off a point with her finger. 'I've forced you, a near stranger, to turn your home upside down to accommodate us—most people would call that being a burden.'

The anger surged and he couldn't keep a snap out of his voice. 'No one forced me, I offered, remember?' *Ten. Ten, count to bloody ten and breathe.* He wasn't cross with her, but he loathed the way she put herself down all the time. It was obvious now where it stemmed from. He reached over and rested his hand on her arm, just the lightest of touches, but he needed to do it. Needed to offer her a little comfort. He hoped she could hear the truth in his words. 'I'm happy to have you here, especially now I've had a taste of what he's put you through.'

Too caught up in her self-deprecation spiral, she ignored his comment and ticked off another point. 'I can't find a job that brings in enough money to pay you any rent. I'm relying on you, and all the others, to help with the children. How is that managing on my own, eh?' There was a suspicious glitter in her eyes, but she sounded furious, not unhappy. Shame her anger seemed directed inwards rather than at the correct target.

'The only thing he's proven is he knows how to push your buttons. He's an arsehole, Kiki; a pathetic bully.' Aaron slung the phone towards the table, unable to bear touching it for a moment longer. He scrubbed his fingers on his jeans, like the filthy words he'd heard had left a mark on his skin. It all felt a bit too close to home. Kiki's self-doubt and willingness to shoulder the blame stirred memories he really wasn't up to facing. The lid on the can of worms of his childhood eased a little bit looser. He couldn't seem to keep it closed these days.

Kiki propped her chin on her raised knees and sighed. 'I kept trying to make it right, and that's what I can't forgive myself for.' All the anger had fled from her voice and she sounded defeated. 'I even made these ridiculous plans that we would join him on his trip, have an extended family holiday, as if a bit of sun and sand would fix things. Right up until the moment I saw those bloody emails between him and his new *Helen*, I was pretending to myself we had something worth saving when nothing could have been further from the truth.'

He tried to pin the bits and pieces of what she was telling him together, but she was talking more to herself than him so he kept quiet. If Neil was a cheat on top of every other awful thing he'd put Kiki through, then Aaron hoped they never came face to face. Never one easily stirred to violence, he would gladly beat the living daylights out of him nonetheless.

She turned her head to rest her cheek on her knees and stared straight at him. 'Why would I do that? Why would I keep trying to be with him when inside I died a little more every day?'

Locked in her gaze, the truth of his own pain rose up from the dark places inside. 'No one likes to admit to failure. Especially not when you're the kind of person who likes to please others.' Hadn't he bashed his own head against the brick wall of Cathy's indifference for a dozen years more than was good for him? 'You know that Luke and I are half-brothers, right?'

A little frown creased her brow. 'I'm not sure I did. Are your parents divorced?'

'Mum died when I was about Charlie's age. Breast cancer.' Aaron swallowed hard around the lump in his throat. *Jesus, would it ever get any easier to say it?*

'Oh, you poor thing.'

He nodded to acknowledge her sympathy, but ploughed on before the words could choke him. 'Luke's mum was my mum's best friend. She was around a lot at the end and then she never left. Dad married her the next summer and Luke came along just before Christmas.' He'd done the maths years ago after a biology class at school and figured out Cathy had been pregnant when his dad married her. Over the years, he'd speculated about whether they would have stayed together once their mutual grief lessened if circumstances had been different. How much of that was coloured by his own dislike of his stepmother, he didn't know. Besides, he wouldn't have given up one single second of having Luke in his life.

Lifting his cup to his lips, he drained the cold dregs of his coffee with a shudder. The bitter taste braced him enough to continue. 'I've never been able to do right in Cathy's eyes.'

Understanding dawned in Kiki's expression and she sat back in her chair. 'My mum used to blackmail me into sneaking her drinks. She'd fix these big, sad eyes on me, and call me her good girl, her helper, her little angel. I knew…' Her voice wavered and she coughed, then carried on. 'I knew it was wrong, but it was the only time she ever said anything nice to me.'

She bunched her fists and knocked them lightly against her knees. 'Mia's right. I need to talk to someone about all this shit. I feel like a dam on the verge of collapse. Everywhere I look, there's another crack spider-webbing across my walls. One more drop and I think I might burst and get washed away by it all.'

Pale, dirt-streaked and shivering with more than just the chill that had fallen as the sun set, she looked so fragile he wanted to scoop her up and hold her tight until every bit of strain was eased from her face. A knight in shining armour, Luke had called him, and damn it, he was right. Aaron had channelled his need to get Cathy to love him into helping women at their lowest ebb. How could they help but love him when he let them cry on his shoulder as he put them back together again?

If anyone needed him, Kiki did. He could help her and it would be no chore to do it. More delicate than Mia, her face held an ethereal beauty that drew him like a moth to the flame. He could snatch her up, give her all the love she'd missed out on, her and the kids both… The need to feel her in his arms built until his fingers turned white from where he gripped the chair. He could make it right for her, shore up her defences and hold back the tide until she could stand on her own again.

And once she was happy and whole again, what then? Once he'd served his purpose would she walk away like all the others? Kiss him softly on the cheek and say she'd always care about him, but it was time to move on? Because they always left in the end. Loving what he did to help them wasn't the same as loving *him*.

A hollow ache spread through his gut. If he got involved with Kiki, he risked losing the little haven they'd created at the cottage. The repercussions would spread, too, beyond the thick, whitewashed walls, creating ripples of disturbance in the friendships he'd made here. Mia and Daniel would stand with Kiki, how could they not? If it came to him choosing between them and Luke, he'd stand by his brother above all else. Madeline and Richard were like family to Mia. He'd be the one who would have to leave, give up his dreams of a quiet life by the sea and head back to the rat race of London or one of the other big cities. Better to let sleeping dogs lie and protect the peace he'd already found.

Being friends with Kiki would be no hardship and would protect the children from any more emotional fallout. It was the pragmatic, sensible choice and at heart that's who he was. Save the wild romance and adventure for the artistic types like Daniel. Some people weren't cut out for crazy, impulsive choices—that's why they became accountants.

Coward.

He stood and gathered their mugs from the table. He needed to get moving before he did something unconscionably stupid. 'It's getting chilly now, are you ready to go in?'

She nodded, uncurled herself from the chair and followed him into the kitchen. Under the harsh strip light the full consequences of her foray into the vegetable patch were clear. Dirt smeared her face and hands, and there were patches of mud on her skirt. After placing the mugs in the sink, Aaron abandoned all his best intentions and reached out to free a strand of hair which had stuck to the mess on her cheek. 'You look like you've been making mud pies.'

Kiki stared at her filthy hands, ruefully. 'I must look a fright.'

Even filthy, with her hair and clothes in disarray, she looked beautiful. 'You look fine, more than fine.' Her head shot up and she gave him a quizzical look. He cleared his throat, casting around for a way to change the subject. 'Did you need to borrow the laptop, do some research or whatever, if you still want to talk to someone?'

She shook her head. 'Madeline already gave me a number. She's terrifyingly efficient once she gets a bee in her bonnet.'

'Efficient? That's the politest term I've heard for her meddling.' Aaron smiled to himself. He hadn't forgotten her sugar-coated threat to make him talk to her about his dad and Cathy. Where Madeline had a will, she'd find a way.

Kiki huffed a little laugh. 'Yes, she certainly isn't backwards about coming forwards with her opinion. You should hear what she said about us.'

'Us?' Even with the cool evening air coming through the still-open back door, Aaron felt suddenly hot and clammy. *What the bloody hell was Madeline up to now?*

He watched closely as Kiki wound her hands in her skirt and nibbled her lip. It was hard to tell with the amount of dirt on her face, but there might have been a faint hint of colour in her cheeks. 'She thinks that you and I should… you know… get together.' She paused and then carried on in a rush. 'Which is ridiculous, and I told her so, because, God, I've barely split with Neil, and there's so much to sort out with the divorce and everything. And of course, we hardly know each other. Two single people living under the same roof doesn't have to lead to anything, right?'

Ridiculous. If he'd had any second thoughts about not entertaining his attraction to Kiki, she'd put paid to them with one word. Given he'd already decided against it for himself, it really shouldn't feel like quite such a rejection. Why would she want to go out with him—go out with anyone, for that matter—when, as she said, things with Neil were barely ended?

Kiki was staring at him now, and he swallowed a curse. He'd been quiet too long; he should have agreed with her immediately. A flutter of panic rose in his chest. If she thought he might *like* her, it would make things awkward between them. Aaron forced a laugh.

'Luke said some idiotic thing when I was with him. He thinks I'm going to fall for you because he reckons I have a fixation with broken girls.'

Her eyes widened in shock and he realised his mistake. *Shit!* 'Not that *I* think you're broken. You're amazingly strong the way you're coping with everything. I told him we're just friends, but I guess people like to put two and two together and make five.' *Stop talking, for the love of God, just shut up.*

He backed up a couple of steps. 'I'm just going to check my emails and then I think I'll get an early night. The deadline for finishing the studios at Butterfly Cove is getting close so I've promised to pitch in with whatever help I can tomorrow.'

Kiki opened her mouth like she wanted to say something then closed it again with a nod. She glanced down at where her hands were still knotted in her skirt. 'I need to take a shower. An early night sounds like a good idea. Do you want me to give you a lift in the morning? Tuesday is my full day at Mia's.'

Damn, he'd forgotten about that when he'd agreed to help Daniel. 'If you need me to stay with the children then I'm sure Daniel won't mind…'

She shook her head. 'No, no. Madeline and Richard are taking them for the day. I assumed you'd have work to do anyway. I don't expect you to run around after them, you already do so much for me. For *us*.'

'I've told you before, I don't mind. You only have to ask.'

There was a certain sadness in the smile she gave him. 'I know, but once Matty starts at the activity club next week I'll need to get into a proper routine. Madeline and Richard have offered to take Charlie two mornings a week and all day on Tuesdays until I get a bit more money coming in, and then I'll find some proper childcare. You have your own work to consider without us disrupting you. Besides, it's not like I can rely on you for ever.'

Aaron wanted to argue that she could indeed rely on him for ever, but that would fly in the face of his decision to let her call the shots. Things would settle down soon enough if everyone just minded their own business and stopped trying to interfere. Once Kiki found some extra work and could contribute more, she'd feel more at home and hopefully get the idea she was being a burden out of her head. Between Madeline's clumsy matchmaking, Neil's poisonous tongue, and Aaron's ability to stick both feet in his mouth at once, it was no wonder she was in a spin.

'Why don't we sit down this weekend and thrash out a timetable together? I've got my appointments for the next few weeks in my diary, and one of the joys of working for myself now is I can do things at times that suit me. I'll go over the schedule with Daniel and Jordy for the studios tomorrow and work out when I can be of actual use to them. It will do me good to get some discipline back into my days as well.'

Kiki nodded. 'I think that's a good idea. I'll call the number Madeline gave me tomorrow and see when

I can get in to meet them. We can add that to the schedule.' She lifted her hand to push her hair back and caught herself just in time. 'Now, I really need that shower. I'll see you in the morning.'

'Jordy's getting to the studios at seven, so you might not. I'll take the bike, I need the exercise.' He patted his stomach. Thankfully, putting in some hard hours with Daniel had kept him fit, but his life in London had included at least four gym sessions a week—and he hadn't had the benefit of Kiki's home-cooking. He needed to get regular exercise back in his schedule as well.

'You look fine to me. More than fine.' Her echo of his previous words sent all his good intentions to the wall. Did she look at him the same way he'd started to notice her? His rugby-playing days might be behind him, but taking care of his body had become ingrained in him. If you ignored the slightly lumpy cartilage on his ears and the bump on his nose from a pile-driving tackle while still at school, he wasn't bad looking.

He didn't have Daniel's brooding intensity, or Luke's angelic dimples and curls, but he could hold his own in the looks department. And why was he even thinking like that? Surely, she was teasing. He met her eyes, expecting to see a glint of mischief. Her mouth had dropped open slightly and that hint of colour glowed through the dirt on her face. She snapped her jaw shut and gave him a bright smile. 'Well, goodnight!'

'Goodnight, sleep well.' He stepped to the side as she scurried towards him and out of the kitchen.

Aaron locked up, taking his time to check all the downstairs windows were secure. He doubted there was much in the way of crime in Orcombe Sands, not compared to London, but he had other people's safety to consider now. Deciding he couldn't be bothered with his emails, he clicked his laptop into sleep mode and turned out the light. The hiss of water through the pipes told him Kiki was still in the bathroom, so he turned down the landing towards his own room.

He stripped his clothes, swapping them for a lighter-weight T-shirt and shorts and lounged back on his bed. Phone in hand, he scrolled through his Twitter feed for a few moments, but soon grew irritated with the endless political wrangling. He tried his reading app next, but the words blurred as he tried not to think about Kiki just a few feet away, naked. *He was going to hell. Or maybe he was already there.*

Chapter Fifteen

Kiki made her way from her latest appointment at the Relate offices through the pedestrian precinct towards the railway station. The sessions had been far more productive than she had expected and Victoria, her counsellor, listened without passing judgement, a refreshing change for Kiki. Once she'd grasped the novel concept that her feelings were neither right nor wrong, they simply *were*, it had given her the confidence and freedom to explore them. They'd also talked a lot about control. Not just Kiki's desire to better control her emotions, but also about taking more control and responsibility for her life. Naturally passive and placating, it had dawned on her during the previous week how much of a passenger she'd been in her own life. Reacting and responding to the behaviour of others had become her default setting. Leaving Neil had been an active choice. She needed to make more such choices if she was to have any hope of living a satisfying life.

The first few sessions had focused on her relationship with Neil and, while Kiki hadn't quite come to terms with her own failure to address their problems sooner, it was growing easier to meet her reflection in the mirror. Victoria had suggested opening a neutral line of communication with him; and Kiki had reluctantly agreed. They would have to talk at some point, about the children if nothing else, so she began sending him weekly updates about what Charlie and Matty had been up to, including a couple of photographs. She made no mention of herself, nor their slightly unorthodox living arrangements—nothing that could provoke a retaliation. He'd not responded to either of her two messages, but, as Victoria had pointed out, that wasn't her problem. Demonstrating to the court a willingness to be reasonable and open with him would do her no harm when it came to settling custody arrangements either.

Today, they'd focused on the complicated tangle of guilt and obligation surrounding Kiki and her mother. It had been a hard hour, with lots of tears on her part. She wasn't doing so well at keeping the promise to herself that she would cry less, but it felt cathartic rather than simply an expression of her disappointment and frustration. Kiki hadn't gone to the hospital after Vivian's accident, and although Mia had told her about the care home she'd helped their father find, she hadn't spoken to him about it herself. Hadn't spoken to him at all since she'd left home a month ago, in fact.

The smell of coffee and sugar wafted on the air as someone exited the Starbucks to her left and Kiki diverted into the shop. Distracted, she found herself persuaded by the smiling young barista into trying something new, and she was soon back on the pavement clutching an enormous iced white-chocolate mocha topped with a huge swirl of cream. Taking a tentative sip, her eyes might have rolled back in her head a little as the caffeine, chocolate and sugar combination hit her empty stomach in a thrilling rush. She'd be high as a kite if she drank the whole thing.

The chilled plastic cup numbed her fingers as she sipped and strolled, letting her eyes roam over the array of shop windows. Nothing caught her attention enough to stop and she soon reached the end of the street and turned towards the road leading to the station. Her train wasn't due for another hour so there was no need to hurry. She considered popping into the museum and art gallery, but it was too nice a day to be cooped up inside. A few hundred feet further on, a gap in the buildings appeared. Following the path, Kiki found herself at the wrought-iron gates of Northerhay Gardens.

Wide paths, planted borders and trees beckoned to her, and she slipped through the gate, heading towards the impressive monument in front of her. The park was quiet. An older couple walked arm in arm some way ahead of her, but, other than them and a pair of chattering young women with pushchairs, the place seemed deserted. She found a spot on a wooden bench and fished her phone out of her bag. Turning it over in her palms a few times, she tried to work out exactly what she wanted to say. Where could she start? *Keep it simple*, that's what Victoria said when she got in a muddle.

Active choices. She repeated the little mantra in her head a couple of times then swiped through the menu and pressed call.

'Hello, Dad.' Simple enough.

'Dikê? Is that you? Are you all right, dear?' She settled back on the bench, caught off-guard by the endearment. George Thorpe had never been one for sentimentality.

'I'm okay. I'm sorry I haven't called earlier but things are a bit complicated.' *Deep breath, no tears*. 'I've left Neil.'

A moment of silence greeted her pronouncement, just long enough for her brain to race in a million different directions. Neil had been something of a protégé of her father's and he hated any kind of disruption to his work. Getting stuck in the middle of his daughter's messy divorce would be George's idea of hell on earth.

'I…' He cleared his throat. 'I heard. Neil sent me an email warning me you were behaving foolishly. His words, not mine, you understand. I didn't want you to think I was interfering, so I called Eunomia and she explained things. Once she assured me you were managing, I didn't want to bother you. I knew you'd talk to me when you were ready.'

She was gobsmacked. Mia hadn't said a word to her about it. Even more astounding was the vein of understanding running through her father's words. 'You're not disappointed?' she half whispered.

George sighed. 'Only in myself for letting you down for so long. I've been a poor excuse for a father to you girls for too long. Sticking my head in my books and ignoring everything else. Not facing up to the difficulties you all were having meant I didn't have to face up to my own. My counsellor helped me recognise that, although I sometimes rather wish he hadn't. Facing one's failings is a painful experience.'

Really, in the almost twenty-seven years of her existence, she'd never had such a revealing conversation with her father. 'Funny you should mention counselling, Dad. I've just come out of a session.'

'Good, that's good. I always thought it was a load of claptrap, but things rather came to a head after your mother's accident…'

Who was this man and what had they done with George Thorpe? Kiki knew communication between him and Mia had improved lately, but this volte-face from taciturn, almost monosyllabic exchanges to a genuine attempt to open up stunned her. If his voice sounded stiff and a little awkward, she could let that go. 'And how is Mum?'

'Not good. Not good at all. They've asked me to stop visiting for a couple of weeks because she gets too agitated.' He paused, and when he spoke again his words were muffled so she had to strain to hear them. 'She pulled her hair, Dikê, and scratched her face.'

'Oh, Dad.' The familiar roil of guilt churned her stomach, but she took a deep breath and swallowed back the words of apology that flew to her lips. It had been nearly ten years since Kiki had stopped giving in to her mother's pleas for assistance after a terrible row with her youngest sister, Nee. She'd promised her sister she would stop and she had. A decade or more for Vivian to seek help, for George to take control and force her into a treatment programme, but neither had acted.

It was too late now. Her parents would have to bear the burden of their responsibilities, not her. Not any longer. Maybe she should hold him closer to account, but she was too damn tired, and if he was willing to try and be a better father, she could meet him halfway. 'Are you taking care of yourself at least, Dad?'

'You have enough on your plate without worrying about me, dear.'

He had a point, but that was a prevarication, not an answer. 'Dad…'

'Yes. I have someone who comes in to keep the house tidy, not that there's much for her to do. She stocks the fridge and freezer, so I'm eating well at least. I never realised until recently how big the place is. It seems a waste of space for just me.'

If he was facing up to everything, how much worse would it be to come home to an empty house full of ghosts and memories? At least Kiki had the luxury of knowing Aaron and the children were waiting for her in a place she'd only been happy in. She would have to go back home at some point to sort through the rest of her things, but it was at the very bottom of her priorities list. 'Maybe you should think about downsizing? Find a flat closer to the university.'

'I wanted to keep the house so you girls would have room to stay, but that's never going to happen, is it? Even at your worst moment, you didn't turn to me for help and who can blame you?'

It was true. It had never entered her head for one moment to consider taking refuge under his roof. 'You had enough on your plate…'

Her father chuckled, a sad little sound. 'Ah, Dikê, even after everything you're still my tender-hearted girl. Don't try and make me feel better about myself, dear. There's really no need. I have no rights or expectations when it comes to any of you. I gave those up years ago through my own selfishness.'

She thought about her own progress with Victoria. 'Dad, it's good to hear you understand where things have gone wrong, but none of us would gain any pleasure from you putting yourself through the mill over what can't be changed. We are where we are. I'm trying to look forwards, and you should do the same.'

'That's kind of you to say and more than I probably deserve. Will… will you keep in touch, let me know how you are and if there's anything I can do for you, Matthew and Charlotte?' She had to smile. He was such a stickler for given names, probably always would be.

'I will, I promise. To both things.' A thought occurred to her. 'If you spoke to Mia recently, did she tell you her news?'

'About the wedding? Yes. I was very pleased to hear about it. Daniel sounds like a fine young man, and it was kind of her to invite me to the ceremony. Things are always busy here in September with the start of the new term…'

Mia and Daniel had settled on 10 September for their wedding date. They'd had only one prior booking and the retired couple involved had been more than happy to change their plans once they heard the reason for the request. She dismissed the little twinge of disappointment at his implied non-attendance. Perhaps it was a bit much to expect George to give up his obsession with his job along with everything else. He was trying to make an effort, which was more than she'd ever expected from him.

She forced herself to speak brightly. 'Well, it would have been nice to see you, but I understand how things are with all the new students.' Neil hated the start of term, said he felt more like a nanny than a tutor as the fresh intake of students tried to find their feet away from home for the first time.

'I don't normally teach on a Friday. I haven't seen the schedule for the new term, but it's a long-standing agreement I have.'

There was something hesitant in his phrasing. And she wondered if there was something else making him reluctant. 'Dad, do you *want* to come?'

'I wouldn't want anything to spoil your sister's day and, with the way things have been, I thought perhaps it would be best if I stayed away.'

'What if I said *I* wanted you to come? That it would be really nice for the children to spend a little bit of time with their grandad?'

George went so quiet, she wondered if they'd lost their connection. She pulled the phone away to check, but she had a full set of bars. Catching sight of the time, she rose from the bench, stretching the stiffness from her back caused by sitting still too long. She replaced the phone to her ear and could hear him breathing. 'Dad?'

'I missed Charlotte's birthday,' he said wistfully.

Kiki's heart gave a funny flutter. 'There were a dozen little girls full of sugar, dressed as Disney princesses. You were lucky to miss it.'

'I suppose you're right. And Matthew will be seven soon?'

August 20 would be upon them before she knew it. Where had the time gone? 'In less than three weeks, yes.' Which meant her own birthday was next week. It had completely slipped her mind. 'He's obsessed with all things to do with the constellations and planets. Aaron is getting him a basic telescope.'

'Who's Aaron?'

She bit her lip as she followed the path back out of the park and towards the main road. How to explain Aaron? Since Madeline had put the idea in her head, Kiki hadn't been able to stop thinking about him.

She'd mentioned Madeline's outrageous comments to him a couple of weeks back, and he'd agreed it was a ridiculous notion. And, of course, it was. But sometimes, in the evening, during those sweet moments between dinner and bedtime when the four of them were playing a game or watching a DVD, she'd catch his eyes upon her and swear there was something there.

It had been so long since a man had treated her with kindness and consideration, she was hopeless in the face of such decency. To say nothing of his smile and the sheer comforting size of him. What would he do if she slid over one evening and tucked herself under his arm? Would he push her away, or pull her close against his broad chest? Things fluttered—around her heart and in other, lower places. She couldn't possibly entertain those kinds of thoughts when her father was on the other end of the phone. *Or at any other time!*

'He's just a friend. Daniel and he have known each other for years, and he's relocated down here recently. We're staying with him until everything with Neil gets settled.'

'I see.'

What? What did he see? 'As I said, he's a friend. I'd rather you didn't mention anything about him to Neil, though. I wouldn't want him to get the wrong impression about things.' Or the right impression, if Kiki was completely honest with herself.

'The only things I might say to Neil about you are not fit for your ears, my dear. You've made your choice and I am on your side, for whatever that may be worth.'

A lump formed in her throat, and she had to blink to clear her eyes as she wound her way through the other pedestrians on Queen Street. 'It's worth a great deal, Dad. Look, I'll have to go in a minute as I need to catch my train.'

She stopped on the steps leading into the station. 'It's been great to talk to you. Please think about coming to the wedding.'

'All right, dear, I will. If you could text me your address, I'll look for something for Matthew's birthday. Constellations, you said? I know of a book which tells the Greek myths behind the names of some of the major ones. What do you think about that?'

'It sounds perfect. Maybe you could read him a story from it when you come and see us?' It would take more than a bedtime story or two to build a relationship between her father and the children, but it would be a start. She would watch him carefully for any signs of the cold, distant George she had grown up with and warn him off. Even if it was just the occasional weekend and birthday visit, it would be more than they'd had with him so far. Kiki had refused to allow Vivian near the children and her dad hadn't shown much interest in them anyway. *Kind of like their own father.*

'I... I'd like that very much indeed,' George said in a voice full of emotion. He coughed, then continued. 'Well, I'd best let you go, Dikê. Goodbye, dear.'

‘Bye, Daddy.’ She tucked away her phone, then retrieved her ticket from her purse. It was time to head back home and relieve Aaron of his babysitting duties. Clutching the tendrils of confidence she’d gained from the talk with her father, Kiki lifted her head and let her shoulders straighten.

An attractive man passing in the opposite direction caught her eye and smiled. Feeling the corners of her mouth twitch in response, Kiki darted her eyes away and kept on walking. She added the thrilling little glow to her collection of positive feelings, weaving them together into a gossamer net of hope. Perhaps there was another conversation she could tackle in the near future.

Active choices.

***

Their arms rested together, the crisp hairs on Aaron’s forearm tickling her every time he shifted against her in the darkened room, sending a little shiver of awareness down her spine. His skin was so warm it chased away the goose bumps on her naked flesh. Kiki swallowed a sigh. It wasn’t exactly what she’d had in mind. When Aaron had acted upon her subtle hint about going out sometime, she’d been over the moon. The bouquet of pink roses he presented her with had matched the blush heating her cheeks when he suggested a date for her birthday.

He leaned in closer, breath tickling her ear as he whispered, ‘Are you having a good time?’

She nodded and his lips brushed the delicate shell of her outer ear. It should have been perfect, a moment of quiet intimacy. The start of something beautiful…

'Mummy, I need a wee-wee.' Charlie wasn't quite as good at whispering as Aaron and a few soft chuckles rose from the seats around them.

'All right, darling.' Kiki lifted the bucket of popcorn from her lap and handed it to Aaron as she stood in a half-crouch and hurried Charlie to the end of the row. A stream of surfer-dude turtles flowed across the big screen and Charlie paused halfway down the steps to clap her hands and giggle. 'Keep moving, poppet,' Kiki urged.

When Aaron had suggested a trip to the cinema, she'd imagined an evening showing, after a nice quiet dinner perhaps. She might have even pictured getting up the courage to reach for his hand as Tarzan swept Jane into a hot kiss, or hiding her face in his shoulder as Jason Bourne dodged another group of determined assassins. The Aaron in her mind's eye had curled his arm around her, tucked her into his side and pressed the first of many kisses to her cheek.

Reality found them with two little chaperones at a matinee performance of *Finding Dory*. The children were already hyped on popcorn and pick 'n' mix, with a promise of McDonald's to follow the film. There would be no sneaking a kiss with Aaron on the landing as they said goodnight. She'd be lucky to end the day without holding one or other of the kids over the toilet as the junk food and excitement took their toll.

Happy bloody birthday, Kiki.

Perhaps she should have been clearer, but her gossamer courage had almost failed her when she'd leaned oh-so-casually against the frame of his study doorway. It had been all she could do to stutter the words, hoping her face wasn't as red as it felt and that he wouldn't flat out laugh at the idea of it.

Kiki sighed. In the face of her vague mutterings about spending a bit of time together outside the house, was it any wonder he'd misunderstood her suggestion? Why wouldn't he assume she'd meant it as family trip? They'd both been so busy, they'd hardly spent five minutes together over the past few days.

The schedule they'd put together was working well, but if she wasn't shuttling the children to and from different places, she was scrubbing toilets or up to her elbows in flour as she met the voracious needs of Mia's guests for cakes, pastries and other sweet treats. The couple of evenings she'd had free, Aaron was invariably buried in his study catching up on work.

Kiki rubbed her arms. The delicate silk vest top she'd teamed with a pair of linen trousers showed the beginnings of her summer tan to perfection, but offered no protection against the Arctic-level setting of the cinema air conditioning. She glanced down and quickly folded her arms across her chest, covering the embarrassing evidence of the chilly air. 'Come on, darling. You're missing the film,' she called encouragingly through the mostly closed door of the toilet stall.

'I can't flush.'

She nudged open the door and shook her head at the sight of her perplexed daughter, shorts and underwear still round her knees as she stared at the wall behind the toilet. 'Pull your pants up, sweetheart. I don't need to see your bottom,' she said, leaning forward to wave her hand in front of the sensor embedded in the wall.

'Ooh, magic!'

'Yes, magic. Now come and wash your hands.'

They eventually made it back into their seats and Kiki let her head flop back against the worn velvet with a sigh. Aaron nudged her shoulder and she rolled her head to peer at him in the gloom. 'All right?' She nodded. Their hands connected as he placed the popcorn back in her lap and she extended her little finger to stroke the side of his thumb. He shied away, then his fingers crept back for their own tentative touch.

Kiki held her breath, feeling the tingle from the top of her head to her neatly polished toes. The little blue fish on the screen danced before her eyes, but she couldn't focus on the story. Couldn't focus on anything but that tiny point of contact. So much hope, so much fear, rested in her little finger. She waited for him to move away, to prove she was making it all up in her head, but he stayed completely still. The heat from his palm, hovering near her thigh, radiated through the thin layer of peach-coloured linen. What should she do? Keep still, press harder, take his hand? The possibilities scrolled through her head.

Active choices.

Stretching her little finger, Kiki curled it over the back of Aaron's, ready to hook their two digits together. At the very same moment, Charlie leaned across her lap, knocking the tub of popcorn flying as she stage-whispered to her brother, 'Matty! They have magic toilets here.'

Kiki dived forward, trying to catch the popcorn, bumping heads with Aaron as he tried to do the same thing. 'Ouch.'

'Shh. You're ruining the film,' a woman hissed at them from the row in front.

'Sorry, sorry.' Kiki slumped back in her seat, trying not to think about the bits of popcorn stuck between her toes. Her head throbbed and she raised a hand to rub the sore spot, catching Aaron on the cheek in the process. 'Oh, God! Sorry!' Hands over her mouth, she could only stare in horror as he clapped a hand to his injured face.

'If you don't be quiet, I'm calling the manager!' The woman in front glared over her shoulder before settling back into her seat like a wet hen trying to settle her feathers.

It was terrible. Just awful. Never comfortable being the centre of attention for the right reasons, Kiki wanted to fold up and disappear under the seat. Not that she could exactly hide there when the seat would flip up as soon as she crouched down. A ripple of silent laughter clenched her stomach at the sheer absurdity of it all.

Her shoulders shook and she pressed her hand tighter against her mouth, fearful of making a sound. Aaron made a kind of half-cough, half-snort and she couldn't help but glance at him. Big mistake. His pale eyes glimmered in the dark and his mega-watt grin shattered the vestiges of her self-control and she started to giggle. Her shoulders shook, and she might have been able to keep quiet had Aaron not cough-snorted again.

As they made their way out of the cinema to a chorus of shushing and loud tuts, Kiki decided active choices might be best left to other people.

Chapter Sixteen

Daniel knuckled the base of his spine to try and ease the ache that had settled there over the past week and refused to shift. He was exhausted, running on coffee, adrenaline and the endless good humour of his friends. *But it's done.* He stared up at the front of the barn and allowed himself a smile of satisfaction. They'd left the outside of the building in a deliberately distressed-looking state, although a clear protective coating had been applied to the worst of the weathering on the boards. He loved the variety of textures and colours the elements had created over time. They also provided the perfect contrast to the sleek, minimalist interiors.

Madeline and Richard had planted beautiful grasses and bright flowering shrubs in the huge earthenware pots he'd found at a local salvage yard. They graced either side of the entrance, and flower boxes full of herbs had been attached beneath the upper-floor windows of each studio apartment. Tending the boxes would be the perfect task for any procrastinating artist, and the summer breeze would fill the rooms with the scents of lavender and lemony thyme.

'You've done an incredible job, mate.' Aaron was sprawled in a groaning heap on the gravel beside him. He'd put everything aside to throw his weight behind the feverish last-minute preparations. Daniel would never be able to repay him, or Luke for that matter. The younger Spenser brother had staggered towards the house a few minutes earlier, muttering about a week-long hot shower and his bed. Daniel couldn't blame him. They'd worked through the night, catching a few minutes' sleep here and there as they checked and double-checked everything was ready for today's grand opening.

He checked his watch. The first batch of artists was due on the late-afternoon train, which would give him a chance to grab his own shower and a quick nap. He just needed to double-check the downstairs studios were all properly stocked…

'Leave it.' Aaron pushed himself to a seated position, a knowing grin on his face. 'Everything is done. All our lists have been ticked. Leave the ladies to tweak the curtains and straighten the already perfectly placed toiletries.'

Daniel gave him a rueful grin. 'You know they're going to move stuff around.'

Aaron shrugged. 'Of course they are. They're better at the finer points than we are.'

It was true. Mia had added the perfect accents and accessories to the rooms in her guest house, transforming them from functional to special with a light hand and skilful eye, which was all the more impressive considering her lack of any kind of interior design training. She just had a knack for seeing the complete picture. Even now, she and Madeline were giving the barn the benefit of their eagle eyes. He paused. 'Hey, where's Kiki? I thought she'd be with them.'

Aaron picked up a handful of gravel and let it trail out through his fingers. 'It's Friday morning – she's got her thing.'

Ah, yes. Wednesdays and Fridays Kiki took herself off to Exeter to see her counsellor. Mia was relieved about it, so Daniel trusted it was a good thing. He glanced down at his friend, although Aaron didn't seem too convinced. 'Problem?'

'What? No, not really. I think it's doing her some good. Even on the days she comes back and it's obvious she's been crying, there's still a lightness about her. Like she feels better for getting it off her chest. I hate seeing her upset, it rips me to shreds. I think she's being incredibly brave, facing up to the past. It's just… bloody Luke.' The last was barely muttered, as though not intended for Daniel's ears.

He crouched down beside his friend. 'What's Luke got to do with anything?'

Aaron shook his head. 'Nothing. He just made some sarky remark a few weeks ago about me only liking broken girls and I can't get it out of my head. I like Kiki. I like her a *lot*, but I can't decide if it's her, or if Luke's claim about me having a hero complex is true. We had this thing, this moment when we took the kids out for her birthday. It was nothing, and everything.

And now I think she likes me, too.' He sighed. 'It would be so much easier if she didn't...'

Daniel liked Kiki, but she always had a vulnerability about her that made him tread carefully in case he hurt her feelings. His Mia had been through the mill, too, but she had a fire in her spirit. Daniel cast his mind back over the women he'd seen Aaron with over the years. He'd never really thought about it, but they were a tad on the fragile side. There'd been a girl at uni with them—all thick black eyeliner and Sylvia Plath poetry. He shuddered at the endless hours she'd spent bemoaning the futility of the world. 'Whatever happened to Kerry Davis?' he mused aloud.

'Kerry? She's doing something incredibly complicated at some tech firm in Silicon Valley. I had an email from her a couple of months back and she was about to go on maternity leave with her second kid.' Aaron cast him a wary look. 'What made you think of her after all these yea... oh, bollocks!' He buried his hands in his face and groaned.

Daniel laughed and patted him on the back. 'There you go.'

'Just don't say anything to Luke; he's insufferable when he's right. Mate, it's screwing with my head. I feel like I'm second-guessing myself all the time around her.'

It was hard not to laugh at the anguish in his friend's muffled voice, so he didn't try too hard to stop it. It was as plain as the nose on his face that Aaron had it bad for Kiki, and from what Mia had hinted, her sister felt the same way. It sounded like neither of them was in a hurry to do anything about it, though. And there was no way Daniel was getting in the middle. He had enough on his plate without turning his hand to bloody matchmaking. They'd work it out at some point, or they wouldn't, but he wasn't about to push it.

Clapping Aaron's shoulder again, Daniel straightened up, his laughter cut off by his own pained groan as his knees protested. 'God, I'm getting old. Why don't you go home and have a kip? I'm sure Madeline and Richard can keep the kids occupied until the barbecue this evening.'

They were planning their first big outdoor event to welcome their first guests to the barn as well as those who'd come to the guest house for a long weekend. A couple Aaron had befriended were bringing their children along, too, so there would be about thirty mouths to feed. The fridge was packed out with salads and side dishes and he knew Aaron and Kiki's fridge was similarly laden. A huge gas barbecue sat under a gazebo in the garden.

The shiny beast was Daniel's new pride and joy and he couldn't wait to fire it up. They'd set a couple of big tubs out on the lawn ready to be filled with cold water and ice so people could help themselves to drinks. An array of old tables and mismatched chairs were scattered around, some in the shade, others where they would catch the evening sun. Luke had already declared himself DJ for the evening and had created a special playlist on his iPod. Tired as he was right now, Daniel was looking forward to it. Things were finally coming together and he might manage to go a day without dust in his hair and grime under his fingernails.

His eyes drifted to the row of old garages running adjacent to the barn. *Maybe not.* He still really liked the idea of turning them into a gallery-cum-teashop, although how they'd find the time to run three businesses was beyond him. Unless…

'Hey, Aaron?'

'Whatever you want me to do, the answer is no.'

Daniel chuckled. He'd never actually asked Aaron to do anything in all the weeks he'd been helping, but he'd never refused either. 'How's Kiki getting on with finding more work?'

Aaron sighed. 'Not good. The only things around were a couple of cleaning jobs the other side of Exmouth. By the time she'd paid for the petrol, it would hardly have been worth the effort. The hours were crap too—mostly evenings, which isn't ideal with the kids and all. It's stressing her out not being able to contribute more towards the household costs, but she needs to hang on to as much of her savings as possible. That bastard changed the passwords on all the bank accounts, so she's only got what she transferred before she moved down here.'

Daniel shook his head. Kiki's husband was proving himself to be every bit as awful as Mia had warned him. 'You know her better than me. Do you think she could handle running the teashop and gallery if we cracked on with the conversion works?' He wasn't sure what work experience she had and he needed the business to succeed. Giving Kiki a project she couldn't handle might destroy the little bit of confidence she'd grown over the past weeks.

'Hmm…' Aaron heaved himself off the ground and wandered towards the rundown buildings. Daniel joined him and they cupped their hands to shield their eyes as they peered through the dusty windows. 'I set her up with a couple of spreadsheets to help manage the costs of the baking she's doing for Mia and she's an absolute whizz with them. It would be much the same, just on a bigger scale. She's smart as a whip, was studying classics at university before she got married and dropped out. I'd say it's been lack of opportunity that's held her back.'

'Well, we know she can cook.' Aaron had pitched up the day before with a box stuffed with cakes and sandwiches to keep them going overnight. Daniel would go to his grave before he admitted it out loud, but Kiki's baking was even better than Mia's… and Mia's made him want to lie at her feet and beg for treats.

'And the opening hours wouldn't interfere with her housekeeping job…' Aaron mused.

'That's true. We could also work out a rate so guests wanting afternoon tea take it here, which would give Mia a bit more spare time in the afternoons…'

'What are you two up to?' Mia's voice called from the left. They stepped back from the window, both blinking as their eyes adjusted from the gloomy interior to the bright sunshine. Exchanging a conspiratorial look, the two men turned to face her. His little Spitfire stood there, hands on her hips, giving them both her best evil eye. He couldn't fight the grin spreading across his face when she began to tap her foot. *God, she's magnificent.*

'Nothing, dear,' Daniel said in a sing-song, innocent voice which made Aaron snort. Elbowing his friend in the side, he tried to force a serious expression as she marched towards them.

'Please tell me you're not going to start knocking this place apart next? If I hear one more drill whirring I might scream.' Though her brows were drawn down, he didn't miss the glint of humour in her chocolate-brown gaze.

'I'm saying nothing.' Aaron backed up to where his bike rested against the wall, hands raised in mock surrender. 'I'll see you two love birds later.' He mounted up and rode down the driveway, leaving Daniel to face his fiancée alone.

'Coward!' he yelled at Aaron's back and was rewarded with a jaunty two-fingered salute.

Daniel turned back to Mia. 'So, what do you think? Everything all set for my first guests?' He couldn't keep the nerves out of his voice. He wanted things to go well, needed them to go well, to prove he'd made the right choice in giving up his photography career for the new venture. The thought of going back to London still filled him with terror; he wasn't convinced even Mia would be able to prevent him sliding back into his formerly seedy lifestyle if he had to sell his soul through his art once more.

She pushed up on tiptoes to cup his face and press a sweet kiss to his lips. 'It looks perfect. You've done such an incredible job and I am so proud of you.'

Sincerity shone in every word, easing the tension in his spine. His Mia believed in him, just as much as he believed in her. Their future together grew more promising every day.

Keeping her hands on his cheeks, she teased the short hairs of his beard with her fingers. 'Are you sure you want to take on another challenge so soon?' Her eyes drifted past him to study the garages.

He knew what she meant. The temptation to sit back and let both the guest house and the studios bed in was high. They had time. It could wait... But if they could get the place up and running, then wouldn't the aching muscles and stress be worth it to give Kiki some extra income and the stability that went with it? 'A few weeks more and all the disruption would be over for good. Wouldn't you rather have it all finished?'

He watched her thought process play out across her expressive, beautiful face. There was no side to Mia and it was one of the many things he loved about her—what you saw was what you got. She bit her lip. 'I'm just not sure I've got the time, Daniel. Getting to grips with the guest house is taking longer than I anticipated and with the wedding planning...'

'I was thinking we could get someone to manage the place for us. Someone we know and trust, who bakes like a dream and needs a decent job. Someone like...'

'Kiki?' A wondering smile spread across her face, chasing away the clouds of worry. 'You want to push on with opening the teashop to give Kiki a job.'

'It's a thought.'

She closed the distance between them and flung her arms around his neck, peppering his beard with kisses. 'It's a wonderful thought. I love it, I love you!'

His arms curled around her waist and he held her close, relishing the feel of her curves pressing against him. They'd hardly taken any time for themselves since they'd met, and lately it felt like the only quality time they spent together was in bed. Speaking of which… he checked his watch. 'I was going to take a shower and then grab a couple of hours' sleep. Can I tempt you to join me?'

Her cheeks flushed and she bit her lip in that way that always heated his blood. 'Madeline's gone home to help Richard look after Charlie. They're going to collect Matty from his activity club, so I don't have to worry about that.'

He let his hands shape her hips, drawing her in closer still. He tugged her lip free and teased it with the tip of his tongue. 'So, are you saying you can find room for a little afternoon delight in your busy schedule, love?'

With a breathy sigh, she sank into him and he lost himself in the warm, soft heaven of her mouth. They were both panting a little by the time they came up for air and the roses on her cheeks had spread to heat the delicate skin of her décolletage. 'I thought you needed to sleep?' she teased.

'I'll sleep when I'm dead.' Sliding his grip lower, he boosted her up until she wrapped her legs around his waist. He carried her across the gravel yard, pausing every few steps to claim another kiss.

It took them longer than expected to get to their room on the top floor, and by the time they reached the upper landing, neither of them was wearing much more than their underwear and a pair of matching smiles. The door to the spare room opposite theirs stood half open and Daniel froze, a silent curse on his lips. In their haze, they'd forgotten about Luke. He placed a hand over Mia's mouth to stifle her giggle, and held his breath to listen. A loud snore rent the air and he sagged against the wall in relief.

Grabbing Mia's hand, they tiptoed over the creaky floorboards and into their room. He eased the door closed behind them and swiped his brow in an exaggerated gesture, which sent Mia off into a fresh round of giggles. With an arm hooked around her waist, he dragged her across the room and tumbled backwards onto the bed, tugging her down on top of him. Her giggles faded into soft moans and Daniel lost himself in the scent, taste and feel of her.

***

Daniel frowned critically at his reflection in the bathroom mirror as he used his clippers to finish tidying up his beard. 'I'm going to stop trimming this. I swear I'm just cutting out the black and leaving the grey behind.'

'It's very distinguished, darling.' Mia's slightly absent-minded tone said she wasn't paying attention. He turned around and leaned against the edge of the sink. Up to her chin in her favourite bubble bath, her eyes were fixed on another of her myriad notebooks. He flinched at the sight of it—the infernal wedding book.

Getting married was great, he was a big fan of it. It was the actual wedding itself that stressed him out. Yes, he'd been busy getting the barn up to scratch, and yes, women traditionally did the majority of the planning, but he couldn't help a pang of guilt. He'd done bugger all towards organising what should be, what *would* be, the most important day of their lives together so far.

Finally noticing his silence, Mia turned towards him. 'What are you staring at?' Her lips curved in a sweetly cheeky grin.

'Tell me about your dress.'

Her eyebrows rose. 'You want to talk about the wedding?' *Shit.* The surprise in her voice proved he had every reason to feel guilty.

'Yes. Please. I need to think about what I'm going to wear and I have no clue. I thought if you told me about your dress it would give me some idea.'

She sat up a bit higher in the water, sending a delicious waft of cherry blossom his way. Her favourite bubble bath just happened to be his favourite, too. It left her smelling like a sexy Bakewell tart. Sweet and sinful. He checked his watch; their first guests were due to arrive at the station in the next half an hour. Not enough time for the plans he had in mind. He pushed them aside with a pang of regret and turned his focus back to the matter in hand.

Mia pursed her lips. 'I can't show you my dress because it's bad luck, and there's also the small matter of Madeline's still making it.'

She was getting her dressed made? Damn, he'd missed way too much. Covering another pang of guilt, he put on his best innocent expression. 'I'm sure Madeline will do a grand job. Those curtains she made for the bedrooms are lovely.'

'Wanker.' Mia laughed and threw a handful of bubbles at him.

He bent down to mop them up with a towel then remained crouched beside the tub so they were nose to nose. 'I've been rubbish, leaving everything to you. I'm sorry.'

'Don't worry about it. I think I have it mostly under control.' She rubbed their noses together in an Eskimo kiss.

'Can you make me a list of the stuff you don't have organised? The garages won't take nearly so much work to sort out. I've got time.' He stroked her damp fringe back from her forehead. 'I'll *make* time.'

'Thank you.' She sounded just relieved enough for him to know he should have made time sooner. 'Nothing in the magazines appealed so Madeline and I put a design together from the bits and pieces I did like. It's not a meringue! One of those is enough for any bride.'

Daniel grinned. He'd seen a photo of her and Jamie's wedding. Her dress had been an elaborate confection of silk with a train, which had gone well with the traditional morning suit her first husband had worn. 'So, no top hat and tails for me?'

'Lord, no! Comfort is the watchword. I'm going to be barefoot. It's about us, Daniel. Who we are, what our life is about. Just our closest friends and family. No performance.'

Jamie's parents, Pat and Bill, were travelling down, and Mia had been quietly pleased to let him know her dad had decided to come with them. He didn't have much in the way of family, but Aaron and Luke would be there and he'd invited Maggie Sinclair, the gallery owner who'd done so much for him at both the beginning and end of his career as a photographer. Family was what you made it, and he wouldn't change his for the world.

He stood up and let his gaze travel out of the bathroom window across the garden to the waves dancing on the beach beyond. This was his place—their place. He didn't know what lucky star had shone down on him, but he would count his blessings, every single one, and be thankful for them.

Water swished behind him and a few moments later he felt Mia at his back. Lifting his arm, he made room for her to cuddle close. The smell of cherry blossom filled his senses and he turned into her. Content. Happy. Home.

Chapter Seventeen

'This place, man. I knew Daniel was close to the edge, so it was no real shock when he dropped off the grid, but you?' Leo Taylor shook his head as he looked around the small crowd spread across the back lawn at Butterfly House. 'You're the least impulsive person I know. It's one of the reasons I trust you with my money.'

Aaron sipped his beer and tried not to let his irritation show. This was the second conversation on the theme of how bloody boring his clients thought he was. Leo meant no harm, so he kept quiet and let the chatter flow over him. The ten per cent stake he had in the studios project would only pay off if Leo and the other guinea pigs went back to town raving about their amazing experience.

Leo took an exaggerated breath. 'The air here, it's incredible. And the colours…' He raised his head to stare at the porcelain-blue sky. 'I get it, man, I get it. I wish I'd booked longer than a week.'

Aaron allowed himself a little smile. It had taken less than an hour for Butterfly Cove to weave its spell. 'I'll speak to Daniel and check the schedule. We have some space in the autumn. Daniel's got some fantastic pictures of the sea in the middle of a storm. You feel the full fury of nature just looking at them.'

'Yes. *Yes*.' Leo's eyes glazed a little and Aaron knew he was lost somewhere in his imagination. He didn't get some of the art a few of his clients produced—abstract and highly modernist things left him cold. Leo's stuff, he almost understood. He worked with oils and produced what would be considered traditional landscapes were it not for the outlandish colours he favoured. Luke, even more of a philistine than Aaron, had compared them to Oz and claimed all that was missing was a few Munchkins.

Aaron liked him—liked his work, too. He'd started working for him when Leo was fresh out of college and had barely had two pennies to rub together. His first payment had been a small original, which now held pride of place on Aaron's study wall. It was worth more than his current pension pot and he'd offered it back when Leo's career took off. His friend had refused—thanks to Aaron's steady guidance, he had a broad portfolio which would protect him from the fickle vagaries of the art world.

'You should set up a house-hunting service.' Leo's blue eyes sparked with excitement.

'How do you mean?' He'd floated the refurbishment business with Luke, but so far his brother seemed set on staying in London. It was selfish of him to expect Luke to move just because he had, but they'd never been more than half an hour from each other since Aaron first went up to university. Not satisfied with his job and crippled by the sky-high London prices, he couldn't understand what the attraction was. Maybe Aaron was just the country versus town equivalent of a reformed smoker—and just as zealously annoying with his constant pressure on others to quit.

'Think about it. If I'm like this after an hour, imagine how in love with the place I'm going to be in a week's time. If you had a picture-perfect little cottage lined up to show me, I'd probably bite your hand off.' Leo winked. 'I'll back you.'

Aaron laughed. A frisson of excitement stirred in his belly, but he knew his friend was only teasing. 'Don't even joke about it or I'll hold you to it.'

Leo took a draught from his own bottle, then levelled Aaron with the most serious look he'd ever seen on his face. 'No joke, man. Think about it. The rates on a couple of my accounts are so piss-poor it wouldn't do any harm to draw some out. It wouldn't take much—a decent website and you on the ground to scout for places as well as advise on mortgages. Daniel must have some good trade connections after all the work he's done on this place, if any refurbishments are needed.' Leo nodded over his shoulder at the barns.

It wasn't exactly what Aaron had in mind for his longer-term plan, but it was pretty bloody close. 'As your financial advisor, I can't recommend it. Too risky.' He couldn't hide his excitement, though.

'Ha! Sod that. At least think about it. Let's sit down before I go back and have a proper talk about it.'

Aaron nodded. 'All right. You might hate it here by then.'

'I seriously doubt that. Well, hello…'

There was something in Leo's tone that made Aaron raise his head to see what had caught his eye. His friend was staring at a small group gathered close to where Daniel held court behind the barbecue. Mia and Kiki were talking to Madeline, Richard and a couple of guests staying at the house for the weekend. Aaron immediately scanned the area for the children, relaxing when he saw them sprawled on the ground in front of where Simon and his wife were sitting chatting to Luke and Alison, the celebrant Mia and Daniel had found to carry out their wedding. Getting a venue licence from the council had proven too complicated, so they'd compromised: Alison would host the wedding they wanted in the garden and they would follow it up with a quiet 'official' ceremony at the local registry office.

Aaron's attention turned back to Kiki, and stayed there. Dressed in a shocking-pink sundress, hair loose and held off her face with a pair of large-lensed sunglasses, she looked glamorous and very different from her usual understated style. The colour choice suited her more than the neutrals and pastel tones she favoured and there was something about it that tickled a corner of his memory.

Tearing his eyes away, he glanced at Leo. With his shaggy blond hair, stubble and paint-spattered clothes, he looked every inch the bohemian artist. The expression on his face suggested he might have found the perfect muse. Aaron swallowed and tried not to think about planting his fist in that too-handsome face. Maybe he wasn't looking at Kiki. Maybe it was just Aaron's own attraction to her that made him assume every other man would be drawn to her as well.

'Who's the brunette?' *Or maybe he was looking at her.*

'The short-haired one? That's Mia, Daniel's fiancée.' It had to be worth a try, right?

'Not her. She's pretty, but I like my face too much the way it is, thanks very much. The one next to her. The one with the hair.'

Damn. He could lie and claim he didn't know her, but what would be the point? If Leo decided to talk to her, he'd find out soon enough. Aaron forced a polite smile. 'That's her sister, Kiki. Struggling with a nasty divorce.' She wouldn't thank him for sharing her private business, but he really didn't like the way Leo was looking at her.

'Really?' His friend raised an eyebrow in his direction then turned his gaze back towards the sisters. 'She doesn't look like she's struggling. And if she is, I've a shoulder she can cry on. Unless you can think of a reason why I shouldn't offer it to her?'

Leo's eyes were back on him and Aaron fought to keep his features relaxed. *No white-knight routine, remember*? Kiki was an adult. If she wasn't interested in Leo's attentions, she could let him know herself. 'Knock yourself out.'

The painter grinned. 'You sound like you want to do it for me.'

Aaron straightened. 'She's a good friend. If you hurt her, or upset her in any way, you'll be sorry. Consider that your only and final warning. I'm going to grab another beer, you want one?' He walked off without waiting for a reply. Not because he was in a huff or anything, Simon and Nancy were his guests and he needed to make sure they were having a good time.

He fished around in one of the tubs of ice and grabbed a handful of long-necked beer bottles on his way across the lawn. Reaching the group, he offered them around then claimed a spare seat next to his brother. If it afforded him a side view of where Kiki was standing, that was merely coincidence. Leo strolled across the grass, and he threw a knowing grin at Aaron before he reached his target. Aaron ground his teeth and tried to pay attention to those around him.

Luke was regaling them with some outlandish story about a new client his firm had landed. The gentleman, of Russian extraction with a murky past, had buckets of money and absolutely no taste. 'I don't know if I can bring myself to do it,' Luke said. 'When we took him to the samples room, he made a beeline for the marble and stayed there.' His brother shook his head. 'His wife had on more jewellery than that fella with the mohawk who does those ads on telly. Calls everyone a fool…'

'Mr T?' Simon sputtered on an inopportune mouthful of his beer. 'Oh God! How did you keep a straight face?'

'I kept telling myself to think about the commission. Even if it's not my taste, they want high-end stuff and the mark-up on the materials alone is more than my annual salary. I never considered myself a snob before, but it's like the more money they have, the more they need to show everyone.' He sighed. 'All that history, all those beautiful mansions gutted for apartments or transformed into tarts' palaces.'

'The commission, Spud, think of the commission,' Aaron reminded him, and everyone raised their drinks.

'The commission!' They toasted Luke and he joined in their laughter with a rueful grin.

***

Aaron eased back in his chair and glanced towards the group by the barbecue. Leo had them all enthralled, hands waving as he described something, face animated. The others were transfixed, clearly enjoying the tale he wove. Kiki's laughter rang out, a melodic cascade that should have lifted Aaron's heart. Black, bitter bile stung the back of his throat and he was halfway out of the chair before he realised it. He cursed himself silently, told his feet to turn away as every step took him closer.

'…And she was just waiting for you in your room?' Kiki sounded part shocked, part thrilled.

Leo grinned. 'Yup. Naked as a jaybird.'

Daniel stopped in the middle of flipping the burgers laid out on the grill to brandish a set of metal tongs at Leo. 'Now tell them the rest of the story, Stud.'

Aaron had seen this routine before. Knew the performance word for word. He folded his arms across his chest, and inched closer to Kiki, giving Leo his best dirty look. Ignoring him, Leo ducked his head, casting his best aww-shucks look at Kiki. 'I turned on my heel and ran. Mo Farah couldn't have outkicked me during that sprint down the corridor.'

Kiki and the others laughed in delight as Daniel chipped back in. 'I'm out like a light. We'd drowned our sorrows pretty heavily in the hotel bar and at first I thought the banging in my head was from too much brandy. I stagger out of bed, open the door, and Leo nearly knocks me flying trying to get in the room. Spent the night in the spare bed.'

And just like that, he won them all. The story was perfect—Leo set himself up as a braggart, reeling them in with a story of conquest, only to turn the tables at the last minute and make himself the butt of the joke. Not only that, but it showed the nice guy beneath the confident, cocky artist. Aaron sighed. That was the worst thing. Leo *was* a nice guy. He watched him soaking up the attention and teasing from the others, and there was no artifice to him. God had gifted him with good looks, natural charm and a healthy dose of modesty. *Bastard.*

He couldn't stand by a moment longer. Reaching out to touch the warm skin on her bare arm, Aaron drew

Kiki's attention away. 'Hey, can I borrow you for a minute?'

Her smile fell instantly. 'Is everything okay?' She was already looking past him, seeking out the children.

'Yes, yes. Everything's fine. I just wanted to show you something if you have time?'

Ignoring the collection of knowing and curious looks from the others, Aaron placed his fingers on the small of Kiki's back and steered her away from the group. She paused to double-check the children were okay and only let him continue to lead her away once she saw they were engrossed in watching Luke play the thumb trick. It was a silly thing their dad had done when they were little, and Aaron couldn't help but smile. They'd pestered him for hours, fascinated as he appeared to pull the tip of his thumb off, then put it back on again. Funny how, even with all the bells and whistles of modern technology, it was the simplest things that never went out of style.

'Watch your step.' Aaron placed a hand under Kiki's elbow as her wedge-heeled sandals crunched across the gravel of the driveway.

'Where are you taking me?' She sounded intrigued as the noise and chatter of the guests fell away behind them.

'Just hang on.' He ran his fingers along the top of the doorframe to locate the key, then unlocked the door to the garages. The old lock had seen better days and it took a grunt of effort to force the rusted mechanism open. Taking a step inside, he kicked aside a broken wooden pallet and checked the rest of the floor was clear. 'Come on.' He held out his hand and beckoned her inside.

Kiki took a tentative step over the threshold. Folding her arms across her chest, she gave a little shiver. The warmth of the sun didn't reach inside the dank space, and there was a marked difference in temperature. She rubbed her hands on her arms as she looked around with a puzzled frown. 'You wanted to show me a dusty old garage?' A shy smile lit her face. 'Or was that just a ruse to get me alone? I saw the look on your face when your friend was flirting with me. Did he make you jealous?'

Aaron blinked, surprised at the directness of her comment. 'Yes. No, I mean. Yes, I wanted to show you the garage.' Needing a ruse to get her away from Leo, he'd decided to see what she thought about Daniel's idea for the teashop and gallery. Now they were alone, it seemed like a mistake. It wasn't his news to tell; he didn't even know if they'd finally decided to ask Kiki to run it.

She took a step closer and the warm, sweet citrus fragrance from her shampoo filled his senses. In her heels, she stood barely a head shorter than him. With her head tipped back, and her dark eyes filled with promise, he couldn't remember why he'd brought her in here, nor why keeping his distance from her had seemed like the right thing to do.

Her tongue darted out to wet her lower lip, and everything inside him went hot and tight. 'I'm not very good at this,' she murmured.

He shouldn't ask. He needed to get back on track, remember what it was he wanted to show her. *Tell her about the conversion plans.* Other bits of his body overruled his brain and instead he asked, 'Good at what?'

Time slowed. He felt like the rest of the world ground to a halt as she went up on tiptoes and closed the distance between them. She inched closer and her breath teased his lips as she whispered, 'This,' and brushed his mouth with a soft kiss.

A million sensations bombarded him at once: shock, hope, fear and a huge bolt of lust. Not sure which to react to first, Aaron froze. He watched, helpless, as her thick lashes fluttered up and saw his lack of reaction register in her eyes. A crease furrowed her brow as a rush of colour turned her face ruddy, even in the shadowy light. Her lips formed a little 'O' of surprise, and she took a step away.

The loss of her heat spurred him into action, and he banded his arms around her waist, dragging her back against him. He swallowed the shocked gasp on her lips and dove into the sweet, wet warmth of her open mouth. She tasted faintly of peaches, from the Bellini she'd been drinking, like summer and rich, ripe fruit. Shifting one hand, he plunged his fingers into the thick mass of hair cascading down her back and gripped her neck to angle her head better.

Her hands rose to grip his shoulders, the neat, short nails pricking his skin through the thin cotton of his polo shirt. A greedy noise escaped her throat and she stretched her lips wider to accept the press of his tongue, curling hers around it in an eager dance. He'd expected her to be shy, and her enthusiasm spurred him on. He slipped the hand on her waist lower to cup the curves of her bottom, drawing her closer against the aching front of his body.

Breaking free, she tipped her head back, gasping in air, offering the tender skin of her throat for his claiming. 'Aaron.' Her fingers curled into his hair, pressing his head down, encouraging him to explore the exposed skin between the thin straps of her sundress.

He traced the delicate line of her collarbone to her shoulder, easing the strap down to reveal a familiar scrap of flamingo-pink lace. The last time he'd seen her bra it had been wrapped around his foot as he tried to stop the crammed belongings from tumbling out of the boot of her car. She'd been so embarrassed, so vulnerable and scared, he'd sworn to do whatever it took to protect her. *Even from himself.*

'Kiki,' he groaned her name into the hollow of her shoulder. 'Kiki, we can't, we mustn't.'

'Please, Aaron, please. The children are fine and no one will come looking for us for a while. Kiss me.' She tugged the back of his hair, an insistent urging for him to lift his face.

He resisted. 'This is a mistake. We're friends.'

Kiki's hands slipped from his hair to his shoulders. 'What's that phrase everyone uses, "friends with benefits". Why can't that be us?' She nuzzled his cheek, pressing soft kisses next to his ear.

He twisted his face away from her mouth. ‘Stop. We shouldn’t.’

Her body language changed, the languid press of her curves fading into rigidity. ‘You’re serious.’

She leaned her weight back against his hands, and he forced his fingers to uncurl and release her. As she stepped back, her heel caught on some of the rubbish littering the floor and she staggered. Aaron lunged for her, but she raised her arms to ward him off and righted herself. ‘Don’t.’

‘I’m sorry.’ Aaron stuffed his useless hands in his front pockets before he did something foolish like pull her back against him.

‘I thought…’ Kiki paced a couple of steps away, turned back and raised a shaking finger at him. ‘You kissed me back. I mean, you *really* kissed me back.’

‘I know, I’m sorry.’

She wrapped her arms around her middle. ‘Stop saying that. Why are you sorry? I thought you wanted this, too.’

Aaron closed his eyes against the disappointment and confusion on her face. *What a mess.* If he didn’t find the right words to explain, he might risk everything he was fighting so hard to preserve. ‘I like you, Kiki. I think you’re beautiful and brave and I admire you so much for taking control of your life.’

A bitter laugh rent the air. ‘There’s a “but” coming, isn’t there? What is it? Is it the kids? I thought you cared about them, too.’

'I do. God, I do. They're brilliant. Living with you all is the best thing that's ever happened to me.'

'So, it's me then.' The hurt in her voice sliced him like a knife. 'It must be me, that's the problem.'

He couldn't have that, he couldn't have her blaming herself; that would make him as bad as Neil. 'It's not you. This might seem like a good idea right now, but what happens further down the line? You'll get things together. Once this place is up and running, you'll have more financial independence—'

'This place? What are you talking about?'

'Daniel and Mia are going to convert this into a gallery and teashop. They want you to run it for them. Things won't always be like this. They'll settle down and then you won't need me any more. If we act on these feelings it will just get messy when whatever this is between us runs its course.'

Kiki turned her back on him. 'You've really thought it all through, haven't you?'

The strap of her dress still hung halfway down one arm, displaying the frivolous lace of her bra. Damn, he wished things could be different, that there wasn't so much at stake. 'It's all I've thought about for the past few weeks. I want you, Kiki. I want to be with you, but I can't see how this doesn't end badly for all of us.'

She laughed again, a bitter, angry sound without an ounce of warmth, and swung back to face him. Anger blazed in her eyes. 'You're so convinced things will go wrong, you won't even give us a chance. How flaky do you think I am? That I'm so pathetic and needy I'll just latch on to the first man who enters my life, but only until a better offer comes along?'

Kiki stormed towards the half-open door. 'You really don't get it, do you? You *are* the better offer, Aaron. You're the best offer I've ever had in my life. It's just a shame you don't feel the same way.'

'Wait!' He couldn't let her go back to the party, not in this state. People would notice, and then she'd never forgive him. How could trying to do the right thing end up going so wrong?

Clenching her hand around the dusty wooden frame of the door, she glanced back at him over her shoulder. 'Wait for what? For you to humiliate me even more? No thanks.'

'Let me go first then. Take a couple of minutes and really think about it and you'll see that I'm right.'

Her hand slid down the frame and she pulled it back with a curse. 'Damn it.' She poked at the centre of her palm and winced. 'Bloody splinter.'

'Here, let me look.' Aaron took her hand, holding it when she would have pulled away until she dropped her shoulders and stopped struggling. Tugging gently, he led her forward until he could better see by the light spilling through the open door. A dark sliver stood out against her pale skin and he pressed his nails down on either side until it eased free. He lifted her hand close to his mouth and blew the splinter away.

Her fingers curled around his. 'Why are you so sure this won't last?' She didn't sound angry any more, just curious and a little sad.

He kept his eyes fixed on the delicate lines webbing over her palm. If he looked into her eyes, he might weaken and try to delay the inevitable. 'Because you'll leave me. Everybody does.'

Chapter Eighteen

Mia leaned across the kitchen table, eyes wide as saucers. 'And then what did you say?'

'I didn't say anything. What was the point? He's made up his mind and I'm too tired to try and persuade him to be with me if that's not what he wants. I won't beg him; I won't beg for anything from any man ever again.' Kiki forced the vehemence into her tone. By preference, she wouldn't have talked to anyone about what had happened, or rather *hadn't* happened, between her and Aaron. She wanted to curl up in a ball and maybe cry for a week until her bruised pride healed. Two children didn't leave a lot of room for self-indulgence, so she'd tugged on her big-girl pants and got on with things instead. Not talking about it hadn't been an option, however, when Mia practically pounced on her the moment she'd arrived for work.

Saturday morning had been pretty excruciating until Aaron had taken himself off on a bike ride, giving them both some well-needed breathing space. She'd thought she'd made a good attempt at putting a brave face on things until Matty had sidled up to wrap his arms around her waist and ask why she was sad. It had been the kick in the backside she'd needed to shake off the disappointment. The children came first, last, always, and they'd been through enough emotional turmoil. Giving them a safe, comfortable place to live was more important than any hurt to her feelings. Being around Aaron was good for them, especially Matty. A little embarrassment wouldn't kill her.

Things had been easier once she'd made up her mind to act like nothing had happened. Aaron had seemed relieved at the lightening of the atmosphere, and between them they'd made a damn fine job of pretending everything was normal. She didn't feel normal, though. If she'd had a time machine, she would have jumped inside in a heartbeat. Knowing the taste of him on her tongue, the feel of his hands in her hair as he pressed her close, was torture. She'd been hyperaware of his every movement, caught herself watching him out of the corner of her eye too many times to count. That would stop soon, though. Once the memory of that kiss started to fade, they'd go back to being just good friends. If it didn't stop, she didn't know what she would do.

'Bloody hell, Kiki Dee.' Her sister sat back in her chair and huffed out a breath. 'Aaron seems so sensible and put together. Talk about still waters! I never would have encouraged you if I'd thought he'd reject you.

Stupid bugger, I could brain him. Can't he see how perfect you'd be together?'

Kiki shrugged. 'Maybe that's the problem. Madeline sowed that stupid idea in my head in the first place and we all got carried away with the fantasy. Real life isn't like that, and I should have remembered that better than anybody.'

'Hey, don't be down on yourself, or Mads for that matter. Yes, she pointed out how well suited the two of you are, but if you hadn't already been attracted to him, it wouldn't have made any difference.' Mia was right. It didn't help much.

She tugged on the end of the braid trailing over her shoulder. An area of high pressure had settled over the country, bringing with it a stifling heat. Not for the first time, she regretted the mass of her hair. Maybe if she cut it, she wouldn't keep thinking about the sensation of Aaron's fingers sifting through it.

Enough. There was work to be done. Mia might be her sister, but she didn't get paid to sit around drinking tea. She stood up. 'It is what it is. I'm going to make a start upstairs.'

Mia rose, too. 'I'll lend you a hand. Daniel's rooting around in the garages looking at some design sketches Luke did for him.' She sighed. 'It won't be long before the hammering starts again.'

She didn't want to think about the garages. Not now, maybe not ever. Which might make things a bit awkward if Mia and Daniel really did want her to manage the place. Mia hadn't said anything when

Kiki explained Aaron's reason for taking her in there. Maybe Aaron had misunderstood and they intended to run the teashop themselves after all. *Or maybe Mia has other things on her mind right now.*

Kiki shook herself. The wedding was just over a month away. With everything going on, she couldn't understand how calm Mia seemed. Maybe she wasn't the only one wearing a brave face. She linked their arms as they headed towards the stairs. 'Now, surely we can find something better to talk about.' Kiki tapped her lip and made a big play of searching for another topic. 'Anything going on with you? Any future plans? Anything, Bueller, Bueller?' The silly quote from one of their favourite films sent them both into fits of laughter.

Mia leaned back against the wall and wiped her eyes. 'Madeline says another week and she'll be finished with my dress. I can't wait to see it.'

'Oh, Mimi, we should have a fitting party for you!' Kiki led the way into the forest bedroom and they began to strip the bedding. 'If you can wait until next Saturday, we could make a girls' night of it.'

Her sister bundled the dirty sheets together and dropped them on the floor by the bed. 'But it's Matty's birthday next Saturday...' She shook her head. 'I can't believe he's going to be seven. When did he get so big?'

Kiki laughed. 'Too big! He's declared his birthday a girl-free zone—including me. He and Aaron are camping out in the garden so they can go stargazing. He doesn't know about the telescope yet, nor about the book Dad sent for him. He wants to ask Richard and Daniel to join them.' Her heart skipped. Her darling boy had so many good men in his life and he was thriving under their watchful care. *Another reason not to let this hiccup with Aaron get in the way.*

Mia bustled out, returning moments later with an armful of fresh linen. 'Well, if they're going to have a boys' night, then we should have a girls' night.'

'Exactly! I'll make some treats and pick up a bottle of champagne. We could make it into a bit of a hen night. I know you said you didn't want one, but we should do something to celebrate. The bank holiday weekend will be mayhem here and the weekend after will be too close to the wedding if you want any alterations made to your dress.' She could picture it already. Yes, there would be guests staying, but they had a separate lounge next to the dining room and were largely self-sufficient in the evenings. 'I'll make a few extra bits and we can put them out in case any of the guests fancies a snack.'

'That would be great. The honesty bar in the lounge is working really well, and most people are happy to stroll on the beach or take a bottle back to their rooms after dinner.' Mia walked around the bed and wrapped her arms around Kiki. 'It's a lovely idea. Thank you, Kiki Dee.'

Kiki held her tight. They'd come so close to losing each other; probably would have done if she'd stayed with Neil. A lump tickled the back of her throat. 'You're the best sister a girl could ever have.'

Mia pulled back and Kiki could see she was blinking back a few tears of her own. 'One of the best sisters.' She sighed. 'I wish Nee was here.'

'Me, too, but the opportunity in New York was too good for her to pass up. Did you get in touch with her about the wedding?' Kiki had sent her an email letting her know about her change in circumstances and had received a chatty reply. It sounded like their little sister was having a ball and learning a lot during her art residency. 'Is there any chance she might make it back for the wedding?'

'She's not sure, but she said she'd try. We'll make a room up for her just in case. That's something else we need to sort out, who's sleeping where.'

Seizing the opportunity, Kiki decided to press a point they'd been arguing back and forth. 'I still think you and Daniel should go away for the night.'

Mia shook her head. 'I don't see why. This is our home and there's nowhere else I'd rather be. Daniel said the same when I asked him.'

'But you should have something special.' Kiki racked her brain as she straightened the plants on the dressing table and wiped everything down with a duster. Of the four guest suites, this was her favourite. She loved the cool, fresh colours and greenery everywhere. She ran the duster gently over the thick leaves of a rubber plant which filled the corner by the window. Madeline had selected plants hardy enough to survive Mia's brown thumb. Little African violets lined the windowsill in the bathroom, and a hanging cascade of baskets held a riot of ever-sprouting spider plants. The only other room with live plants in was the harem…

'Of course!' Kiki clapped her hands together, forgetting she still held the duster. Coughing through the little cloud of dust, she grinned at her sister. 'I've got the perfect solution!'

***

Kiki looked around the happy chaos in the back garden and tried not to think about the mess four grown men and two small boys were likely to generate. Simon and Christopher, Matty's new best friend, had been added to the sleepover party. Richard had accepted with an alacrity that surprised her, going so far as to furnish a selection of fizzy drinks and enough sweets to make them all sick as dogs. Matty and Christopher were racing around the bottom of the garden, drenching each other with a pair of fluorescent Super Soakers. Charlie darted between them, squealing with shocked delight every time one or other of the boys aimed a stream of water at her. The sheer joy on her son's face was enough to lessen the pang caused by her impending banishment.

Daniel had sweet talked the company providing the gazebos for the wedding and he and Aaron were wrestling with an array of poles and guy ropes. A groundsheet and a pile of sleeping bags sat nearby. She glanced across to where Richard had made himself comfortable in a garden chair, his Panama hat tipped at a jaunty angle. 'You're not going to give them a hand?' she asked.

A broad grin creased the older man's face as he waved the booklet in his hand. 'I'll give them another half an hour or so. It's too much fun watching them struggle.'

'You have a point.' Kiki checked her watch. 'Matty's cake is in the fridge. Can you remind Aaron to take it out about half an hour before you're ready to light the candles?' She choked on the last word and fanned her face with her hand to try and ward off the silly tears which suddenly threatened.

Richard leaped from his chair and wrapped his arm around her shoulder. 'He'll miss you before the sun sets, wait and see.' He kissed her temple.

Kiki gave a watery laugh. 'I hope not. I don't want anything to spoil tonight.' She leaned into the comfort of Richard's shoulder. 'He's just growing up so fast.'

They watched the boys run around for a few more moments. When Richard spoke next, he sounded as emotional as her. 'I wouldn't wish on anyone what you've been through, but it brought you and the children into our lives. Whatever happens in the future, I hope you'll always keep in touch with us.'

She raised a hand to pat his chest. 'I'm in no hurry to go anywhere, believe me.'

'Good.' He squeezed her shoulder and they broke their embrace as Matty came barrelling towards them.

Kiki crouched down to receive a very damp hug, and ducked her head to avoid getting whacked with the squirt gun. 'Mummy! Simon says I can keep the gun, that it's my birthday present. Isn't that cool?'

Gee, thanks, Simon. 'Yes, darling, it's very cool. Did you offer your guests a drink?'

Matty stepped back, a crease furrowing his brow. 'I forgot.'

She chucked his cheek. 'That's okay, but all this exercise has probably made Christopher thirsty. Why don't you ask him? And let Charlie know we're leaving in five minutes.' He gave her a sunny grin and zoomed away, yelling for his sister at the top of his voice.

She straightened up and almost bumped into Aaron, who'd appeared from nowhere. 'Hey, steady now.' He grabbed her arm and she couldn't help but shy away. Things were growing easier between them, but she missed the effortless, friendly contact. It was her own fault, but she couldn't have him in her space without images of that bloody kiss threatening to overwhelm her.

'Sorry.' He stepped back and shoved his hands into his pockets.

'It's okay, you just startled me.' She ignored the heat the lie brought to her face and turned away. 'I need to get going. Can you round up Charlie for me?' Not waiting for a response, she made for the relative safety of the house.

Footsteps creaked on the stairs and she called out as she finished zipping up her overnight bag. 'Charlie, darling? I've left you some dry clothes on your bed. I'll be with you in one second.'

'She's downstairs with Richard.'

Kiki closed her eyes and prayed for strength. 'She needs to get changed, we're going to be late. Can you fetch her?'

'We need to talk, Kiki. Things can't go on like this. You jump every time I come anywhere near you.' His deep voice made things curl deep inside her and she cursed her own weakness for him. It wasn't his fault, but anger didn't make people rational and, damn it, she was so *bloody* angry.

Swinging around, she clamped her hands on her hips. 'Poor Aaron. I'm sorry if I made things awkward for you and shattered your perfect little fantasy here.'

He took a step inside the room and pushed the door shut behind him. 'They'll hear you. You don't want to upset the children.'

He was right, of course. They'd heard too many raised voices in the past and she'd sworn not to shout at or around them. Him being right just fanned the flames of her anger. 'Don't you tell me what to do about my own children. You don't have the right.' She lowered her voice to a hiss nonetheless. 'We're friends, Aaron, nothing more. You're not their father, not their stepfather either. You've made it clear where the boundary lies, so stick to your side of it.'

His face paled, leaving him looking sick beneath his tan. 'Kiki, I'm sorry I hurt your feelings. It was the last thing I intended. Can we just talk about it?'

The air caught in her lungs and she sat heavily on the edge of the bed. 'I don't want to talk about it.

I'm so bloody tired of talking about everything. I just wanted one uncomplicated thing in my life, and I thought you were it.'

'Kiki...' He took a step closer, but she shook her head.

'No, Aaron. I don't have it in me right now to make you feel better. You made up your mind about us without even giving me a chance.' She threw her hands up. 'If you didn't feel the same way about me as I do about you, then I could get over it. A little embarrassment, a few new bruises to my ego, nothing I'm not already an expert at dealing with.'

'Don't do that. Don't compare me to him.' Aaron's voice cracked and he slumped back against the wall to cover his face with his hands. 'This isn't what I wanted.'

It wasn't what she'd wanted either. 'What we want and what we get aren't always the same things.' She picked up her bag, stood and crossed the room towards the door. Pausing beside him, she glanced down. 'You should talk to someone, Aaron. Just not me. Not right now.'

She fiddled around, putting her bag away in the boot, double-checking the bag of toys she'd put together to keep Charlie amused at her sister's. Once she knew she could keep her composure, she fixed a bright smile on her face and returned to the kitchen.

The boys were sitting at the table with glasses of fizzy pop so pink she had to bite her lip against a protest about e-numbers. Richard glanced up and she snorted at the sight of a pink moustache curling from the corners of his lips. 'Cherryade?' she guessed.

'Strawberry ice cream soda, nectar of the gods,' he said with a beatific grin.

She shook her head. 'You'll never sleep.'

'That's the plan, right, guys?'

He held out both his hands and received a high-five slap from each boy and an affirmative, 'Right!'

'And that's definitely my cue to go. Where's Charlie?' Kiki stood on tiptoe to peer out of the window. Daniel was crouched down, his face a picture of concentration as her little chatterbox explained something to him. She tapped on the window. 'Come on, poppet, let's go and see Aunty Mia's dress.'

***

Two glasses of champagne, a large slice of lime cheesecake and a whole lot of giggles later, Kiki finally relaxed. She stroked the hair back from Charlie's forehead and pressed a kiss to her cheek. 'Is she asleep?' Mia whispered from the open doorway.

'Out like a light.' Kiki rose from her crouch and drew the door partially closed behind her. 'Oh, Mimi, you look amazing.'

The champagne-coloured lace brought a glow to Mia's skin, even under the harsh light of the hallway. The neckline cut straight across, leaving the tops of her shoulders bare. Kiki's eyes traced the delicate flower pattern of the lace down to the wide silk band circling her waist and over the simple chiffon fall of the skirt.

Madeline stepped out of the bedroom opposite, a couple of pins stuck in the arm of her shirt. 'Hold still.' She straightened Mia's shoulders then bent to place the pins in the back of the gown. 'Almost perfect. Just a couple of adjustments here and we'll be cooking on gas.' She smoothed her hand over the chiffon skirt. 'Just don't lose any more weight, dearest.'

Mia twirled around, letting the skirt flare out. 'I love it, Mads. I love it so much.'

'It's beautiful. You look radiant.' Kiki caught her sister's hand and held it. 'I'm so happy for you.'

Mia gave her a misty grin. 'Thank you.' She shook her head. 'No tears, no tears! Let me get changed and we can have some more champagne.'

Kiki grinned. 'And cake. Madeline's worried about you getting too thin, after all.' Halfway down the stairs her phone started to ring. Expecting it was Matty calling to say goodnight, she pulled it out of her pocket and answered without checking the screen.

'Hello, Kiki.'

Her knees gave out and she sat on the stairs with a thump. 'Neil.'

'I'm home. Imagine my disappointment to find you not here.'

She bit the inside of her cheek and counted to ten. Footsteps creaked behind her and she held up her hand to silence whoever was approaching. 'You had my solicitor's letter. I wasn't bluffing. It's over.' Soft fingers touched her shoulder and she reached up to grip them tightly. The raised edges of a large ring told her it was Madeline and she clung to her hand like an anchor.

'Really, Kiki, how foolish of you to believe so.' She shuddered. Calm, seemingly reasonable Neil was so much worse than furious, ranting Neil. Calm Neil was the one who hit her, who vented his anger with fists rather than words.

'Why can't you accept this and move on? I'm settled here, and the children are happy.' Her voice started to waver, so she clamped her mouth shut. She wouldn't give him the satisfaction of her fear.

'Speaking of the children, I'd like to talk to Matty and wish him happy birthday.' *Oh God.*

'It's late, Neil. He's in bed.' She crossed her fingers against the lie, a childish habit she'd never grown out of.

'He's my bloody son! Get him on the phone, or you'll be sorry!' The change in his demeanour was as swift and ugly as a squall rolling in from the sea.

There was no way she'd let him speak to Matty like this, even if she could. 'You can talk to him in the morning.'

'Are you denying me access to my child?' Calm Neil. Sly Neil. Her stomach rolled as a sense of dread struck her.

Stay strong. 'Not at all. As I already said, you can speak to him in the morning.'

The jaws on the trap snapped closed. 'And why exactly can't I speak to him now? It's Friday night, not even an hour past his usual bedtime, on his birthday. My solicitor will be keen to hear the exact details of your unreasonable behaviour.'

Shit! 'He's having a sleepover with some friends. I'm at Mia's for the evening. She's getting married in a couple of weeks so we're having a celebration.' It was too much information, but mention of his solicitor set her fear running like a hare from the trap. She placed her free hand on her chest to try and calm her racing heart. Madeline squeezed her fingers and pressed a kiss to the top of her head, but didn't speak.

'A celebration?' Neil paused so long, if she hadn't heard his breath in her ear she would've thought they'd been cut off. When he spoke again, she wished they had been. 'Let me get this straight. It's my son's birthday and you're out drinking with your *sister*? If neither of you are with him, then who the hell is looking after my children? Where's Charlotte? Christ, I always knew you were unstable, just like your mother.'

There was no way she was letting him get away with that. 'Charlie's here with me. She's asleep upstairs and absolutely fine. I'm nothing like my mother, Neil, and you damn well know it!'

'I don't know anything of the sort. You're irrational, you've clearly been drinking in front of my daughter, and you're neglecting my son. It's just as well I've decided to sue for custody. You're obviously incapable of taking care of them.'

The rolling in her stomach ramped up to full-blown nausea. 'You can't be serious. You haven't spared them a thought for the best part of three months while you soaked up the sun with your new girlfriend. There's no court in the land that'll let you take them from me.'

'What's going on?' Kiki shook her head at the sound of Mia's voice; she couldn't afford to be distracted now. She felt Madeline's warmth leave her and the two women moved further up the stairs and began whispering to each other.

Neil gave an exaggerated sigh. 'So, that's what all this nonsense is about? There's no need to be jealous, Kiki. Emily is a colleague who developed a bit of a crush on me, nothing more. Come home and we can sort this out.'

The blatant lie fed her anger and she stoked it further, feeding every slight, every slap, every putdown he'd given her into it. The anger gave her strength and she stood up, not willing to crouch before him even if he couldn't see her. 'I've seen the emails. I've *copied* the emails and given them to my solicitor. This is my home, here with people who love me. Who treat me with kindness and respect.'

'You'll be sorry for this,' he spat. 'I'll make you pay for defying me, you stupid bitch.'

A bitter laugh cracked from her mouth. 'I'm already sorry. Sorry for the years I wasted on you. I'm done paying. You'll get nothing more from me, you bastard. Not another tear, not another flinch, and definitely not my children. I'm never coming back, so get used to it!'

She dragged the phone from her ear. The adrenaline flooding her body made her hands shake and it took her two attempts to end the call. Footsteps clattered on the stairs and she found herself enveloped in two sets of arms. Resting her head on her sister's shoulder,

Kiki breathed deeply, refusing to cry. She'd told Neil he wouldn't get another tear from her and she bloody well meant it.

She'd also told him she was never going back, but she knew the truth. There was no way to fight him from a distance, and he would do everything in his power to make things as difficult for her as he could. Knowing all too well how charming and persuasive he could be, she couldn't afford to be so far away. Her visit to Butterfly Cove had helped her heal, given her strength and repaired the ties to her family.

It was time to go back. But not to him.

Chapter Nineteen

Aaron slid the air con switch in Kiki's little car all the way to the right and rested his head back against the seat as icy cold air blasted in his face. The past week had been hellish, not least because of the spike in temperature. Luke's train wasn't due in for another quarter of an hour, but there was no way he was going to pass up the chance to sit in the cool air for a few extra minutes. From the filthy look Daniel had thrown his way when he'd left him stringing fairy lights through the trees, his friend knew exactly what he was up to.

Holding a wedding in the beautiful gardens at Butterfly House had sounded idyllic when Daniel had told him about it. It was a terrific spot, and between the beach and the lush grounds, there would be no shortage of spots to take memorable photos of the wedding party. From the comfortable rooms at the guest house to the gorgeous setting, Mia's idea of branching out into hosting weddings made perfect sense. *Unless you were the poor saps trying to erect the marquees in the middle of a heatwave.*

The installation company were brilliant, fielding their bombardment of questions with good humour and endless patience. Aaron had been fascinated by how sophisticated the set-up was, especially the flooring. The main marquee had a laid wooden and carpeted floor, with a special section set aside for dancing. They'd also erected a handful of smaller, round marquees—some with coconut matting and others with carpet directly on to the grass so they could test out how the different surfaces fared over the evening. It might be Daniel and Mia's special day, but they were taking the opportunity to do some market research for their future business enterprise.

Thunderstorms were predicted overnight, which everyone hoped would break the worst of the heat, but after that the weekend weather promised to be fine and dry. They'd consulted every forecasting service known to man bar sacrificing a chicken and reading its entrails, but there were no reports of strong winds so the marquees were going up regardless. There would be too much to do on Friday as it was. The lower floor of the barns was stacked high with tables, chairs, boxes of cutlery, tableware and all the other 'essentials' needed for Saturday.

He closed his eyes with a sigh. The white noise of the fan whirring couldn't drown out the thoughts spinning through his brain. Groping for the radio, he cranked the volume and an obnoxious pop song filled the interior. It didn't help. He'd been on autopilot for the past few weeks, ever since Kiki had walked through the door the morning after Matty's birthday and told him she would be leaving Butterfly Cove. Knowing he'd been right not to rush into things with her did nothing to ease the gaping hole in his heart, nor the sense he'd let the most precious gift slip through his fingers. *Too late now.* He had no choice other than to play the hand he'd been dealt. Be the friend he'd told her he was, and help make her return trip as pain-free as possible.

Going back was the right thing to do—he knew that; they both knew. Neil had decided to play dirty so Kiki would need to keep her wits about her. Her dad had offered to take them in, and they were travelling back together after the wedding. Which meant Aaron had to hold his brave face in place for another seventy-two hours. Poor Matty had been beside himself until they'd been able to make him understand that going back didn't mean going home to live with Neil again. Charlie had grown increasingly clingy, attaching herself to Aaron the moment he walked through the door. Feeling pretty damn needy himself, Aaron had indulged her need for comfort, and his own as well.

The song ended, and Aaron sat up to switch off the radio as the local DJ blathered on about making the most of the gorgeous weather and enjoying the calm before the storm. He hoped, for the guy's sake, Mia wasn't listening or she'd probably unleash a curse on him for the reminder. Climbing out of the front seat,

Aaron stared up at the wide expanse of Wedgwood-blue sky. Maybe the forecasters had got it wrong, because there was barely a wisp of white to be seen. He shoved the car keys in his pocket and strolled across the patchy gravel car park towards the tiny station which served Orcombe Sands.

He arrived on the platform at the same time as the guard, and the man gave him a friendly wave. 'More guests coming in?' he asked with a smile. 'You lot are keeping me in business now the holiday season is coming to an end.'

'My brother.'

The guard nodded. 'Ah, yes. He's one of my regulars now. Nice lad.'

Aaron grinned. 'He has his moments.' They shared a laugh before the guard moved away to complete his final checks.

The train easing into the station was an older style one with drop-down windows built into the doors. Luke's head stuck out of one towards the back, and he could make out the wide grin on his face from where he stood. Aaron rolled his eyes; he looked like a bloody Labrador hanging half out of a car window with the breeze blowing in his face. He grabbed his brother's bag and dropped it on the ground before sweeping him into a tight hug. 'All right, Spud? It's good to see you.'

Luke squeezed his ribs and planted a kiss on his cheek. 'Good to see you, too. How's things?' A concerned look creased his brow.

'Bloody awful.'

'Thought they might be. We'll have a beer tonight, eh?' Luke picked up his bag and slung his free arm around Aaron's shoulders, offering comfort without censure. Aaron raised his hand to pat his brother's where it rested on his shoulder and they strolled down the platform towards the car park.

The guard had his back to them, talking to someone. He turned as they drew level. 'These lads might be able to help you. This young lady's trying to get to Butterfly Cove.'

Aaron stopped immediately, speaking before he'd even got a good look at the woman. 'We're headed that way, we'll be happy to give you a lift.'

She glanced up through a choppy, peroxide-blonde fringe and he would have recognised those chocolate-brown eyes anywhere. *The infamous third sister.* Kiki had mentioned Nee knew about the wedding but they weren't sure if she'd be able to make it back from the States to attend. Apparently, she had.

Stepping forward to offer his hand, Aaron froze at the look of abject horror on her face. Her attention was fixed at a point past his left shoulder. Raising a shaky hand to her mouth, she choked out a single word. 'Luke?'

'Shit.'

Confused, Aaron spun towards his brother. The unhappy expression Luke wore matched Nee's to perfection. 'You know each other?'

Luke pursed his lips. 'You could say that.'

He stepped forward, a mocking smile on his face. 'Aaron, allow me to introduce you to my wife. Nee, this is my brother, Aaron. He's in love with your sister, but she's about to leave him. Must run in the family.' Luke turned on his heel to walk off without a backward glance.

'Well, if you'll excuse me, I've things to do.' The guard's flustered words of departure barely registered with Aaron as he watched the colour drain from the already pale woman's face.

Grabbing her arm, he held her steady until she stopped swaying. 'Take a breath, I've got you.'

She blinked up through a shimmer of tears. 'How is he here?' Her eyes drifted past him again.

'Luke, you mean? Your sister Mia is marrying my best friend, Daniel. We've been coming here since the winter to help with the renovations on the guest house and the studios. I live here now. With Kiki. Not *with* her, you understand. Just under the same roof. Well, until Sunday, and then she's moving back to your dad's. Neil's giving her a hard time. You know about her leaving him?' The flood of explanation sounded ludicrous to his own ears, but was nothing compared to the questions screaming in his head. How? How could Luke be married to Nee and he not know about it? How could his little brother be married to *anybody* without him knowing about it?

Nee glanced over her shoulder at the stationary train. 'I... I should go. This was a mistake.' She tugged against his hold, tears brimming over her lids to spill down her cheeks, but Aaron didn't release her. The train wouldn't be going anywhere for a couple of hours and he couldn't leave her on her own in this state.

'Shh. Don't cry. Let me take you to see your sisters, okay? You've come all this way, it would be such a shame to turn around now.' He pulled a folded handkerchief from his pocket and handed it to her.

'All this way?'

She was obviously in shock, poor thing. Hours on a plane followed by a surprise confrontation with Luke. *Her husband!* the inner voice in his head screamed. Aaron shoved it away and tried to focus on the immediate situation. 'Come on, my car's just around the corner. Let's get you back to Mia's and the rest will come out in the wash.'

This time, when he tugged on her arm, she didn't resist. He grabbed the handle on her rolling suitcase with his free hand and led her off the platform. There was no sign of Luke in the car park, although his bag sat on the gravel beside the car. He stowed it beside Nee's suitcase then helped her into the passenger seat. She didn't mention his brother, and he thought it best not to. Orcombe was little more than a one-horse town so there weren't many places he could be. As soon as he delivered Nee, he would double back and look for Luke. His eyes rose to the large white building on the other side of the road. The pub would be as good a place to start as any.

The ten-minute drive from the station to Butterfly Cove seemed endless, and Aaron couldn't help but heave a sigh of relief when he pulled up close to the kitchen door of the house. Daniel stood in the shade, holding a cold can of lemonade to his forehead. 'About time you slackers got here,' he greeted Aaron as he climbed out of the car. 'Hey, who's your friend? Where's Luke?'

Aaron shook his head. 'Is Mia about? Can you fetch her?'

'What? Hey, sure. She's just throwing some sandwiches together.' He leaned back towards the open door and called out. 'Mia, love? You've got a visitor.'

Mia appeared from inside the house, wiping her hands on a tea towel as Aaron opened the car door and held out his hand to help Nee out. 'What's all the racket? Luke isn't exactly a visit... *Nee?* Oh my God, Nee! Kiki! Kiki, come see who's here!'

Nee flew past him like a tiny whirlwind and threw herself at her sister. The two women clung to each other, joined almost instantly by a third as Kiki gave a cry of delight at the sight of her little sister. Laughing and crying, the three women stumbled towards the house in a tangle of arms and legs.

Daniel popped the tab on his drink and downed several huge swallows. Wiping the back of his hand over his mouth he glanced at Aaron. 'So that's Nee, is it?'

He nodded his head. 'Yup.'

'And where's Luke?'

Aaron scrubbed a hand over his eyes. 'The pub, I think. I dunno. I need to go and find him.' He glanced towards the open door. 'What a bloody mess.'

Daniel followed his gaze. The chattering voices inside had dropped away, leaving it ominously quiet. His best friend swung back to frown at him. 'What's going on?'

Aaron shrugged. 'I don't even know where to start. Let me go and find Luke first.' He rounded the car and slid into the driver's seat. The forecast hadn't been kidding when it predicted storms on the horizon. In the light of developments, perhaps his own plans for Saturday should be put on hold. *Or maybe he was desperate for an excuse.* Whatever. His own problems needed to wait their turn, Luke needed him and nothing else could come before that.

It was with no small sense of relief when Aaron pulled up outside the pub and found Luke waiting for him on the pavement. He leaned over and popped the handle to let his brother in. 'All right?'

Luke laughed. 'Anything but. I know it'll be a bit of a squeeze tonight, but can you find room for me at your place?' The original plan had been for Luke to stay in one of the studio apartments tonight before he and Daniel stayed over on Friday night. They might be already living together, but Mia wanted to respect the tradition of the bride and groom not seeing each other on the morning of the wedding. Kiki and her children were staying over at Butterfly House, and Honeysuckle Cottage would become a bachelor pad for one night only.

Aaron rested his head on the steering wheel, wishing the errant thought away. After Sunday, the cottage would revert permanently to a bachelor pad. Meals for one, no slalom course of toys and games to negotiate on the living-room floor. Tears burned the backs of his eyes and he bumped his head against the wheel. The horn blared, scaring the crap out of him, and he jerked upright. Laughter filled the car and he punched Luke in the arm. 'It's not funny.'

'No, Bumble, it's really not.' Luke stared at him, straight-faced for a moment before they both burst out laughing.

It hurt, Christ it hurt, but the cathartic nature of their shared pain helped Aaron purge the cancer of doubt that had been eating away inside of him. Kiki might be leaving, just as he'd predicted, but in his self-indulgent wallowing he'd forgotten one important fact—she wasn't leaving *him*.

Breathing easily for the first time in days, he turned in his seat to regard Luke. 'She's the girl you told me about, right? The love-at-first-sight girl from The George?'

His brother nodded.

'Why didn't you tell us; tell me at least?'

Luke shrugged. 'At first, I didn't want to talk about it. It didn't seem real, you know? Like I'd been living in this dream world and I woke up.' He coughed, a raw painful sound, and Aaron reached out to clasp his shoulder. The space in the car made it awkward, but now Luke had started talking, he didn't want to interrupt him by suggesting they relocate to the pub, or back to the cottage. He notched the air conditioning up with his other hand to ease the stifling atmosphere.

'When I opened my eyes, the first thing I saw was an empty champagne bottle with one of the roses from her bouquet sticking out of the top of it. Bouquet sounds grander than it was—we grabbed a bunch of them from a street seller on the way to the registry office. She had this lilac dress on, and she'd painted her nails to match it…' Luke shook his head as though trying to dislodge the image from his mind. 'The bottle, the rose, I thought my heart would jump right out of my chest as I raised my left hand and saw the band on my finger. I was married, and happier than I'd ever been in my life.'

He looked away and Aaron schooled himself to wait. Forced himself to ignore the tide of anger rising inside him. The anger wasn't directed at Luke, not even at Nee, though she'd surely broken his brother's big heart. He'd let Luke down. Been too busy playing hero to a girl who didn't really need him, and for what? His need to apologise rode him hard, but he swallowed it down.

'I thought she was in the bathroom, or maybe in the kitchen getting a cup of coffee, so I waited. I'd persuaded someone to take a few photos of us after the ceremony. I reached for my phone and knocked something onto the floor. It… it made this noise when it hit the floorboards, and I heard it roll under the bed.' Luke glanced over at him and the raw anguish on his face ripped his guts to shreds. 'I knew. That thud and roll. I just knew what it was.'

Jesus Christ. 'Her wedding ring?'

Luke nodded. 'That's all she left. No note, no trace she'd ever been in my flat other than that fucking ring I'd slid on her finger twelve hours earlier. I didn't even know she'd left the country until Mia mentioned something about New York.'

He'd opened the door, so Aaron felt able to ask the question that had been weighing on him. 'When did you realise Mia and Nee were sisters?'

'Not for ages. I thought Mia looked familiar, but I was so obsessed with Nee I saw her everywhere, in the face of every woman who looked even remotely like her. I chased one poor girl down the street, thinking it was Nee, and the fear on her face when I grabbed her arm broke something inside me. So I did my best to forget. To pretend she never existed.' And it worked for a while.' He sighed. 'It was the weekend we were trying to finish the harem room. Mia had ordered some fabric for the curtains, but it hadn't arrived. The order was on that big corkboard of hers, the one in the kitchen…'

Aaron nodded. The board was Mia's lifeline—an overspill of her endless notebooks and crammed with recipes, bills and other things she didn't want to lose.

'I lifted a piece of paper, and there was this photo underneath it. Three girls, long hair flowing as they laughed together, and the pieces clicked into place.'

'You went home early that weekend, said you had a bad head.' It had been a busy weekend for them all and Luke had been pale enough for Aaron not to think twice about it. He'd been doing that a lot, accepting excuses and taking everything his brother said at face value. Guilt jabbed him below the ribs. 'I wish I'd been there for you. That you would have talked to me. Why didn't you say anything?'

'At first I was too shocked and then it just felt too awkward. What could I say to Mia? *By the way, I'm married to your sister.* I found myself listening for any hint of Nee, and that made it worse, like I was stalking her or something. My contact details haven't changed in the last year so she could have reached me if she wanted to. The message was loud and clear.'

His heart ached for Luke, but he must have known things would come to a head eventually. As usual, fate had picked the worst timing possible. 'What will you do now?'

His brother shrugged. 'It's not up to me. Nothing's changed.' He grabbed Aaron's arm, his face creased with intensity. 'If I'd thought for a moment she'd be here, I would have said something, I swear. The last thing I want to do is screw things up for Mia and Daniel. I should go home…' He looked past Aaron in the direction of the train station.

'No. No way. I'm not letting you out of my sight, Spud. Not when you're so upset. I'll talk to Daniel and we'll work something out. You can stay at the cottage and if you don't want to see her, you won't have to.'

'That's not fair on you. Not fair on them either, I came here to help, to celebrate my friends finding a happiness they both desperately deserve. I've accepted the fact she doesn't want me in her life.' Luke took a deep breath. 'I'm not looking for a big confrontation.

I don't even care any more why she left me.' Aaron wondered if his brother could hear the lie in his words, but he kept quiet.

Luke glanced up. 'I can handle it, if she can. If she can't, then I'll go back to London. I don't want to spoil things.'

Aaron didn't think he'd have the same strength if their situations were reversed, but his job right now was to let his brother handle things however he needed to. 'Do you want me to find out what's going on?' At Luke's nod, he climbed out of the car and placed a call to Kiki.

'Aaron? Hold on a minute.' He heard the faint sound of a door closing, and her voice blurted in his ear. 'Oh my God, did he tell you?'

He paced along the pavement to make sure he was out of earshot should Luke open his window. 'Yes. I don't know what to make of it, to be honest. What did Nee say?'

A soft sigh echoed down the phone. 'Not much. She was pretty hysterical at first. Just kept saying she'd made a terrible mistake.'

He wondered if Nee was talking about getting married to Luke or leaving him, but he kept quiet. It was a discussion for the two of them, and no one else. 'Luke told me he didn't think she would make it to the wedding or he would have said something. I think he was in denial over the whole thing. He'd like to stay, but he doesn't want to cause any more upset, so if Nee can't handle seeing him, he says he'll go home.' Aaron scuffed a stone on the pavement with his foot. 'He's my baby brother, Kiki. I can't let him leave, certainly not tonight.'

Her response was instantaneous and went a long way to easing the tightness in his chest. 'Of course he can't! He can stay with us tonight. The kids can double up, or come in with me even. Take him home and I'll try and find out what's going on.'

Relief flooded him. 'Thank you. I... tell Mia and Daniel that I'm sorry.'

'For what? None of this is your fault, Aaron.'

He could see the logic in her statement, but it didn't do anything to ease his guilt. He should have seen, he should have known Luke was upset about something. He said as much, and Kiki cut him off with a rude noise. 'Bollocks to that, Aaron Spenser! If it's your fault, then it's surely my fault—Mia's, too, for that matter. We let our little sister slip away from us; we were too caught up with our own struggles to pay proper attention to her.' Her voice softened. 'It happens. That's life. We can't control everything.'

A smile stretched his lips. 'When did you get so smart?'

She laughed. 'Too damn late for it to do any good, it seems. I've got to go.'

'Okay. I'll get Luke settled in and make a start on dinner. Ring me when you're ready and I'll come and pick you and the kids up.'

'Okay. Don't worry, we'll sort things out.'

He ended the call, hoping like hell she was right.

Chapter Twenty

Friday dawned bright and fair. Birds sang in the hedgerows, and a tractor turned a lazy circle in a nearby field. If she hadn't spent the night with Charlie and Matty, cuddled close as thunder roared and lightning flashed outside the window, Kiki would never have believed there'd been a storm overnight. Tension rolled off Luke from his position in the passenger seat in front of her. She lifted her eyes to meet Aaron's via the rear-view mirror and offered him a weak smile. Both Luke and Nee had sworn they could deal with the other's presence; that their only concern was making sure Mia and Daniel had the best day possible. They were both terrible liars.

Kiki turned her attention back to the passing countryside as Aaron steered them over the little crossroads and down the hill towards Butterfly Cove. The sea glittered in the distance, a shimmering carpet of blue edged with the last traces of pink from the rising sun. She caught her breath, knowing it would be one of the last times she would enjoy the spectacular vista. Blaming the burn at the back of her eyes on a lack of sleep, she pointed out the small triangle of a sailboat bobbing on the bright-blue water to Matty and they spent the rest of the short journey imagining where the boat might be travelling to.

Aaron parked the car out of the way next to the garages and they all piled out. 'At least the marquees survived.' The relief in his voice was palpable and she met his eyes over the roof of the car. He flicked his gaze to Luke, who stared out across the gardens, then back to her. 'We'll head for the barns and make a start with the furniture.'

Kiki nodded. 'I'll take the children in and get them sorted out. Madeline and Richard should be here shortly.' Madeline had offered to supervise the little ones and keep them occupied while she put together the table decorations. It had been suggested Nee could help her and she'd agreed readily enough. It would keep her and Luke out of each other's way at least. When she entered the kitchen, her younger sister was the only person present. The dark circles beneath her eyes and her scruffy hair told Kiki enough about how Nee's night had been that she didn't need to ask.

'Hey…' Nee offered a weary smile. Spotting the children, she crouched down and forced a brighter expression. 'Hey, kiddos. Are you ready to help me make some pretty things for tomorrow?'

Shoving her worry down, Kiki urged the children closer to their aunt. They'd seen her the previous day, but that had been the first time in a couple of years. 'That sounds like fun, doesn't it, Charlie?'

Her daughter clapped her hands. 'Can I do painting?'

Nee reached out to brush her cheek. 'You can do whatever you want, Chicken. What about you, Matty? What would you like to do?'

'Madeline wants me to polish things. She said it's a very reasonable job, and she only trusts me to do it.'

A glimmer of mischief glinted in her sister's eye at Matty's verbal mix-up, the first sign of anything other than pain, and it gave Kiki hope. Nee nodded at Matty. 'Polishing is a very *reasonable* job indeed, something only a big boy like you can do for sure.'

Matty's chest puffed up with pride. 'I'm seven now. I just had my birthday.'

'Oh, that's right. I'm sorry I missed it. I'll have to get you a present. What do big boys like?'

Kiki ran her hand over her son's head. 'Matty's a stargazer these days, aren't you?' She caught Nee's gaze, deciding now might be a good time to raise another issue which had preyed on her mind in the early hours. 'Aaron gave him a telescope, and Dad sent him a book about the Greek myths connected to the constellations.'

Nee started. 'Dad?'

Kiki nodded. 'Things have moved on while you were away.'

Her sister pushed to her feet, glaring at her. 'Just like that, all is forgiven?'

Ignoring Nee's outburst, Kiki sent the children into the living room to watch cartoons whilst they waited for Madeline. She leaned back against the closed internal door and tried to check her anger. 'Look, Nee, I get that things are bad for you right now, but I won't have you raising your voice in front of the children.'

'I'm sorry, but...'

She held up her hand. 'Let me finish. Neil is fighting me for custody so I have to move back. Things are nowhere near resolved with Dad, but he's trying and I need him on my side more than I need to hang on to old hurts. We're going to stay with him while I try to get everything sorted out. He's on his own now, with Mum in the care home.' Vivian not being there was the only reason Kiki had considered moving back home. *Needs must when the devil drives* was her new motto. If the summer had taught her anything, it was that she had more strength than she'd ever realised. There wasn't much she wouldn't face down these days when it came to protecting the future she wanted for her children. And for herself, too.

Adopting a more conciliatory tone, she closed the distance between them and put her hands on Nee's arms. 'Mia wants him at the wedding, and that's good enough for me. You've got about six hours for it to be good enough for you.'

Nee shook her head. 'I can't forgive him; I won't forgive him. How can you even bear to set foot in that house again?'

Kiki drew her close. Nee had always been the one who'd raged against their father for not doing enough to get help for Vivian. She'd been too young to remember George as anything other than a remote figure, more interested in work than dealing with the problems at home. He'd been in denial. Adult Kiki could see that, could look back and remember the harsh insults Vivian had thrown at him as often as she threw glasses and china. It didn't excuse his behaviour, but hadn't she exposed her own children to an equally destructive and insecure household?

She stroked Nee's hair. 'No one is asking you to forgive him, Nee. As for the rest, I'll do what I have to until the divorce is settled. I'm not asking for your blessing. I don't need anyone's permission to do what I think is right for my family. When it comes to Dad, just try and be civil. Or steer clear of him, if you can't manage that.'

Nee's bitter laughter tore at her. 'At this rate, you'll have to put me at a table on my own.' She leaned into Kiki's hug for a long moment then drew back. 'I'm the fly in the ointment here. I shouldn't have turned up unannounced.'

Kiki cupped her face. 'You're here, that's all we care about. You travelled all this way for our sister's wedding. We understand how important New York is to your future.'

'My future, right,' Nee said dully. She leaned back and Kiki let her hands drop, though the bleak look on Nee's face made her want to snatch her back and hold her tight. She knew that hopeless look, had seen it in her own reflection too many times.

'Nee...'

'Hello, darlings!' Madeline swept through the back door like a force of nature. She took in the bleak scene with one swift glance and clapped her hands together. 'Right, you two. No moping! There's too much to do and Mia needs all the smiles we can give her.' After putting down the bags she was holding, she slung her arm around Nee's waist and gave her a quick squeeze. 'I'm parched. Be a darling and put the kettle on. I'll get things set up in the dining room while you make the tea. White, no sugar for me!'

Nee sagged back against the sink as she watched Madeline grab her bags and leave the kitchen. 'Is she always so bossy?'

Kiki laughed. 'Oh no. Most of the time she's much worse.' The thought of watching her stubborn little sister butt heads with the implacable, spirited Madeline was almost tempting enough for her to stay and watch. She took in her sister's wan complexion, the prominent bones of her too-thin frame, visible through the thin material of her shirt, and swallowed a sigh. There was more to this than a bit of jetlag and the shock of seeing Luke again. Nee looked exhausted, worn away to almost nothing. A dose of Madeline might be just what the doctor ordered.

***

A horn toot-tooted from the driveway and Kiki pressed her hands into the small of her back as she straightened up from placing the final touches on the top table. She wasn't sure what Mia's agenda was for that evening, but she hoped it involved hot baths and early nights for everyone. A quick glance at her watch told her they'd made decent time, and as she surveyed the interior of the largest marquee, a frisson of excitement shivered through her. With the tables and chairs all dressed in sweeping cream coverings and crisp, apricot-shaded linens, it looked beautiful.

The long table was set for sixteen and would serve the attendees of the wedding—the family, Aaron and Luke, Madeline and Richard, Pat and Bill, and Maggie. Over the course of planning their ceremony, Mia and Daniel had grown close to Alison, their celebrant, and she'd been invited to join them for the meal, together with her wife, Sue. They'd originally planned to split the group across three tables, but neither she nor Mia had come up with a solution which would keep certain people away from each other without making one of the older two couples sit apart. The single, long run of seating made it easier to spread Luke, Nee and their dad out amongst the group, and hopefully help keep the peace.

Smaller, round tables had been set out on either side of a square, parquet dance floor, and a small table near the entrance would hold Luke's iPod and docking station, which he'd brought with him. He'd elected himself DJ for the night as part of his gift and had spent weeks putting together playlists for the event. Everyone had been required to send him a list of their favourite songs, even her dad. Kiki couldn't wait to find out what he had in store for them all.

'Oh, my dear, it looks lovely.' Pat paused on the outside of the marquee, her hands clasped together and her face wreathed in smiles.

Kiki rounded the table and held out her hand. 'Hello, Pat. It's so good to see you. Come in and have a proper look.'

The older woman's eyes lit up. 'Do you think it'll be all right?'

'Yes, of course.' They met in the middle of the dance floor and Kiki sank gratefully into the warm hug from Mia's former mother-in-law.

'You're looking well, darling. This sea air seems to be doing you the world of good,' Pat said, as Kiki led her up to the top table. 'Oh, look at this, it's adorable!' She plucked one of the place cards from the table with a delighted laugh. Nee and Charlie had made them together, and the elegant, curling script of each person's name was surrounded by lopsided flowers and glittery butterflies. Kiki loved the playfulness of them and they provided a sweet contrast to the formal tableware.

Each knife, fork and spoon shone with mirror-brightness and had been placed with absolute precision by Matty. He'd refused to let her help, beyond telling him which order things went in, and he'd even worn a pair of gloves so there would be no smudges on the handles. They'd both worked so hard on the jobs Madeline had given them, wanting to make things just right for their Aunty Mia. A pang of regret struck; leaving Butterfly Cove would be a terrible wrench for them, but she hadn't come up with a better solution.

Her expression must have betrayed some of her inner turmoil, because Pat reached up to tuck a stray strand of hair back from her cheek. 'Has it been awful? Your dad told us about Neil being difficult over custody.'

She welcomed the touch, marvelling at how lucky she was to have so many people to lean on in her life. They'd always been there, she'd just been too afraid to ask before. 'It's had its moments, but I don't regret leaving, not for one moment.'

Pat leaned over to kiss her forehead. 'I know you don't want to come back, but Bill and I will be glad to have you and the children nearby again. We'll help you and your dad in any way we can.' She shook her head. 'He's having a terrible time of it with Vivian. I know you've got enough on your plate, but I think you should prepare yourself for the worst.'

'Dad said her condition had deteriorated. It seems like a terrible thing to say, but it'll be a relief. I can't bear to think of her so lost and confused.' Even on her worst days, Vivian had been perfectly turned out and made up. She would hate the loss of that perfect veneer more than anything, so perhaps her lack of awareness was a blessing, even as it cursed the rest of them. Kiki would bear the scars of her mother's manipulation for the rest of her life, but they would no longer define her.

‘Ah, lovey, I didn’t mean to upset you. Let’s put all that away for now and enjoy the weekend. Where’s your sister? I haven’t seen her yet.’

Kiki linked arms with Pat and they strolled towards the house. ‘Which one?’

The older woman stopped, eyes rounding as her mouth dropped open. ‘Nee’s here?’

She nodded. ‘Yes, and, oh my goodness, she’s brought some drama with her. I’ll let Madeline tell you about that, though.’ The two women had become firm friends over the past six months. ‘As for Mia, we sent her for a lie-down about an hour ago. I saw Daniel sneaking off after her, so I doubt there’s much resting going on, though.’

‘Ah, young love.’ Pat clutched her hand to her breast with a dramatic sigh, sending them both into a fit of giggles. ‘And what about you? I know Madeline had hopes for a certain gorgeous blond and you...’

Kiki shook her head. ‘Don’t go there.’ She’d mostly come to terms with her disappointment over things with Aaron, but she couldn’t suppress the sharp edge in her tone. If the timing had been different, or if there wasn’t so much at stake, then maybe it would have worked out between them. ‘It’s... awkward.’

Pat hugged her arm as they reached the back door. ‘There’s plenty of time for things to come right.’ Something in her tone made Kiki pause and look at her. A glint of determination shone in Pat’s eye.

‘Oh God, no,’ she groaned. ‘One meddling old bag in my life is more than enough.’

Madeline arrived on the threshold in time to catch her comment. 'We prefer fairy godmothers, remember?' The three of them laughed and exchanged hugs of greeting.

Bedlam was the word that came to mind as she entered the kitchen. There were people, bags and boxes everywhere and at least four different conversations going on. A slightly rumpled-looking Mia and Daniel were chatting to her dad. Bill and Richard had magicked a bottle of red wine from somewhere and were toasting each other. Luke swung a screeching, laughing Charlie upside down by one foot while Aaron knelt next to him, an intent look on his face as he nodded at whatever Matty was telling him. The only notable absence from the noisy group was Nee.

Her heart did a funny squirm in her chest; watching Aaron lavish all his attention on her son undid all her good intentions. Fate was a bitch and Neil was a bastard for tearing them all apart just as things were starting to come together. Kiki sighed. Blaming others for things would only make her feel better in the short term. Her circumstances were of her own creation and she had to face down the past before trying to create a better future. Growing up really sucked sometimes.

Leaving Madeline and Pat to whatever plots they were stirring up, Kiki slipped across the room to stand next to her dad. She didn't interrupt his conversation with Daniel about his journey down, just took his hand in hers and gave it a quick squeeze. His fingers lay limply in hers for a moment before closing tight.

It might have been twenty years or more since he'd last held her hand, but the hard callous on the side of his middle finger from years of clasping a pen felt exactly the same as when he'd gathered them close to cross the road. She'd forgotten until just then that he used to take her and Mia to school, always making sure they used the Green Cross Code.

Daniel and Mia excused themselves to say hello to Pat. She got a proper look at George when he turned towards her and the strained lines on his face told their own tale. 'How are you, Dad?'

'A bit tired, but glad to be here. He seems like a good fit for her.' He nodded towards where Daniel stood behind Mia, his arms around her shoulders, and Kiki smiled.

'He certainly is. I didn't think I'd ever see her glow like that again after Jamie.'

George squeezed her hand. 'And how about you? Are you coping all right with everything?'

Kiki sighed. 'Just about. Trying not to think about Sunday too much.' She hesitated. 'Sorry, that sounds ungrateful to you, but I'm not looking forward to uprooting the kids now they're happy and settled.'

'Not at all. Why would you want to leave all this and move back in with me if you didn't have to? Too many unhappy memories.'

He was right, but how much worse for him to be stuck in that place on his own with the ghosts of the past. 'Well, we'll have to try and make some new ones, some happier ones this time.'

'You're a good girl. Too good by half. Look, I was going to wait until later, but can you spare me a few minutes to talk?'

She glanced over at Aaron and found him watching them. The concern in his brown eyes helped and hurt in equal measure. If only her circumstances were different; if only he'd been willing to take a chance on them; if only she could stop thinking about if onlys. She looked at the children and then towards the door behind her and he nodded. 'We can find a quiet spot through here,' she said to her dad before leading him into the relative quiet of the rest of the house.

After peeking around the door to Mia's little sitting room to check Nee wasn't hiding in there, Kiki walked in and took a seat on the large L-shaped sofa. George closed the door behind him and settled himself at the other end. He brushed some non-existent fluff from the neatly pressed leg of his dark trousers, then folded his hands nervously.

Kiki found herself nibbling her lower lip between her teeth and scolded herself silently. She'd almost broken the habit, but she couldn't help picking up on the worry coming from her father. Perhaps it had been too much to expect him to take them all in. George saying he wanted to do right by them all and facing up to the reality of what it would entail were two different things. She took a deep breath. Better to know now if he'd changed his mind so she could try and make other arrangements. Maybe Pat and Bill would help out for a few days until she could find a hotel.

'Look, if there's a problem with us coming to stay, I'll understand. You've got used to your routine and the prospect of a couple of noisy children under your feet can't be appealing.'

Her dad's head reared up, the shock in his eyes giving way to a pained smile. 'I wouldn't blame you for thinking I'm about to let you down, dear, not after everything. The thought of having you and the children live with me has been something of a lifeline these past couple of weeks, but I realised it would probably benefit me more than any of you.' He cleared his throat. 'I... umm... I went to speak to Neil.'

'Dad, you didn't have to do that.' She couldn't help the tinge of frustration in her tone. She knew George meant well, but his interference would likely do more harm than good. Neil's reputation at work meant everything to him and he would no doubt blame Kiki for falling out of George's good graces.

George leaned down to his feet, drawing her attention to the soft leather attaché case he carried everywhere, which was currently resting against the side of the sofa. It was so much a part of him, she hadn't even noticed he'd brought it into the room with him. He flipped open the gold catch, the movement worn smooth with years of use, and removed a sheaf of papers, which he slid across the empty cushion between them.

Kiki's eyes swam, the words blurring in and out of focus as she stared at a copy of her divorce papers. A Post-it flagged one of the pages and she lifted the sheets in front of it with trembling fingers. She gasped at the bold, black scrawl at the foot of the page and glanced up at her father. 'What did you do?'

'I gave him something he wanted—my job.'

She slumped back against the arm of the sofa, trying to comprehend the enormity of those two simple words. George had defined himself through his work for her entire life. He *was* Professor George Thorpe, Head of Ancient Greek Studies, before everything. 'But your job means everything to you…'

Her father lifted the papers aside to slide along the sofa and rest his hand on her leg. 'And that will always be my biggest mistake and my deepest regret. I was a fool to put my career first, to use it as a way to hide from my problems with your mother. I've missed so much time with you and your sisters, and now with the little ones, too. Your mother's illness has made me realise how skewed my priorities have been. Your boy is seven years old and I've never read him a bedtime story…' He trailed off, moisture spilling over onto his cheeks.

'Oh, Daddy.' Kiki sat up and flung her arms around him, holding him tight as he shuddered through a couple of deep breaths. 'It's too much, I don't know what to say.'

George leaned back and smiled at her through his tears. 'It's not nearly enough to repay what I owe you, but it's a start. You've a chance at a new life here and I want you to make the most of it. Aaron and the children look like they get on well…'

She couldn't smother the laugh bursting out of her. Lord, he was about as subtle as Madeline and Pat. 'We're just friends, Dad.' Her face sobered and she squeezed his hands. 'Don't be looking for something that isn't there. I already made that mistake once.' She tilted her head towards the signed divorce papers. 'Can we keep this between us for now? There's so much going on and I don't want to be another distraction from the wedding. The kids have barely got used to the idea of leaving. Come for breakfast with us on Sunday morning like we've already planned, and we can tell them together.'

George patted her hand. 'If that's what you want, dear. You'll tell Aaron, though?'

She shook her head. 'Not yet.' Her relief at not having to leave Butterfly Cove was tempered with a deep realisation. Continuing to live under the same roof as him was out of the question. Seeing Aaron, sharing everything with him but her heart, needing him and being rebuffed, would break her as surely as the years spent with Neil had.

One step forward, two steps back.

Chapter Twenty-One

Aaron shuffled through the pale-blue prompt cards he'd prepared for his best man's speech one last time, checking he'd covered everything on the helpful list of what to include he'd found online. A separate stack of yellow cards rested near his elbow. The blank one on the top of the pile mocked him, and he knew he would have to tackle it if he was going to go through with things properly. He just wanted to run through his speech once more before he dealt with it.

A tap on the doorframe saved him from the silent lie burning his tongue and he cast Daniel a grateful smile for the distraction. 'Shouldn't you be in bed? Your ugly mug needs all the beauty sleep it can get.'

Daniel's white teeth flashed through the darkness of the beard covering his chin. 'Cheeky bastard. I could say the same for you, though nothing's gonna rescue those cauliflower ears of yours.'

Aaron raised a hand and traced the slightly bumpy edge of his left ear and grinned back. 'Adds character.

The ladies like a sportsman.' His smile faltered. He'd never been a ladies' man and he was on the cusp of losing the only one he wanted. The yellow cards beside him might be his last chance to put things right. He sat back in his chair. 'You're absolutely sure Mia's on board with this?'

Daniel folded his arms and leaned against the frame. 'She said, and I quote, "if that stupid arse *doesn't* do something about it, I'll never feed him again."'

With Kiki's imminent departure, the loss of access to Mia's comfort food was a deadly serious threat. 'And you don't mind?'

'Mate, as long as I get that ring on her finger I couldn't care less what else happens tomorrow.' Daniel softened. 'Do it. You've got my support. One hundred per cent.' He nodded towards the stairs. 'You coming up?'

'Soon. Just got one more thing to do. Don't forget to set an alarm.'

Daniel laughed. 'Already done. Watch, tablet, I've even borrowed that Minnie Mouse clock from Charlie's bedside table. G'night.'

'Night.' He checked his watch. Perhaps it was too late to call... 'Bloody coward,' he said out loud and snatched his mobile from his pocket.

'Bumble? Is something wrong?' His dad answered on the second ring.

Aaron took a deep breath. It was now or never. 'I'm fine, Dad. Sorry to call so late. I... I'd like to talk to Cathy if she's around.'

'She's just rinsing out a couple of things in the kitchen. What's this about?'

'A friend told me recently I should talk to someone about a problem I've got.'

'And you think Cathy's the right person to talk to?' Brian Spenser sounded incredulous.

'I expanded on the original suggestion and I've talked with a lot of people. Cathy's the last one on the list. I don't want to upset her, Dad. I don't want to upset either of you, but I have to ask her something. *Please.*'

The past few weeks had been a humbling, and occasionally humiliating, experience, but Aaron felt better for it. He had most of the answers he needed, enough to be sure about the next step he wanted to take. But if he didn't cross this final item off his list, it would hang there. A loose thread he couldn't pluck, a thorn in his side that would continue to prick and bleed him.

'Hold on.' The phone went quiet long enough for his stomach to turn queasy. *Leave it. Just leave it.* He'd almost convinced himself when there was a muffled sound in his ear and then…

'You've got your dad all worried, Aaron. What do you want?' Strangely enough, the sharp edge to her words eased his worry.

'I won't keep you long, Cathy. I just have to ask you one thing and then I won't bother you again—what did I do wrong?'

She huffed out a breath, sounding aggrieved. 'What are you talking about? When?'

Aaron sighed. He didn't believe for a moment she didn't know what he was talking about. 'Always. What was it about me that made you treat me the way you did when I was growing up? The way you still do now. I tried my best, but nothing was ever good enough.'

Silence greeted him, stretching out long enough for him to wish he hadn't bothered. She would never see things from his point of view, so why keep picking at the scab? He'd just about reached the point of hanging up when she responded, in the barest of whispers. 'I couldn't forgive you for being *hers*.'

The air left his lungs in a rush, like he'd taken a punch to the gut. Luke had been spot-on, apparently. 'This was all about Mum?'

Her shrill laugh hurt his ear. 'Of course it was. Everything's always about her. Always has been, always will be. I tried, Aaron. God knows, I tried, but how could things move on with you staring at me with her eyes? Every smile you gave me showed the same dimples, the same sweet nature. And you never let me forget.'

Sick and shaken, Aaron closed his eyes. 'Forget what?'

'That I would always be second best. For you, for Brian. It wasn't me either of you really wanted. I thought once I had Luke things would be better, that I'd have something of my own, but you took him from me, too!' Her voice choked off, and he could hear his dad murmuring in the background.

Aaron rubbed his forehead, trying to make sense of the scramble of words. 'I was just a little boy, Cathy. I didn't ask for any of it. I would have loved you if you'd let me.' He tried to fight the rising hysteria in his voice, but the lonely little boy he held so deep inside was so needy, so desperate for her reassurance, even now.

It was his father who responded, though. 'Bumble? My poor boy, I'm sorry.'

'I loved her, Dad. I only wanted her to love me back.' Jesus, he couldn't stop crying.

'I know you did, Aaron. And Cathy knows that, too. This isn't your fault, son. Isn't hers, really. It's mine. I felt so guilty over your mum, over the depth of my feelings for Cathy and moving on so soon, that I tried too hard to hold on to her memory.' Brian sighed. 'I haven't done right by either of you.'

Aaron raised his hand and scrubbed the snot and tears from his face. He sniffed loudly, the disgusting sound enough to make him laugh at himself. He wiped the gunk off his hand on the front of his T-shirt. 'What a bloody mess.'

He wasn't the only one crying. He could hear Cathy's sobs and his father talking quietly to her. 'Dad?'

'I'm here.'

'Tell Cathy it's okay. And tell yourself the same thing whilst you're at it. All this guilt and hurt, where has it got any of us? I'm so tired of it; God knows you both must be, too. I'd like to start again. If and when she's ready, let me know.' It hurt, but it was a good, clean pain. The poison in his childhood wounds had been lanced, and he knew they'd finally start to heal.

'You're such a good lad, Bumble. Hold on one moment for me.' The phone rustled and Aaron could picture his dad pressing it against his chest the way he always did. It rustled again and he caught the end of a question not directed at him. '…If you're sure?' Another brief pause, followed by, 'Cathy wants to know if you'd like to come for Sunday lunch next weekend?'

The olive branch surprised him. It was one thing to say he was ready to start again, another to actually take the risk of being hurt if Cathy changed her mind. He thought about Kiki, about the way she kept opening herself up, to him, to her dad, when there was every reason to pull down the shutters and lock her heart safely away. Time to see if he had an ounce of her courage. 'I'd like that.'

Aaron ended the call and took the blank yellow card from the top of the pile. He wrote a couple of lines then shuffled it to the back. He placed the stack next to the ones for his speech and turned off the desk lamp. Faint light from the landing drifted down the stairs, calling him to bed. Feeling drained, but ready for the morning, he headed up to his room, stripped off his filthy T-shirt and collapsed face down onto his bed. Sleep came quickly, and he didn't stir.

***

Beep. Beep. Beep. Aaron rolled onto his back, blinking to free the sticky mess clinging to his lashes. He fumbled for the off button on the side of his phone.

Although Daniel had assured him he'd set multiple alarms, Aaron hadn't wanted to leave anything to chance. *Beep. Beep. Beep.*

'Bloody thing.' He glared at his phone before realising the noise came from one of the other bedrooms. Desperate for a drink of water, he forced himself up and out onto the landing, coming face to face with a groggy-looking Luke. His brother rubbed his eyes then suddenly looked a lot more awake.

'Dibs on the bathroom!' Luke made a dash for the end of the corridor.

'Git. I'll go and put the coffee on and then see if Daniel's awake.' Shrill bells rang from what was usually Kiki's room – Minnie Mouse was on the case already, it seemed. He shuffled towards Matty's room and tapped on the door. 'You awake, little man?'

The door swung open and Matty grinned up at him. 'Is it time?'

Aaron grinned and ruffled his already messy hair. 'Time for breakfast. You want cornflakes?'

Matty shook his head.

'Scrambled eggs?'

'Nuh-uh.'

Aaron wracked his brain as he made his way downstairs with the little boy hopping and skipping after him. He could do with some of the energy Matty seemed to be brimming with. 'Roast beef and Yorkshire pudding? Fish fingers? Apple pie and custard?' He listed the unlikeliest of breakfast dishes and was rewarded with a giggle.

Entering the kitchen, he flicked the switch on the coffee machine and opened the fridge. He glanced back over his shoulder at Matty and waggled his eyebrows. 'Jelly and ice cream?'

'Pancakes!'

'Pancakes? Sounds like a great idea.' Daniel wandered into the kitchen, clad in a pair of boxer shorts and a T-shirt. He slid into a free chair and Matty pulled one close to him and sat down. 'Hello, squirt, you all ready for today? Know what you need to do?'

Matty nodded solemnly. 'I have to keep the rings safe until the lady asks for them.' He'd been thrilled to be asked to be the ring bearer. Charlie was equally excited about her job as flower girl.

'That's right. You're the only man I can trust with the job.' Daniel slung his arm across the back of Matty's chair and the little boy squirmed closer to lean against him.

Fighting a lump in his throat, Aaron made himself busy, pulling milk, butter and eggs out of the fridge. He opened the cupboard Kiki used to store her dry ingredients and the lump grew a little bigger. Soon, there'd be no more scents of baking wafting through the house, no more high-pitched voices or little footsteps clattering up and down the stairs. Giving himself a shake, he dug around for plain flour, and sugar for sprinkling.

He'd just poured the first of the batter mix into a hot pan when Matty spoke up. 'If you're marrying Aunty Mia, does that mean you'll be my uncle?'

The things kids came out with. Aaron glanced over as Daniel shifted in his chair so he could turn to meet Matty's inquisitive gaze. 'That's right. You'll be able to call me Uncle Daniel, if you'd like to.'

Matty nodded. 'I used to have an Uncle Jamie, but he died and Aunty Mia was very sad. You won't die, will you?'

Daniel pulled the little boy close and stared wide-eyed over the top of his head at Aaron. The panic in his eyes said he wasn't sure what to say. Aaron raised his shoulders helplessly. What could one say to a question like that? His friend pulled back and gripped Matty's chin gently. 'I love your Aunty Mia very much and I promise to do everything I possibly can to stay safe so I can look after her for a long, long time, okay?'

'Okay.' Apparently satisfied, Matty moved on to his next topic. 'I'm going to have Nutella on my pancakes, what are you going to have?'

Bloody hell. If any of them made it through the day without bawling, it would be a miracle. Aaron turned back towards the pan, just as it began to smoke. Grabbing a spatula, he loosened the edges and managed to flip the pancake over without dropping it on the floor. The bottom looked a little singed, but he didn't think his breakfast companions would complain. He shook the pan a few times and flipped the finished pancake onto a plate. 'Who's first?'

***

'I appreciate your help with this.' Kiki smiled at the older woman arranging a pair of exquisite crystal flutes on a scallop-edged, silver tray on the chest of drawers beside the bed. Maggie had arrived late the previous evening, looking immaculate after three and a half hours on a crowded train. Even this early in the morning, her hair was styled into a neat French twist. Kiki raised a hand to her headful of heated rollers with a rueful shrug.

Maggie placed a single pale peach rose on the tray then glanced over her shoulder at Kiki. 'It's my absolute pleasure, my dear. I adored your sister from the first moment we met, and Daniel has always been more to me than a client. When he told me they were engaged, I couldn't have been happier.' She bent and drew a white box with a lilac ribbon wrapped around it and held it up. 'Here or in the bathroom?'

Kiki crossed to take the Molton Brown bath products from her. 'I'll put this next to the tub. If we leave the gifts in different places it will give them more surprises.'

'That's a wonderful idea. Where shall I hide these fabulous chocolates?' Maggie did a slow circle and her eyes lit up as, through the open door to the adjoining sitting room, she spied a low table next to the plush velvet couch. 'What about in there?'

'Perfect.'

A tap on the door drew their attention. Madeline poked her head around the door. 'Oh, it looks wonderful in here. Hello, Maggie, how are you?' The two older women exchanged kisses and hugs. Although her hair was a sleek, shiny bob, Madeline's face was bare and her Capri pants and T-shirt looked a little too casual. She followed Kiki's glance down at her outfit and grinned. 'I've brought my dress with me. I couldn't stand waiting at home a moment longer in case I missed out on anything.' Her blunt admission set them all smiling.

'Why don't you put your things in my room?' Maggie offered. 'I'm in that gorgeous country cottage room. We can get ready together once everything else is done.'

'That would be lovely. Richard dropped me off and he's gone over to the cottage to see how the boys are getting on.' Madeline smiled. 'He couldn't bear to miss out either. So, what else do we need to do in here?'

Kiki popped into the bathroom to put the luxury bath products on the side of the tub. She couldn't resist brushing her hand over the thick cotton towels hanging neatly on the rail. Pastel-coloured tea lights lined the windowsill and a glass shelf above the sink, ready to provide some romantic lighting. Pulling the door closed, she ran through her mental checklist. Other than the champagne, which she would sneak up to put in the ice bucket later, the room was ready. 'I think we're all set.' She checked her watch. 'I'm going to go and wake Charlie and see how Mia is getting on.'

Madeline laughed. 'I passed Charlie and your father in the kitchen. She was giving him a lecture on the proper way to cut toast.'

'Poor Dad. I take it he did squares instead of triangles?' She pictured her father trying to deal with her precocious three-year-old. She supposed it was something he'd have to get used to again. 'Did he look like he needed rescuing?'

Madeline shook her head. 'Pat and Bill were keeping him company and he looked to be taking instruction well. She'll have him wrapped around her finger in no time.' Her smile turned serious. 'I didn't see any sign of Nee.'

Kiki glanced towards the window. A solitary figure stood on the edge of the surf line, facing out to sea. 'She went for a walk on the beach.' Nee had still looked tired and drawn this morning, but she'd waved off any attempts at conversation.

A soft touch on her arm turned her from the window. 'Give her some time, darling. Let Butterfly Cove work its magic on her for a few days.'

She leaned into the comfort of Madeline's shoulder. 'It's not like her. From the moment she could talk, she couldn't keep quiet for two minutes. This…' She waved a helpless hand towards the window. 'This isn't like her. We emailed regularly whilst she was away and there was never any hint about a man in her life.' Kiki shook her head. 'Which I should have noticed before. Nee always lived her life to the full and she always had a boyfriend in tow. She used to joke it was her duty to play the field because Mia and I had settled down so early on. I think she was just worried about making the same mistake I did.'

Maybe that was the answer to why Nee had abandoned Luke so abruptly. None of the marriages she'd been witness to had exactly been happy. Between their parents' dysfunction, Mia's loss and Kiki's own issues with Neil, they hadn't set her a great example. It didn't excuse what she'd done, but perhaps it might go some way to explaining it. There wasn't a cruel bone in Nee's body, so there *had* to be a reason.

Madeline kissed her temple. 'You go and see how Mia is, and Maggie and I will make a start on the salads.' The wedding breakfast would be a cold buffet, with a barbecue planned for the evening when the other guests arrived. They'd done as much preparation as possible, but some things still needed to be put together.

They parted on the stairs after Kiki had elicited a promise from the others to send Nee up if she came back in. She tapped on Mia's bedroom door and peeked round the edge. 'How's the bride doing this morning?'

Mia swung around on the stool in front of her dressing table. 'Bored!' She waggled her pearlescent fingers and toes. 'I've done my hair, my nails, moisturised every inch of my skin, and it's still only nine-thirty.'

Kiki laughed and perched on the end of the bed nearest her sister. 'If you need something to do, you can help me with these infernal curlers.' She'd never been one for over-styling and the weight of the curlers had started to make her scalp ache. They swapped places and Kiki closed her eyes in relief as Mia began to unravel her hair.

'You've always had such beautiful hair, Kiki Dee.'

She opened her eyes and met Mia's reflection in the glass. 'Do you regret cutting yours?' Her heart stuttered at the memory of a distraught Mia with her hair hacked off to just a few inches. It had been part of her grieving process, a form of self-punishment she'd said afterwards.

Her sister ducked her head so they rested cheek-to-cheek. Her usual haphazard style had been tamed with a pair of straighteners and feathered about her face in soft tendrils. 'Lord, no! My ears get a bit chilly in the winter, but a hat soon fixes that. I'm different now, and this suits me.' Her eyes misted up, and Kiki felt an answering lump in her throat. Mia pressed a kiss to Kiki's cheek. 'I just got used to you being around. What will I ever do without you?'

Kiki raised her hand to clasp Mia's where it rested on her shoulder and gave her a teary smile. 'You won't have to.' Mia sank back on the bed, mouth open in surprise as Kiki explained to her about the deal George had struck to get Neil off her back. By the end of her tale, they were gripping hands and laughing through their tears. Kiki raised her thumb to wipe a streak of mascara from Mia's cheek. 'Look at the mess we've made of your face!'

'He really did that? Dad gave up his job for you?' Nee's husky question came from just inside the open bedroom door. She held a small tray with three glasses balanced on it. She hovered uncertainly on the threshold, the distance between the three of them palpable. 'Madeline sent me up with these.' Her white-blonde hair served only to highlight the purple shadows etched deep beneath her eyes. Fragile had never been a word Kiki associated with her younger sister, but she looked as pale and breakable as a china figurine.

Mia stood up and held out her hand. 'Come in, darling. I didn't dare hope that the three of us would be together this morning.' She handed a glass of Buck's Fizz to Kiki and took a second for herself. Nee took the remaining glass and laid the tray aside. Mia looked at each of them in turn. 'Knowing Kiki doesn't have to leave tomorrow is the best news I could have hoped for.' She smiled at Nee. 'The only thing that could top it was if you didn't have to rush off back to New York.'

Nee bit her lip. 'I... I can stay for a little while.'

Mia shook her head. 'No, no, darling. I'm being selfish. New York is a dream come true for you and your career. Go with my blessing, just try not to forget about us when you hit the heights.'

Nee swayed on her feet, would have spilled her drink had Kiki not steadied her hand. Beneath that pale, pale hair, her skin had turned ashen. 'What is it?'

'I don't want to talk about it. Not today.' Nee sucked in a deep breath. 'New York didn't work out.'

Five words didn't seem enough to hold such stunning impact. Kiki's mind raced as she recalled their email correspondence over the past year, seeking out a clue, a hint of the unhappiness clearly written on Nee's face. Maybe she'd been too caught up in her own misery to notice. 'Why didn't you tell us?'

'I shouldn't have said anything. Look, I'm okay.' Kiki didn't need to see Mia's face to know they were both wearing the same look of scepticism. Nee shrugged. 'All right. I'm not okay, but I want to try and be. Today isn't about me. *Please*.'

This time Kiki did look to Mia. It was her day, her choice. Whatever she decided, Kiki would follow her lead. Mia opened her mouth, closed it, then nodded. 'Okay. But you're not going anywhere, you hear me? Your place is with us. We're going to help you.' *Whether Nee liked it or not*, her firm tone implied.

'Come here.' Kiki moved to the right so the three of them faced each other and curled her free arm around Nee's waist. Nee did the same to Mia, and Kiki felt her elder sister's hand on her hip. They raised their glasses to the centre of the little circle they'd formed. There was so much left to unravel, so many bumps in the road ahead, but, in that one quiet moment, the Thorpe sisters were reunited and there wasn't anything they couldn't face together.

'To Mia, wishing you every happiness on this most special of days,' Nee said softly.

'To Mia, thank you for finding this beautiful place and sharing it with us.' Kiki added her own toast.

Mia's hand shook a little, rattling their glasses together. 'To my sisters. Thank you for being here with me today. I hope Butterfly Cove can bring you as much joy as it has me.'

They clinked their drinks together. 'To Butterfly Cove.'

Chapter Twenty-Two

The weather gods had come through; a few fluffy white clouds decorated the bright sky. Aaron turned his face into the light breeze blowing in from the sea, savouring the scent of salt. As they'd hoped, Thursday night's storm had freshened the air, lifting the oppressive temperatures of the previous days. A few of the more delicate flowers had suffered a little in the downpour, but the grey army had done a sweep through the garden and staked up any straggling blooms. The leaves on the bushes gleamed as though polished, any sandy traces from the beach washed clean by the rain.

Everywhere his eye rested, bright colour greeted him. From the crisp, cream marquees set out on the right-hand side of the lawn to the lilac and purple blooms coating the Buddleia trees behind him. The cove lived up to its nickname, with fragile blue butterflies he didn't know the name of and bold Red Admirals dancing from blossom to blossom. He'd meant to get

Charlie a book on butterflies so they could learn the names of all their pretty visitors together, but time had run away with him, and now it was too late.

It's not for ever. There would be other summers, he had to hold on to that hope. His hand dropped involuntarily to cover the pocket of his beige, tailored trousers where he'd tucked the small stack of yellow cards. He checked his watch; five minutes to go.

***

'Stop fidgeting or I'll never get this on straight.' Madeline patted Daniel's chest to soften her admonishment.

'Sorry, Mads.' Daniel stood still to allow Madeline to pin the peach rose buttonhole to his white linen shirt. Aaron bit the inside of his cheek to hide the grin twitching at the corners of his mouth.

Madeline stepped back to eye her handiwork and gave a nod of satisfaction. 'You'll do.' She turned to Aaron next and he bent his knees to bring himself nearer to her short height. 'Cheeky sod.' She gave him a gentle poke in the stomach and his grin broke free.

'You're looking mighty fine this morning, Mads. I hope Richard understands how lucky he is.' Her primrose-yellow shift dress looked cool and elegant. The wicker-soled wedged sandals on her feet added a couple of inches, but she was still petite enough for Aaron to tuck her under his arm once she'd finished pinning his rose.

Her rich laugh rolled across the open garden, turning heads, drawing smiles. 'He knows. I remind him every day.' She leaned into his hug for a moment and Aaron marvelled anew at the difference this livewire of a woman had made to his life. Things might work out with Cathy; they more likely might not, given the bitter void between them. He would try one last time—for Luke, for his dad, for the promise he'd made to himself to stop the past from holding him back—but everything he needed from a mother was right there tucked against his side.

He pressed a kiss to her cheek, careful not to mess up the sleek curtain of hair framing her face. 'I love you, Madeline.'

Daniel took her hand and pressed a kiss to the back of it. 'Me, too, Mads.'

'Me, three!' Matty threw his arms around Madeline's waist and Aaron dropped his free hand to the little boy's shoulder.

'My boys.' She rested her head against Aaron's chest for a moment before drawing away with a laugh. 'You'll have me watering like a pot if you keep this up.' She fanned her face with her hand, eyes glittering. 'I'd better take my seat.'

A small arc of chairs had been set up so everyone had a front-row view. A wide aisle divided the seats, leading to the French windows of the dining room, which were currently closed. Sue, the celebrant's wife, slipped from around the side of the house, crossed the grass and took her seat at one end of the arc. She gave Alison a discreet nod to signal everything was ready. The celebrant touched Daniel's arm. 'It's time.'

His friend swallowed hard then set his shoulders back. 'I'm ready.'

Aaron glanced down at Matty. 'You remember what to do?' The little boy raised the black velvet box holding the matching rings, and nodded. 'Good boy.'

Luke left his seat at the opposite end of the arc, moving quickly to the table just inside the main marquee. The soft strains of an acoustic guitar filled the air with 'Storybook Love', the theme song from *The Princess Bride*. The French doors opened.

Charlie stepped out of the dining room, and Aaron wasn't the only one who chuckled at the sight of her. Clutching a basket of rose petals in one hand, she adjusted the gold crown nestling in her hair then strode forward, the low heels of her bright-red boots tapping on the stone patio. She'd been given her choice of princess costumes, and it appeared that Wonder Woman had won out over Belle in the final decision process. With the gold stars on her blue tutu glittering, she made her way down the aisle, tossing the petals from her basket with more enthusiasm than finesse.

Kiki came next, and Aaron's breath caught at the sight of her beautiful hair tumbling around her shoulders in soft curls. The coral satin dress she wore shaped her figure as she turned to offer a hand to help Mia step out of the door. She pressed a quick kiss to her sister's cheek, then began her own procession towards them. Traditionally, everyone had eyes only for the bride, but Aaron would have to beg Mia's forgiveness later because he couldn't look away. If he'd only seized the chance Kiki had offered him, those wild curls would be spilling over his pillow later as they snuggled together and recalled the highlights of the day. She took her place on the other side of Alison and gathered Charlie's free hand.

At last, Aaron tore his gaze away, just in time to catch the stupid grin on Daniel's face as Mia took her last couple of steps towards them. A flowered clip held up one side of her short hair, the cream roses matching those of the simple bouquet she clutched before her. Kiki reached out to take the flowers, leaving her sister free to grasp Daniel's outstretched hand. The couple turned to face Alison, who offered them an encouraging smile, then raised her arms to encompass everyone present.

'Friends. You are here today to support Mia and Daniel as they take the next step in the beautiful journey they have chosen to make together. They want to thank you all for bringing them this far, and hope to share the many years of love and happiness to come with you. In your presence, they will pledge themselves to each other with words and symbols of their union.' Alison lowered her arms. 'Are you both ready?'

They nodded, and Mia cleared her throat. 'Daniel. It's no secret that I was less than happy when you showed up on my doorstep.' Aaron smiled across at Madeline, and she winked back at him. She'd been directly responsible for the couple's unorthodox meeting.

Mia glanced over her shoulder at the house, then back to Daniel. 'You helped me bring this place to life, and in doing so you managed to bring me back to life, too. I gave you a week, and you took for ever. I love you.' A soft sniffle rose from the seats, and Pat raised a handkerchief to dab her eye while Bill patted her other hand. Aaron couldn't deny the scratchiness in his own throat.

Daniel raised his hand to graze the backs of his fingers down Mia's cheek. 'I'm not a great one for words so I've borrowed a bit from traditional vows. When I came here my life was at its very worst. Every moment I've spent at your side has only made it better. Many would consider me rich, but before I met you, my heart was empty, my soul was poor.' He laughed. 'I was literally sick, and you helped me recover my health. I love you and will cherish you always.'

Aaron bent at the waist. 'You're up, bud,' he whispered to Matty. The little boy nodded solemnly then took his place opposite Alison. It took him a couple of attempts to lift the stiff lid on the velvet box, and Aaron steeled himself not to step forward and help him. A collective sigh of relief rippled around when he prised open the lid and proudly offered up the rings nestled inside.

Mia and Daniel each removed one of the slender platinum bands, taking turns to slide them on each other's ring finger as they made their pledges. Matty continued to hold up the now-empty box until Kiki reached out and gently caught his arm, tugging him to stand beside her.

Alison smiled. 'Mia and Daniel have shared their love and commitment with words and symbols. It gives me great pleasure to pronounce you husband and wife.' She nodded to Daniel, who cupped Mia's cheek as though he handled the most delicate porcelain, and pressed a soft kiss to her lips.

The celebrant waited until the couple drew apart then placed her hands on their arms to turn them towards the arc of chairs. 'Ladies and gentlemen, I present to you all, Mr and Mrs Daniel Fitzwilliams.'

***

With everyone pitching in, the buffet had been laid out on the long dining-room table. People wandered back and forth, helping themselves to whatever took their fancy. Inroads had been made into the large bucket of ice sitting in the shade of the tent that held a mixture of soft and alcoholic drinks.

Bill rested his hand on Kiki's shoulder as he topped up her glass of white wine. 'Are you having a good time, lovey?' he asked, and she nodded.

'It's been wonderful. Better than I could have imagined. How about you?' She'd seen Pat having a few tears earlier. It can't have been easy for them watching Mia get married again, knowing she was only free to do so because of their son's passing. Kiki had experienced her own conflicting emotions, particularly when Aaron had offered his arm to escort her to the table. It was so close to the fantasy she'd imagined of them, yet miles away from where she'd hoped they would be.

Using the children as an excuse had felt a bit shabby, but she'd taken their hands to avoid having to walk too close to him. She hadn't missed the flicker of hurt in his eyes, but he only had himself to blame. Their once-easy friendship, which had led her to hope for her own happy ending, felt strained to the limits. Coronation chicken and white wine stirred uneasily in her stomach. Perhaps if she tried hard enough, she could put things behind her and they could get back to how things had been before that stupid kiss in the garages. *Perhaps not.*

Bill gave her a pat. 'We're all right. I won't deny I'm missing my boy something fierce today, but Daniel's a good man and it does my heart glad to see our Mia happy again.' He reached down to stroke Charlie's head. 'Save me a dance later, poppet?'

Charlie bounced in her chair. 'Can we dance now?'

Bill laughed. 'Soon, darling. Aaron needs to give his speech first. I'd better finish filling these glasses so he can get started.' He moved up the table, offering red and white wine as he went.

Madeline and Pat returned to the marquee, having cleared the last of the plates away, and Kiki glanced around to check everyone else was present. She lifted Charlie to sit sideways in her lap, and turned her chair to shift it closer to Matty, who sat on her other side. He gave her a sweet smile and bent his head to rest it on her knee.

A soft tinkle filled the air as Aaron stood and tapped his glass with a spoon. All eyes turned towards him and an expectant quiet settled around the table. A lock of blond hair tumbled over his forehead as he shuffled the prompt cards in his hands. He raised his head to look at Mia and Daniel, and Kiki felt her heart flutter as his mega-watt smile lit up his whole face.

'You'll be thrilled to know I have not one, but two speeches to give today.' A chorus of jokey groans and boos rose up, and Aaron ducked his head as a bread roll flew through the air from Luke's end of the table. He held up a hand. 'I know, I know, but I'll try and keep it short and sweet.'

He scanned the blue cards and his expression sobered. 'There was a time not so long ago when I feared I might lose my best friend.' His eyes flicked to Daniel, and Kiki could see his Adam's apple bob as he swallowed hard. 'Daniel, I feel like I didn't do enough to help you when I should have. I walked away when things got bad, and I'll carry the shame of that with me.'

Daniel reached up to grasp his arm, his voice gruff as he said, 'No, mate. I wasn't ready to accept anyone's help. Let it go.'

Aaron nodded. 'I'll try. Luckily, a wonderful woman succeeded where I failed.' He turned his eyes to Mia. 'From the first moment I walked into your kitchen, I knew everything would be okay. I saw the connection the two of you had, I think, even before either of you were really aware of it, and I can't tell you how happy I am to see you moving forward together. You make an incredible team and I don't think there's a person around this table who doesn't know you'll make a success of your marriage. The work you've put into renovating the house, converting the barns, creating a solid foundation for your future, is awe-inspiring.'

He paused to turn over a card and Richard raised his glass. 'Hear, hear,' he said and the toast rippled around the table. Kiki caught her sister's eye and raised her own drink in tribute and they shared a wobbly smile.

'You'll be relieved to know I'm almost finished…' A cheer went up and Aaron gave a laughing shake of his head. 'With this *first* speech,' he added.

'I want to dance!' Charlie piped up, and Kiki shushed her with a little squeeze.

Aaron mock-sighed. 'Everyone's a critic. I don't have much more to say other than to wish you both every happiness for the future. Butterfly Cove wouldn't be what it is without the two of you at its heart.' He raised his glass. 'To the bride and groom.'

The children were too settled on her lap for Kiki to stand along with the others, but she joined in the rising chorus of the toast. 'To the bride and groom!'

She watched Mia and Daniel exchange a tender kiss, which went on long enough to raise the colour in her sister's cheeks. They broke apart with a laughing gasp, and then Mia turned to Kiki with a glint in her eye. She held out her arms to her niece. 'Come and give your Aunty Mia a cuddle.' Charlie scrambled down, disturbing Matty, who sat upright in his seat. With the startling lack of loyalty only children were capable of, he shifted his chair so he could snuggle into Mia's side.

Kiki pouted, then winked at her children, who grinned back, but stayed put. The light tinkling sound of Aaron rattling his spoon against a glass quieted the table once again. 'Oh, this is going to be good,' she heard her sister mutter. A feeling of trepidation crept up Kiki's spine as she saw the cards Aaron held were now yellow instead of blue.

He looked up from them, his eyes meeting hers, and began to speak. 'A few weeks ago, a friend and I had something of a falling out.' Kiki's face flushed with heat, and a shiver sent goose bumps racing over her skin.

Keeping his focus fixed on her, Aaron continued his speech. 'That friend told me I needed to speak to someone about my issues. I took that advice, only I didn't just speak to one person. I spoke to all of them. Kerry was my first serious girlfriend. When I asked her why she left me, she said…' He paused to glance down at the first card. "Because I knew you didn't really love me, but you were too nice to say anything."

A sympathetic chuckle rose from the group. Kiki raised a hand to cover her mouth. *He couldn't have…*

Aaron looked up. 'She has a point. I couldn't even bring myself to tell her I really hated Sylvia Plath.' Daniel snorted with laughter as Aaron turned to the next card. 'After Kerry came Lisa, and I asked her the same thing. Her response was, "You never let me in. You knew everything about me, but there was this wall between us. A sweet, stubborn, implacable wall and I knew you'd break my heart against it."' He gave a self-deprecating shake of his head. 'Wow, I'm a catch, huh?'

Oh, Aaron. Kiki forgot all her good intentions and drew her lower lip between her teeth. What must it have taken to not only put himself through this, but to stand up in front of the people he was closest to and share it. The list went on, Aaron reading out point after point of criticism from his ex-girlfriends. None of them had anything bad to say about him, but they were all in the same vein—he had never let them feel really close to him. Her heart ached for him.

Aaron paused to take a sip from his glass. 'You'll be relieved to know there's only a couple more to go. My final girlfriend was Natalie. We were together last summer, which is one of the reasons I was distracted from other things.' His gaze travelled down the table to meet Luke's. 'I should have been there for you, Spud.'

Luke smiled and waved his comment off. 'Forget it. This litany of relationship disasters is doing my soul the world of good. At least I didn't keep sticking my hand back in the fire.' A soft gasp sounded behind Kiki, but she forced herself not to look round and risk drawing attention to where Nee was sitting.

Aaron grinned. 'I'm here to help. Anyway, back to Natalie. She's doing great, by the way, recently engaged to a mutual acquaintance who I'm sure will make her very happy. I asked her the same question about why she'd left me and she said, "You were wonderful, and I'll always be grateful for the help you gave me. You changed my life, but once I stopped needing you and started wanting you it was like you weren't there any more.'"

He looked straight at Kiki and there was no trace of humour in his expression. 'She was right. I never trusted she wanted me for who I was and not what I could do to help her. Same as all of them. I never let myself be truly vulnerable with them, because that way they could never hurt me when the inevitable happened and they left me.'

Kiki couldn't stay quiet any longer. 'Aaron, you don't need to do this…'

He raised a finger to his lips and smiled at her. 'Yes, I do, Kiki. For myself as much as any point I'm clumsily trying to make to you. There's just one more card, I promise.' She closed her eyes briefly and nodded, but regretted it the moment he spoke again.

'Last, but not least, is the woman who's been a constant in my life longer than anyone else, my stepmother, Cathy.'

'Don't do this, Aaron,' Luke said, his voice rough with emotion.

Aaron looked at him and Kiki could see the moisture gleaming in his eyes. 'It's all right, Spud, I promise.' He glanced around the table. 'I asked Cathy a slightly different question. What it was isn't as important as her answer, because she made me realise that, when things happen, when things go wrong, it's not necessarily my fault. That not everything is about *me*.'

He left his place at the table and came to crouch in front of Kiki's chair. 'I'm sorry for not being braver, for squandering the most precious thing anyone has offered me. I was too afraid to let you in, because what I feel for you is too big, too all-encompassing, and it scares me to death. I thought being near you would be enough and I was wrong. It'll never be enough.'

Kiki could do nothing to stop the tears spilling down her cheeks, and he reached out to catch one on his fingertip. 'I know you have to leave, darling. I also know you're not leaving *me*. I'll be waiting for you, for all three of you, if it's not too late to say that. If I haven't made too much of a mess of things between us.'

'It's not too late,' she whispered. 'I'm not…' He didn't let her finish, as he leaned forward to brush his mouth over hers.

'I love you, Kiki. Be mine.' He turned and held his arms out to where the children were sitting with Mia. 'You, and Matty and Charlie. Be mine. Be my family.'

Matty hurled himself from his chair and into Aaron's arms, Charlie right behind him. Aaron held them tight, eyes fixed on Kiki's over their heads. So much love, so much hope brimmed in his gaze.

Raising a shaking hand, she cupped his cheek. 'We already are.' He closed his eyes, an expression of sheer relief on his face as he leaned into her hand. This man, this gorgeous man, had placed his battered heart in her hands. She would keep it safe. Protect it with everything she had—with everything she was. He deserved nothing less.

Charlie lifted her head. 'Can we have dancing now?'

Chapter Twenty-Three

Kiki made her way back from putting the bottle of champagne on ice in Mia and Daniel's room. She'd added a bottle of sparkling apple juice to the bucket, in case they preferred something non-alcoholic. He didn't make a big deal of it, but she knew Daniel was still very conscious of what he drank.

The evening was in full swing, the garden alive with voices, laughter, and the smell of steak and sausages wafting from the barbecue. Fairy lights glittered in the trees and around the edges of the marquees. Solar torches lining the flowerbeds began to flicker into life as dusk fell. Kiki rubbed her arms, grateful she'd found a thin cardigan to match her dress. It wasn't cold, but she could feel the difference in temperature now the warmth of the sun had started to fade.

A lot of noise and giggling was coming from one of the smaller marquees and she paused, recognising Matty's sweet laugh. The tent had been designed as a quieter chill-out space for guests wanting to get away from the music. Huge, square cushions covered the floor, with a couple of low tables scattered between them. Someone had closed the curtains which served as a door, and she pulled one aside to peek through.

Children littered the space, sprawled across the cushions on their bellies, chins propped in their hands as they faced in towards the centre of their circle. All eyes were fixed on her dad, who held a large picture book in his hands. Oblivious to anything but their rapt attention, George continued to read the story, putting on silly voices and pulling faces to make the children laugh and gasp as he led them on an adventure through the Labyrinth to face the dreaded Minotaur. Maggie sat on the cushion beside him, every bit as enthralled as the little ones.

A warm arm encircled Kiki's waist, followed by the familiar scent of Aaron's favourite aftershave. She tilted her head back to look up at him, and he kissed the tip of her nose. 'I thought you'd had a change of heart for a moment.'

Releasing the curtain with a laugh, she turned in his arms to lean against him. 'No chance of that, I'm afraid. You're stuck with us. With me.'

He lifted her hair away from her nape as he ran his mouth along the top of her shoulder. 'That's good to know.' He worked his way into her neck and she couldn't suppress a shiver.

'Behave.' It might have had more effect on him had the word not ended on a breathy moan.

'No chance.' Flashing her a grin full of such promise it sent her insides fluttering, he took her hand and led her away from the busy garden to a quiet spot in the shade of the sprawling barns. The tang of salt from the sea filled her lungs as he pressed her into the sun-warmed wooden boards of the old building.

Curling the thick weight of her hair around his hand, he gave the faintest of tugs as he urged her to tilt her head. His lips returned to their lazy exploration, and she clutched at his shoulders when her knees threatened to give out. He spoke between kisses. 'Madeline and Richard are taking the children home with them tonight, and Luke's crashing in a spare room here.'

She laughed and squirmed as his mouth found a ticklish spot. 'You've been busy.'

'Mmm.' He nuzzled her neck again. 'As tonight's all we're going to have for a while, I want to make the most of the little bit of time we have together.'

They'd been so busy dancing and celebrating, Kiki hadn't quite got around to mentioning her rather important change of plans. It wasn't really her fault. Aaron had become *very* distracting since they'd resolved matters between them. His hand at her waist crept higher up her ribcage, proving her point. She eased away before her brain shorted out again in the flurry of new sensations. 'Aaron, wait…'

His brows drew down, shadowing his features until she could barely make them out in the fading light. 'I don't mean to rush you. I'm not expecting anything from you tonight. I just want to take you home and hold you while I can.'

Her belly flip-flopped. People would say they were rushing into things, that it was too much, too soon, given her circumstances, but she didn't care. Her heart *knew* this man, recognised him as the right one for her, and her body was in perfect agreement. It didn't matter what had gone before, what indignities she'd suffered in the past. The slate had been wiped clean with that first tender kiss.

Kiki stepped into him, rising on tiptoes to press her soft curves into all his interesting, hard places. 'That's disappointing to hear, because I have very high expectations of you tonight…' She pressed a kiss to the underside of his jaw. 'And tomorrow night, and all the rest of our nights to come. It's time to put your money where your mouth is, Aaron, because I'm not going anywhere.'

He cupped her face, drawing her higher up as he lowered his face to meet hers. 'What are you saying?' he breathed against her mouth.

'Neil signed the papers.' She kissed him. 'Dad sorted everything out so we don't have to leave after all.' She found his mouth again, and his arms banded around her back as he returned the kiss. His tongue traced the seam of her lips, and she welcomed him in with a sigh.

The rattle of footsteps on gravel broke them apart. Aaron eased them deeper into the shadows, and Kiki pressed her face into his shoulder as she fought the urge to giggle. Her mirth at the idea of being caught snogging at their age vanished at the sound of her younger sister's voice.

'Luke, please.'

The footsteps halted. 'Leave it, Nee.'

Stones crunched again, softer this time. 'I just want to talk.'

'You've had the best part of twelve months to do that.' Footsteps sounded again, followed by the heavy creak of the barn door.

'Please wait, at least let me tell you I'm sorry.' Nee sounded ready to cry.

'That doesn't help me. Just leave me alone.' The bitterness in Luke's voice stole Kiki's breath, and she wished the ground would swallow them up so she didn't have to bear witness to their pain.

'Would it help if I told you I'd made a terrible mistake? That leaving you was the worst decision I've ever made in my life?'

'Fuck, no,' Luke snapped. 'It doesn't help at all.' The door of the barn slammed, making Kiki jump. A flurry of steps on the gravel didn't quite mask the sounds of her sister's sobs as she ran away.

Kiki pressed her face deeper into Aaron's shoulder, feeling like the worst kind of eavesdropper. His arms tightened around her back as he muttered a soft curse against the top of her head. It had been too much to hope that the weekend would pass without a confrontation between their younger siblings, but Kiki would have paid any money not to have heard it.

Both Luke and Nee would be horrified if they ever found out they'd been overheard, and there was a little part of Kiki selfish enough to want to push it away before it completely ruined what should be a special night for her and Aaron. Her conscience pricked her and she lifted her face to try and read the expression on Aaron's face. 'Should we go after them?'

He brushed his lips against her temple. 'We probably should, but I'm not sure they'd thank us for intervening.' He kissed her again, his mouth catching the corner of hers. 'And I'd much rather stay here with you.'

Kiki dropped her head back against the side of the barn with a soft thud. 'Oh God, me, too. Does that make us awful people?'

Aaron leaned into her. 'Awful,' he agreed, softening the word with another kiss. 'Terrible.' Kiss. 'The worst.' Kiss. She couldn't help but laugh, and he took advantage, claiming her mouth until every thought flew from her head other than her *need* for him. The problems between Luke and Nee would have to be faced by all of them, just not tonight. She and Aaron deserved tonight.

'So, you're staying here in Butterfly Cove?' he asked when he finally let her up for air.

'Hmm?' She rested her head on his shoulder. A thousand tiny sparks flickered under her skin, culminating in her centre. Her hands traced the width of his chest, and down the flat plane of his stomach. All hers, to touch, and taste, and tease whenever she wanted. Her eyes rolled back in her head just at the thought of it.

He laughed, catching her hands before they strayed too far. 'Focus, Kiki.'

She nestled into him. 'I can't, you're too distracting. What was the question?'

His hand curled under her chin to tip her head up. 'I asked if you're staying here at the Cove.'

Hadn't she already told him that? Kiki wound her arms around his neck and tugged his head back down towards hers. 'Yes,' she whispered against his mouth. 'We're staying right here with you for ever. Now take me home and distract me some more.'

Turn the page for an exclusive sneak peek at the next book in the enchanting Butterfly Cove series, *Christmas at Butterfly Cove*!

Chapter One

Nee Thorpe stared at the brown oblong of modelling clay sitting on the workbench in exactly the same spot she'd dropped it two hours earlier. The tactile material had always been her favourite medium to work with, but these days the earthy scent of damp clay did little more than bring bile to the back of her throat. After a month staying with her sister, Mia, and her new husband, Daniel, she'd run out of excuses as to why she wasn't working on anything. Daniel had recently opened a set of bespoke artist studios in the old barns adjacent to his wife's guesthouse in the idyllic coastal village of Orcombe Sands – known to the local population by the far prettier nickname of Butterfly Cove. They were still taking regular bookings, even this late in the season, with sun-worshippers giving way to the hardier walkers who wanted to make the most of the outdoors before winter set in and kept them closer to home.

Perched on the edge of the cove, at the head of a private beach, Butterfly House had provided a welcome haven for Nee's tattered spirits. It had also become the new hub of their family. Her middle sister, Kiki, had relocated to the village in the spring, finally escaping her disastrous marriage. With her two small children in tow, she'd not only made a new start, including running the latest family enterprise – a beautiful little teashop and gallery in what had recently been a scruffy-looking garage block – she'd also found a new love in the shape of Daniel's best friend, Aaron Spenser. Nee swallowed. She should be thrilled Kiki had found happiness with someone who would finally treat her in the way she deserved, and in truth she was. She would just have preferred it if Aaron hadn't been the elder brother of the man whose heart she'd broken, smashing her own to pieces in the process.

Desperate for a distraction, anything to avoid the lump threatening to choke her every time her eyes strayed to the formless block of clay on the worktable, Nee rinsed her still-clean hands at the sink then pulled the studio door shut behind her. Soft music drifted from the open door of the space next door, accompanied by a deep baritone hum which was enough for her to identify the occupant. Bryn was a broad-shouldered, softly spoken car mechanic who also produced the most delicate, ethereal watercolours she'd ever seen. He was staying for a week and appeared to be relishing the calm serenity of the cove. Not wishing to disturb him, or to be caught up in an awkward discussion of what she was working on, or wasn't working on as the case may be, she tiptoed past his door then hurried down the corridor to escape onto the gravel driveway which separated the barns and the house.

A quick glance towards the teashop put paid to her hopes of drowning her sorrows in a cup of tea, and she checked her watch. If she was quick, she might still catch up with Mia and Kiki in the kitchen. Tuesday was turnaround day at the guest house, and in addition to running the teashop, Kiki helped out changing the beds and cleaning the rooms.

Opening the back door, she paused to toe off her shoes and caught their familiar voices deep in discussion over arrangements for Aaron's upcoming birthday. Circumstances had led to her middle sister and her two children sharing a nearby cottage with Daniel's best friend. After a shaky start, the two had finally admitted to feelings that were obvious to everyone around them, and they were a picture of domestic bliss. The kids adored Aaron, and it sounded as though they wanted to throw him a surprise party.

'It's such a sweet idea, especially when you think they came up with it themselves. I just wish things weren't so awkward, with…you know.'

Awkward. Nee stopped short at the word, her call of greeting frozen on her lips. Heart dropping with a knowing premonition, she waited anxiously for Mia's response.

'I know.' Mia sounded sympathetic and resigned in equal measures. 'But we can't keep ignoring the situation.'

Kiki sighed. 'You're right, but I don't want them thinking I've manufactured a situation to force them to face each other. But how can we possibly have a party for Aaron without Luke there?'

Nee sagged against the cool plaster wall, shivering from more than the cool air gusting through the open door behind her. The soft, familiar voices of her sisters continued their discussion, but she couldn't make out the words over the pounding of her heartbeat in her ears. Tightness filled her lungs and the walls of the cloakroom seemed to constrict around her. She had to get out. Had to get away. Reaching blindly for a jacket, she spun on her heel and fled across the grass. A bitter voice whispered in her ear. *That's right. Run away, just like you always do.*

Nee huddled deeper into the padded jacket she'd borrowed from the row of pegs beside the backdoor at Butterfly House. The sleeves hung past the tips of her fingers, and the material smelled faintly of the kind of citrusy scent that spoke of aftershave rather than perfume. She hadn't stopped long enough to examine her choice, just grabbed for the first one her hand reached as she flew out of the kitchen and into the beautiful, sprawling garden behind the guesthouse. Her headlong flight carried her down the flagstone path to the short flight of steps leading to the beach. Only once her shoes sank into the soft, pale sand did she slow her frantic pace.

The thick fleece collar blocked the worst of the wind howling in across the open water, and she narrowed her eyes against the sting of sand whipped up by its fury. The approaching storm transformed Butterfly Cove from a seaside idyll into a wild, desolate space. The normally gentle waters churned and roiled as though a monstrous beast twisted below the surface. Gone was the peaceful blue blanket she'd grown accustomed to over the summer, replaced by a murky, green-grey morass. Dark clouds scudded across the sky, and the first icy drops of rain hit her raw cheeks. It had to be rain because, after the past few weeks, Nee was sure there wasn't a tear left inside her.

The rain fell harder – fat, cold drops that soon plastered her short blonde hair flat against her skull. Her face began to ache, a combination of the harsh bite of the wind and the desperate clench of her jaw. Everything was such a bloody mess, and she had no one to blame but herself. Luke had committed no sin, unless falling in love with her could be considered a sin. A bubble of hysteria formed a tight knot at the top of her chest. He would probably consider it more of a curse. And who would blame him when she'd done the unthinkable and left him alone in their marriage bed without a word.

Her decision to leave had made sense at the time. They'd acted impetuously; wouldn't be the first couple to confuse a heady rush of lust with something deeper. Better to make a quick break, go out on a high before the humdrum reality of life crept in and shattered their perfect fantasy. The hurt would fade, leaving behind fond memories of a foolish summer of love.

All perfectly sensible and rational conclusions, and every one a complete and utter lie. The moment she'd seen him staring at her across the platform, the one hope she'd clung to, that Luke had moved on without her, had been destroyed. She'd put her own ambition before his heart, and ruined both their lives in the process.

'One cannot make true art without first suffering, my dear.' The only voice she hated more than her own guilt intruded on her thoughts, and Nee raised her hands to her temples. She squeezed her fists into the sides of her head, as though applying the right amount of pressure could force him back into the skittering darkness of her deepest subconscious. It didn't help. The moment she let her guard down, he was there.

Staring out across the tossing waves, Nee could almost sense him reaching out across the miles to drag her back over the ocean. 'I won't come back. You can't have me!' She shouted her defiance. The wind swooped to snatch her words away, stealing her strength with it. Dropping to her knees on the wet sand, she lowered her head and acknowledged the truth. Devin Rees had stolen the most important thing from her, leaving nothing but an empty shell behind.

Even if Luke could be persuaded to give her another chance, what could she offer him? She stared down at her shaking hands. Short nails edged with raw skin. Stubby fingers bereft of any traces of dark clay. An artist who couldn't create – was there a more pathetic kind of creature? Putting pen to paper to help her niece make the place cards for Mia's wedding had been an exercise in torture.

Staying in Butterfly Cove, watching week in and week out as her former peers descended on Daniel's studios to paint, carve, sculpt and hammer beauty from nothing had become an exercise in self-flagellation. The thought of sitting in the sweet, cosy warmth of Kiki's new teashop, gorging on slabs of cake which were masterpieces in their own right, as the visiting artists added new pieces to the planned gallery collection, might just break her.

There was nothing here for her. Mia and Kiki tried their best to help her, but she kept them at arm's length. She didn't want their sympathy, feared even more turning it into something harder, colder, if they discovered the reason she'd left Luke. They would continue to love her, of that much she was certain, but Kiki's loyalties were already divided between her sister and the brother of the man she loved. The conversation she'd overheard earlier had made it crystal-clear. It hurt Nee to be the cause of any distress to her middle sister, who'd borne the brunt of so much already. But it hurt even more to watch her unfolding joy and contentment in the arms of the man who reminded Nee of everything she'd lost.

No. Not lost. Thrown away. Lying to herself had caused this ugly mess. There could be nothing but truth from now on. Nee would not become a millstone for her sisters to bear. They'd been happy before she'd shown up, would be happier once she left again, regardless of how much they would protest otherwise.

And, most important of all, she owed it to Luke.

She'd usurped his place here in Butterfly Cove and it was time to give it back. Never one to indulge a sulk for long, Nee gave herself a mental kick in the arse and forced her cramped body to stand. The lower half of her jeans were soaked, and her bones ached from the cold and rain soaking her skin. She folded down the collar of the coat, the once-cosy fleece now wet and clinging unpleasantly to her cheek. Shoving her frozen hands into the depths of her pockets, Nee trudged across the beach towards the beckoning warmth of the guest house.

A hot shower and a change of clothes did wonders for her outward appearance, though they couldn't help much with the growing coldness inside her. Telling herself she needed to leave was one thing, but where the hell could she go? Not back to London, that was for damn certain. She'd find herself making excuses to hang around the places Luke liked to go, the way she had in the intervening weeks between her return from New York and her fateful decision to attend Mia's wedding. Perhaps the answer lay in finding somewhere new...

Energised by the idea, she hurried down the remaining stairs and into the private sitting room Mia had created away from the guest spaces. The large wooden bookcase in the corner was stacked high with myriad different books, and she knew her brother-in-law had an old atlas somewhere around. She'd seen him poring over it with Kiki's little boy, Matty, the other weekend. Bursting into the room, she pulled up short. A white-faced Kiki clung hard to Mia's hand while their older sister frowned and nodded at something the person on the other end of the phone pressed to her ear was saying.

Kiki glanced up and Nee could see the tear tracks on her cheeks. 'It's Mum,' she whispered.

A wave of relief washed over Nee, followed swiftly by a sharp stab of guilt. Of the three of them, her relationship with Vivian was the most fractured, having never known the kindness and care she'd been capable of before her alcoholism had dug its claws deep. The two women sitting opposite her had, to all intents and purposes, raised her. Given her more than enough love to buffer their mother's neglect and their father's indifference. She crossed the room to sit cross-legged on the carpet in front of them, placing a hand on Mia's knee in silent support.

Kiki leaned towards her. 'She's taken a turn for the worse,' she whispered.

'What else did the doctor say, Dad?' They both turned towards Mia, who was staring off into the distance, uttering soothing noises as she listened to George's response. The curve of her shoulders increased, as though the words she heard had a physical weight to them. Nee patted her leg, wishing there was something she could do to help. Mia sat up straighter, spine going ramrod-straight. 'Okay. I need to sort a few things out and then I'll be up first thing.'

Nee closed her eyes. Mia to the rescue, just like always. She dug her fingers into the rich pile of the carpet beneath her. An image of the sitting room, all warm creams and soft browns with splashes of rich red, filled her mind's eye. She thought about the other rooms, the stylish bedrooms, the cosy warmth of the kitchen, each one a testament to the beautiful home Mia had built from the ashes of her past. Love and laughter infused every corner of the guesthouse. Just a few short weeks since their beautiful wedding, Mia and Daniel should be on their honeymoon, but they'd postponed it to throw all their energies into the guesthouse and studios. They had enough on their plates as it was without facing the prospect of spending time apart so soon.

Decision made, she opened her eyes. 'I'll go.'

Acknowledgements

Well, here we are again! This book is for everyone who read *Sunrise at Butterfly Cove* and told me how much they wanted Kiki to get her own story. I hope I've done her (and Aaron) justice.

As ever, I couldn't do this without the support of my husband. Thanks, bun x

My love and gratitude go to my mum, for everything x

To Charlotte and Rayha, who love Butterfly Cove as much as I do and really help make the stories shine – it's a pleasure to work with you both.

To the other HQ Digital authors, thank you for your support. The laughter, the commiserations, and your unflagging support for each and every member of our literary family is amazing. Writing is a lonely business, but I'm never alone with you guys ready to lift me up.

And finally, my thanks to you, the reader. It's such a pleasure to welcome you back to Butterfly Cove. I hope you'll join me again soon when the sound of wedding bells will be replaced by jingle bells as we celebrate Christmas at Butterfly Cove.